The Lost Diary of Snow White Complete Collection

By Boyd Brent

Contact: boyd.brent1@gmail.com

The Lost Diary of Snow White

The Found Diary of Orange Orange

The Return of Snow

Snow & Alice in Wonderland

This diary is the property of Snow White.

Strictly speaking, I'm not supposed to keep a diary. No fairytale characters are. It's *the* unwritten rule of the land. And now I know why: because life here is so unlike anything people in the real world have been led to believe. Once it's finished, I'll have to find a hiding place for it. But if you're holding it now, it means it's been found, and the truth about my life can *finally* be revealed…

Monday

"Mirror, mirror on the wall, who's the fairest of them all?"

"You are Snow White." I've never much cared for this mirror. It's not even supposed to have an opinion – not according to the fairy tale upon which my life is based. It's only my evil stepmother's mirror that's supposed to say what an unrivalled beaut I am. Well, it simply isn't true. I mean, there's pale and then there's PALE. And I'm the kind of PALE that makes me visible from space most nights.

I can't *tell* you what a relief it is to share this secret: you can't believe everything you read in fairy tales. The truth is that all the mirrors in the land (not to mention all the reflective surfaces) are wrong about my fairest-of-them-all status. I caught my reflection in Not Particularly Hopeful's eyes the other day, and his eyes said (you heard me correctly, welcome to my fairytale paradise), "You are without doubt the fairest of them all, Snow White." At this point you may be wondering who Not Particularly Hopeful is. You know there are seven dwarves, and even though you can't name them all, you're pretty certain that none of them are called Not Particularly Hopeful. Yet another misunderstanding about my life. There are *five* dwarves, and contrary to popular belief, none are even remotely Happy. How could they be, with names like Not Particularly Hopeful, Insecure, Meddlesome, Inconsolable and Awkward? According to the little lamb that skips past my kitchen window every morning, the dwarves represent facets of my own personality. Cripes. That's deep. Particularly for a constantly-on-the-go lamb of such tiny proportions.

Then there's Prince Charming. He wasn't supposed to arrive until *after* my stepmother poisons me, and I've been in a coma for a hundred years. As the story goes, that's when he wakes me with a kiss, and after that we live happily ever after. No pressure, then. But the other day, when the little lamb hopped, skipped and jumped past my kitchen window, it bleated something about a hunky prince on a white stallion coming into my life. “Really?” I replied. “Stop the press. We're talking in a hundred years' time, once I'm fully rested and up to the challenge of living happily ever after.”

“No,” replied the little lamb. “His arrival is imminent.”

“Imminent?”

“Any second now.”

“Did you swallow a dictionary? Imminent? I don't think…” And there he was, a hunky prince riding a white stallion. He looked me up and down, smiled and said, “Reports of your beauty have not been exaggerated. You are indeed the fairest in the land.” Prince Charming isn't the only one who can look a person up and down. And once I'd made a point of doing just that – minus the smile, of course – I said, “What are you *doing* here? You're over a century early. Please. Leave me alone. I'm not ready to live happily ever after yet.”

“Nonsense!” said he. “One so perfect on the outside must also be perfect on the inside. And ready for any challenge. What have you to say to that?”

“That you should never judge a book by its cover,” said I firmly.

As Prince Charming rode away on his horse, he called out, “I intend to win you over, Snow.”

“But why ever would you want to?”

“So we can live happily ever after.”

“Really? No pressure, then!”

The next day as I swept the porch, the little lamb saw me crying. It hopped about in a circle and bleated, “Whatever is your problem?” I rested my chin on the broom handle, and my eyes went up and down as they followed its cute bounce. “My problem? At least I can do stationary. What's with all the bouncing, anyway?”

“I was just written this way: always on the move, and quite unable to slow down.”

“Really? Well, I was just written this way.”

“What way?” asked the little lamb.

“I suppose I'm insecure. And at times such as these, quite inconsolable.”

“Anything else?”

“Well, now you come to mention it, I'm awkward and not particularly hopeful.”

“About what?”

“About living happily ever after with the prince.”

“Why? Is the prince not charming by name *and* by nature?”

"I presume so. But he doesn't understand me at all."

"Then introduce the prince to your dwarves. The clues are in their names," said the wise little lamb.

I began sweeping the porch again and said, "First of all, they aren't *my* dwarves, and secondly the prince is already well acquainted with them."

"Then he's been blinded by your beauty?"

I nodded mournfully, then shook my head. "He must need his eyes tested. I have seen a three-headed toad fairer than I."

Saturday

Today my evil stepmother invited me to tea. Yes, that's right, the same evil stepmother who has hated me ever since she asked her mirror, “Who's the fairest in the land?” and it lied and told her that I was. And ever since that day, she's been trying to poison me with apples. She's quite the one-trick pony in that way: apples, apples, always apples. My friend Cinderella said I should count my blessings.

“*Blessings*?” said I.

“Yes. That your stepmother has absolutely no imagination when it comes to poisoning you.” Cinders also pointed out that I'm related to my stepmother. And that when it comes to our relatives, we must make allowances, even if they do hate us enough to poison us with fruit. Then she reminded me of what she has to put up with with her sisters. Poor Cinders. They give her a dreadful time.

My stepmother sent a sparrow with a message this morning. In between tweets, the sparrow read the following to me: 'I'm so excited about your early engagement! You must come for tea! And a slice of apple pie! I baked it myself only this morning! Especially for you!” As you can see, my stepmother is fond of exclamation marks. In my experience, the more exclamation marks a person uses, the crazier they are. It's really no different from someone shouting all the time for no apparent reason.

I stepped onto the porch, and whistled for Barry the boar. Barry runs a taxi service, and is the fastest boar in the land (ask any mirror). He also has the longest tusks, and they're perfect to hang on to. “Mind that hanging branch, Barry!” said I, lowering my head.

“I see it.”

“Appreciate the ride, Baz.”

“No problem, Snow. Happy to help out. How are the dwarves? Still whistling while they work?”

“Oh, yes. Of course. It helps to keep their spirits up. It's hard work down that mine.”

“If I could, I'd whistle while I worked too.”

“Then why don't you?”

“I can't on account of my piggy lips. Whenever I try, I blow raspberries instead.”

Barry dropped me off outside the palace, and then trotted off, blowing raspberries (at least, I assume he was trying to whistle). And so it was with a heavy heart that I turned and knocked on the door. The palace is very large and the butler very small. The sun had gone down by the time he let me in... and had risen again by the time we reached the parlour, where my stepmother stood over an apple pie, pastry knife in hand. “Pie?” she asked.

“I'll take a rain check on the pie, thank you.”

“Nonsense,” said she, cutting an ample slice. “You're such a waif of a thing. You need fattening up.”

“Oh,” I said, looking at my reflection in one of the parlour's many mirrors. “I'm quite fat enough already, thank you.”

My stepmother slammed the knife down on the table. "Fat, are you? If you're *fat,* then what does that make me?" She turned yellow and green with envy (she does that a lot around me), then she remembered her charm offensive and assumed a more plausible colour. "No matter," said she. "How lovely it is to see you! I so look forward to your visits. Come and sit beside me. Tell me all about Prince Charming. He must be awfully keen. Why else would he turn up so early?"

I sat down, and she placed a piece of pie before me on a plate. I watched as apple oozed from its sides.

"What*ever* is the matter? It won't bite," she said.

I pushed the plate away. "I'm too bloated for pie. And what's more, I don't want to marry Prince Charming. Not yet."

"Why ever not?"

"Because I'm not ready to live happily ever after."

My stepmother rang a little bell on the table to summon a servant. "We'll skip the apple pie," she told her servant, "and have apple strudel instead."

I rolled my eyes.

My stepmother did the same, then she lowered her voice to a whisper and said, "Trust me. If you have a slice of my apple strudel, you won't have to marry the prince."

"Oh? And why is that?"

"Because it's an enchanted strudel," she whispered, like she was confiding a secret. *You mean because it's a poisoned strudel,* I thought. I straightened my back and said, "I'm in no need of enchantment at the moment, thank you very much."

"Ungrateful girl!"

"Is my father home?"

"The king is away on state business."

"Will he be back soon?"

"Just as soon as you eat some strudel."

"I won't do it," said I.

"How about a nice bowl of fruit salad?"

"Are there apples in it?"

"Just the one."

"No, thank you."

"Toffee apple?"

"No."

"Apple fritter?"

"No."

"Tart, then."

"Ex*cuse* me?"

"Apple tart?"

"No way."

"Perhaps I can tempt you with a delicious glass of apple

cider? Seventy percent proof. Promise I won't tell your father."

I couldn't take any more apple offers, I simply couldn't. So I left.

It was cold and dark, and a long walk back to my cottage. I felt a pang of guilt at not being home to make the dwarves their supper. After all, they had taken me in and befriended me in my hour of need. It seems like only yesterday when my stepmother asked her mirror *that* question, and it lied to her. She told the woodcutter to take me into the woods and make sure that I *never* came back. I promised the woodcutter that if he let me go, I would leave the land for good. And that way, my stepmother's mirror would tell her that *she* was the fairest in all the land. The woodcutter must have been a kindly fellow, for he let me go. I walked for many days looking everywhere for the exit to the land, but the land seemed to go on forever. I grew downcast, and that's when I came upon the dwarves. They were on their way home after a hard day down the mine. "Excuse me," I said. "I have been walking for days, and I'm very tired. I'm looking for an exit to the land. Is it close by?"

Not Particularly Hopeful shook his head (I've since discovered that Not Particularly Hopeful shakes his head a lot), then Inconsolable began to cry. I put my arm around the little fellow, doing my best to console him, but it was quite useless. Awkward went bright red and snorted... awkwardly. He looked at Insecure, who said not to ask him *anything* because he didn't know anything. Not Particularly Hopeful spoke up again, and he said that as far he knew, there was no exit to the land. Not anywhere. That everywhere you went, you found more land. And there you had it. Or didn't. Not if you were looking for an exit, anyway.

I sat down on a tree stump and rested my heavy head in my hands. “Do you mean to say that I've spent all this time looking for something that doesn't exist?”

Inconsolable blew his nose, and said it wasn't like it had stopped anybody before. So why should it stop me? Then he pointed in no direction in particular and said the exit was probably that way.

“It can't be. Not if it doesn't exist. Oh, whatever I shall I do! I promised the woodcutter.”

“Can you cook?” asked Meddlesome. “Only, Insecure makes all our meals and he's a terrible cook.”

Insecure nodded his head in agreement.

“I suppose I can cook. I won't really know until I try,” I said.

“What about housework?” asked Meddlesome. “Only, Insecure does all our housework too, and he's terrible at it.”

Again, Insecure nodded.

“I suppose I could do housework. I won't really know until I try.”

The dwarves went into a huddle, and they decided that in return for cooking and cleaning, I would be given a roof over my head. Apparently, I was almost exactly what they'd been looking for.

The early hours of Sunday morning…

So anyway, back to the present. As you may recall, I'd just left my stepmother's, and had begun my walk home in the dark through the woods. I was just feeling peckish (for just about anything other than apple) when I saw a trail of breadcrumbs. The trail was long and winding, and once I'd eaten it, I found myself on my hands and knees outside a cottage – not my own cottage, but one made entirely from gingerbread. I said to myself, "*Dessert*? I like gingerbread, but don't think I could eat a whole abode."

I peered in through a kitchen window. Inside, I saw a small boy sitting beside a sweet old lady. The old lady was feeding him marshmallows by hand. *How lovely,* I thought. I heard someone chopping wood close by, and hoped it might be the woodcutter. I felt guilty about breaking my promise to him, and wanted to explain why I hadn't left the land. *The land is absolutely everywhere,* I would say. *And therefore quite impossible to leave. And if you did, you'd end up precisely nowhere. And how dreadful would that be*? Having rehearsed my explanation in my mind, and being happy with it, I was disappointed to see not the woodcutter, but a little girl chopping wood. She had long brown hair and big brown eyes, and said her name was Gretel. As it turned out, Gretel and I had a lot in common: she had a stepmother of questionable character too. Her stepmother had left her in the woods with her brother Hansel, where she hoped they would starve to death.

"That's pretty grim," I said.

She nodded and asked, "Did your stepmother abandon you to starve in the woods as well?"

"Oh, no. She told the woodcutter to flat-out murder me." I glanced over my shoulder at the gingerbread house. "Thank goodness," I said.

"What do you mean?" she asked.

"That you and your brother found a happy ending after all."

"How so?"

"You came upon a lovely gingerbread house. And a kind old lady who feeds children marshmallows by hand."

Gretel shook her head. "She's not a kind old lady. She's a witch. And she's fattening my brother up."

"But why?"

"So there'll be ample meat on his bones when she eats him. Or so she said."

I tutted.

Gretel echoed my tut and said, "The old witch plans to fatten me up too, and then she's going to eat me. But not before she's worked my fingers to the bone." I reached out and squeezed Gretel's shoulder. "Sorry. That's pretty rough. Whatever does a person have to do to get a break in this land?"

"It beats me," said she.

"I won't have it."

Gretel shrugged her shoulders. "What can you do? What can anybody do? It's just the way our story was written."

“I used to think that way too. And then my prince arrived early, and said he couldn't wait to marry me.”

“You must have been so happy,” sighed Gretel.

I cast my gaze upon the ground and shook my head. “I'm not ready to live happily ever after. Tell me, is there any mention of me in your story?”

“Who are you?”

“Snow White.”

“The fairest in the land?”

I shook my head.

“Well, no,” said Gretel. “I don't believe there's any mention of Snow White.”

I folded my arms and said, “My own story has been changed. And my being here only goes to prove one thing.”

“And that is?” asked Gretel.

I raised an arm and brought my thumb and forefinger together. “That we might change it a *teensy weensy* bit more.”

“How so?”

My gaze fell upon the axe in her hands, then I looked over my shoulder at the cottage where the witch was fattening up her brother.

“Oh!” said Gretel. “Why ever didn't I think of that?”

Monday

I'm back at home now, and you'll be pleased to know that Hansel and Gretel's story ended happily after all. The same could not be said for the witch. I imagine she had quite a shock when Gretel burst into her kitchen, axe raised above her head, and said the story was about to be altered 'a *teensy weensy* bit more.'

Today Prince Charming invited me to the enchanted lake for a picnic. He seems quite convinced that he can change my mind about marrying him early. His invite said that when it came to wooing the ladies his record was flawless. And that even if he had to make an effort to understand my feelings, that's precisely what he would do. His message said I should *fear not* and *brace myself for falling hopelessly in love*, and that if all else fails, *I should get a grip for once in my life.*

I handed the dwarves their lunch boxes and kissed them goodbye at the garden gate – all except Insecure, who was even more worried than usual about hitting the wrong part of the mine and causing a cave-in. “I'll stay with you today, Snow, that's if you don't mind?” Of all my dwarves, I feel closest to Insecure. “Of course I don't mind. I'm going to meet Prince Charming down at the enchanted lake later.”

“Do you mind if I tag along?” he asked.

“You know, I somehow thought you might.”

Insecure and I walked up a steep hill, on the other side of which the sun glistened upon an enchanted lake and leaves rustled upon enchanted tress. At the top of the hill, we stopped and looked down upon the scene as just described. The only difference was Prince Charming. He lay on a blanket beneath the shade of a tall tree, his perfect head placed in a perfect palm, a blade of grass turning slowly between his perfect lips. Placed upon his blanket were all manner of tasty treats to tempt me.

Insecure looked up at me and I looked down at Insecure. “The prince will not be at all happy to see me,” said he. “Of that I'm quite sure.”

“What makes you say that?” asked I.

Insecure sat down and hugged his knees to his chest. “Because nobody is ever happy to see me. I'll keep watch over you from up here.”

“If you're sure?”

Insecure nodded.

“Okay then.”

As I approached the prince, he got up and told me I grew fairer with each visit. “Come and sit beside me,” said he, “and share this delightful picnic.”

Prince Charming and I sat cross-legged opposite each another. He took an apple from a bowl of fruit and handed it to me. “The apple's ruddiness is intense, is it not?” said he. I glanced down at the apple in my hand. Indeed, it was the ruddiest apple I had ever seen. The prince smiled and said, “I chose that apple for you especially.”

“Why?”

“Because it matches perfectly the colour of your cheeks

when you blush."

"Really? Thanks. I think."

"Tell me," said he, leaning closer, "what good and charitable deeds have you performed lately?"

I rubbed the apple against my sleeve to bring out its shine. "What makes you think I've performed any good and charitable deeds?"

"One as fair as you must have charity in her heart."

"Really? Well…"

"Come now, my love, there's no need to be coy about your charitable deeds."

I took a bite out of the apple. As I chewed I said, "I presume my stepmother didn't provide the fruit for this picnic?"

Prince Charming's eyes opened wide, and they filled with wonder. "Not only are you the fairest in the land, you also possess the wisdom of kings."

With a mouthful of apple it wasn't easy to talk, but I did my best. "Are you 'elling me that eye step-um gave 'ou this apple?"

"Yes, my darling. She insisted on supplying all the fruit for our picnic."

I spat out the apple. As I picked bits of it out of his hair and lap, I said, "In the future, if my stepmother offers you fruit… say no."

"But why, my love?"

"She's been trying to poison me with it for years."

"With *fruit*?"

"Apples, to be precise."

"I can't believe *anyone* would wish to harm even a hair on your fair head."

"Believe it."

"I don't want to believe it."

"You must believe it."

"But what if I can't believe it?"

"Then you must try harder."

"But why apples, my darling?"

I shrugged up my heavy shoulders. "Maybe she's just written that way." Prince Charming stood up and hurled the fruit bowl into the enchanted lake. Moments later, a great many fish floated to its surface, all in deep comas from which they would never awaken – well, not unless kissed by a prince who wanted to live happily ever after with a fish. I thought about how unlikely this was, and sighed.

Prince Charming sat down again. "Now," said he, "you were about to tell me of your charitable deeds?"

"But why should I?"

Prince Charming leaned back on the palms of his hands. "I have been led to believe that talking of your charitable deeds will fill you with pride, and make you feel less insecure."

I leaned back on my own palms. “Fat to no chance of that,” said I.

“All the same, please indulge me.”

“Alright. I helped a brother and sister in the woods yesterday. Does that count?”

“I knew it! One so fair must carry out at least *one* charitable deed every single day.”

“If you say so.”

“Tell me of these fortunate siblings whose paths crossed your own, my dearest, most charitable darling.”

“I simply had to help them.”

“Oh, my darling!”

“We had such a lot in common.”

“How so?”

“They have a stepmother of questionable character too.”

“So how did you come upon the unfortunate brother and sister?”

“Their names were Hansel and Gretel. I came upon Gretel chopping wood. She told me how a witch was fattening her brother for her cooking pot.”

The prince looked suitably concerned and said, “Whatever does a person have to do to get a break in this land?”

“Tell me about it.”

“So what did you do?” asked the prince.

“Well, I knew I had to change their story, as mine had been changed.”

“And?”

“And I considered the options available to me.”

“Very wise, my love, very wise indeed. And these options were?”

“Pretty scarce, actually. There was a barn filled to bursting with marshmallows, a well filled with chocolate syrup, and a young girl with a grudge... and armed with an axe.”

The prince twirled his moustache and looked very pleased with himself. “Say no more,” said he. “It's clear that your plan involved marshmallows and chocolate syrup.”

Tuesday

Yesterday, when I described the crime scene that Gretel had created in the witch's kitchen, the prince turned quite pale. I imagined he'd quite fallen out of love with me, but alas, when I asked him if this were true, he looked once again like a love-sick puppy and said, “When faced with evil witches who eat children, charitable solutions are not always possible.”

“You're not wrong, and…”

The prince held up a palm. I'm no palm reader, but even I could read that palm. *Pipe down and let me speak*, it said. The prince smiled, and then finished what he was saying using words, “If there had been a way to escape using only chocolate syrup and marshmallows, then you would have found one. Of this I am convinced, my love.”

I thought about that for a moment and nodded. “I suppose we *could* have thrown the witch down her well and drowned her in chocolate syrup. Oh! Or we could have locked her up in her barn with *nothing* to eat but marshmallows. She'd have grown fatter and fatter and eventually burst. A proper taste of her own medicine. Or…” The prince raised his other palm, and with both palms now raised, I imagined he wanted to play pat-a-cake. While we played, he told me that while he appreciated my ingenuity, he'd quite heard enough alternative endings for the witch.

Anyway, today I'm going to visit my friend Cinderella. I

expect you've heard of Cinders. Her story is as well-known as my own, and like me she is supposed to go through a terrible time before her Prince Charming rescues her. I rode over to her palace on Barry the boar. As Barry trotted through the forest, I said, “Is everything okay, Barry?”

“I mustn’t grumble,” said he.

“Only you seem slower than usual.”

“I never was the brightest boar in the land.”

“That's not what I meant. The spring has quite gone out of your trot. It's my fault, isn't it? I've grown fat.”

Barry shook his head. “Is Cinderella expecting you?”

“Oh, yes.”

“Only she generally has a lot of palace-work to get through,” said Barry.

“Don't I know it.”

Barry snorted. “I can't imagine Cinderella complaining much if her Prince Charming arrived early and wanted to live happily ever after.”

“*What* did you just say, Barry?”

“I said I can't imagine Cinderella complaining if her Prince Charming turned up early. Not with her working her fingers to the bone every day.”

“Barry! You've just given me a brilliant idea! The solution to both mine and Cinderella's woes.”

“How so?”

“All I need do is get my Prince Charming to fall in love with Cinderella. That way, I'll have time to sort out my issues, and Cinders can live happily ever after right away. Do you think my plan might work?”

“It might. I hear that Cinderella scrubs up pretty well. And one Prince Charming is just like any other. There's a factory that makes them. And I hear they're pretty easy to put together.”

“And why is that?”

“Because they're only one-dimensional characters. Gallant and charming.”

I yawned. “That sums up my own Prince Charming to a tee, Barry.”

“There you have it, then.”

“There I have it.”

Barry dropped me off at a side entrance to the palace, and I slipped inside unnoticed. I expect you've heard about Cinderella's sisters: ugly by name and ugly by nature. They don't allow Cinderella to have a social life. What's more, the palace is huge, which means there's always a room in need of scrubbing. But in many ways that's quite handy, as all I have to do to find her is follow the smell of bleach. Today I came upon her in the ballroom. The ballroom is very grand, and Cinders looked out of place in her sackcloth and rags. She was halfway along the ballroom's floor on her hands and knees, scrubbing for all she was worth. I took off my shoes and tiptoed up behind her. “Surprise!” I said.

"Argh!" she cried, and fell flat on her face.

"Do not be alarmed," I whispered. "It's only me. Your good friend, Snow."

She sat for a minute with birds circling her head, and slowly her senses returned. "*Snow*?" said she.

"Hello, Cinders."

She glanced about fretfully. "Do my sisters know you're here? Only, if they find out I have a visitor they will punish me."

"Fear not, good friend of mine. Your sisters' carriage was not on the palace forecourt."

This news cheered Cinders no end. She stood up and extended a hand for me to shake. "Why the formal greeting?" I asked.

"I'm just so pleased to see a friendly face. How are you, Snow?"

"Not so good."

"Is it your evil stepmother? Is she *still* intent on poisoning you?"

I shrugged up my hulky shoulders. "You know how it is. And you? Do your sisters still think of you as a horrid blot on their family tree?"

Cinders shrugged up her beautiful shoulders. "Just look at me. So what's new?"

"Glad you asked me that. My own Prince Charming has

turned up early, and seems keen as mustard to live happily ever after."

"Oh, you lucky thing! Then why the face like you've spent the morning sucking on a rotten lemon?"

"Think about it, Cinders," said I, looking at my reflection in one of the ballroom's many mirrors. While we waited for the mirror to make its predictable pronouncement, I rolled my eyes. "Without doubt you are the fairest in the land," said the mirror.

"Still don't believe the mirrors?" asked Cinders, scraping some dirt from beneath her thumb nail.

"Not just the mirrors," said I. "It seems to me that all the reflective surfaces in the land need their eyes tested."

"But they don't *have* eyes, Snow."

"That explains a lot. Had they eyes, perhaps they wouldn't talk such nonsense. And that's especially true with you standing beside me."

Cinderella looked at her own reflection: her long blonde hair was dirty and matted, and her face smeared with dirt. "Truly, I am a dreadful mess," said she.

"And still more beautiful than I."

Cinderella began to chew a nail. "How'd you work that one out?"

"You just are. And what's more, you're so patient with your sisters. And so accepting of all the awful things in your life."

"What choice do I have, Snow? It's just the way things are

written."

"That's what I used to think, but then my Prince Charming turned up early. And I met Hansel and Gretel in the woods. And neither of these things were in the book."

"What does that prove?"

"That we can change things."

"Not me. But in a year and a bit, give or take, my own Prince Charming will rescue me. And then we're going to live happily ever after."

"What if you don't have to wait a year and a bit for your Prince Charming?"

"But I do."

"But what if you don't? What if my Prince Charming falls for you?"

Cinders cast her gaze the length and breadth of the ballroom. "Is he here?"

"I hope not."

"But why would he fall for me? I'm not the fairest in the land."

"That's just the thing. Barry the boar said there's a big demand for Prince Charmings in stories such as these, and that there's a factory that makes them on demand. One Prince Charming is just like any other, apparently."

Cinders nodded. "Gallant and charming."

"You know, I sometimes think that if my prince was a bit less charming, I'd find him more interesting. I may even think myself more worthy of his attention."

"You mean if he was a bad boy?"

"Whatever is a *bad boy*?"

Cinders lowered her voice. "I sometimes hear my sisters giggling about them. They say they're not in the least bit charming."

"But they are gallant, surely?"

Cinders shook her head. "They are perfectly horrid. I don't understand what my sisters see in them. The worst of all is the Big Bad Wolf. My sisters say he only has eyes for Little Red Riding Hood. I sometimes think they hate her almost as much as they hate me."

"I'm going to arrange a meeting."

"With the Big Bad Wolf?"

"No, silly. Not for me. For you with my Prince Charming."

Cinders looked in a mirror and toyed with her filthy locks. "Do you really think he might prefer me to you?"

"Oh, yes. I'm quite convinced of it."

Wednesday

This morning, I asked Barry the boar about the Big Bad Wolf. “Stay away from that wolf,” said Barry. “That wolf is bad by name *and* by nature. Besides, he only has eyes for Little Red Riding Hood.”

“So I hear. I believe I've heard of her. Although I can't quite place her. Tell me, what ghastly things must *she* endure before she can live happily ever after?”

Barry shook his head. “There is no happily ever after. Not for Little Red Riding Hood.”

“*What*? Not ever?”

“That's right. The Big Bad Wolf gobbles her up.”

“Fair enough. We all have our problems. But *then* she gets to live happily ever after?”

“Not a bit of it. That's where her story ends.”

“That's pretty grim. I mean, that's grim even by fairytale standards.”

“Don't I know it.”

“I won't allow it, Barry.”

“Not a lot you can do about it. It's the way her story was written.”

"We'll see about that. Any idea where I might find her?"

"Little Red Riding Hood?"

"No. The good angel who keeps watch over all good children. Of *course* Little Red Riding Hood. She's clearly in great peril."

"Funny you should ask. I spotted her on my way over here."

"Where was she going?"

"In the direction of her grandmother's cottage."

"What a relief," said I. My relief was short-lived, for Barry shook his head and then explained his reason for doing so. "The Big Bad Wolf has already gobbled up Little Red's grandmother. And now he's dressed in her grandmother's dress and bonnet, and waiting for Little Red in her bed."

"And when Little Red arrives at the cottage?"

"That's when the Big Bad Wolf is going to gobble her up."

I leaped onto Barry's back. "Go! For we must reach Little Red before she gets to her grandmother's cottage!"

"I'm uncomfortable with all this meddling, Snow. If anyone asks, you walked. Alright?"

"Alright. Now we really must get going."

Not long after, we came upon Little Red in the woods. She looked as cute as a button in her red cape and bonnet – way more attractive than me. "Hello, Little Red!" I called. Little Red turned and waved. Then she squinted and asked, "Do I know you?"

"I expect you've heard about me," I said, climbing off Barry's back. "I'm the one that mirrors take a delight in lying to."

"The fairest of them all? But you *can't* be Snow White."

"At last. Someone with exceptional eyesight."

Little Red fiddled with the strap of her bonnet under her chin. "That's not what I meant. You can't be Snow White. She isn't a part of my story."

"Well, she is now. Speaking of your story, do... ah, do you know how it ends?"

"Well, no. Not exactly. I presume I'm going to live happily ever after."

"I'm sorry to be the bearer of dreadful news, but the Big Bad Wolf is waiting for you at your grandmother's cottage… and when you arrive, he's going to gobble you up."

Little Red nodded bravely. "Maybe so," she said, "but after *that,* I'm going to live happily ever after."

I shook my head.

"Really? Then whatever is to become of me?"

I shrugged. "You're to be digested, presumably."

"You mean that's *it* for me? Digestion!"

I nodded politely. "That's why I'm here."

"To tell me happily ever after was never an option. And that I'm to be digested. You're supposed to be the fairest of them all, not the cruellest."

“I'm neither the fairest nor the cruellest. My only claim to fame may be that I'm the most average.”

“Then what *are* you doing here?”

“I've come to help.”

“Help? If that's how my story has been written, then what can you do?”

I glanced left and right to check that nobody was around. Nobody was. Even Barry was gone. I lowered my voice anyway. “The thing is, Little Red, I've already made one or two *tiny* changes to other stories.”

“To minor stories perhaps. Look,” said she, taking off her bonnet and shaking out her red curls. “I have no wish to blow my own trumpet, but my story is one of the most famous.”

“And the story of Hansel and Gretel isn't?”

Little Red looked suddenly downcast. “Oh, don't. Those poor siblings.”

“Not anymore,” said I, proudly.

“You mean to say they're okay?”

“Oh, yes.”

“And what of the witch?”

I held the back of my hand to my face and looked at my fingernails. “The same could not be said for the witch.”

“Dead?”

"Very much so."

"Oh! So what are you saying?" Little Red lowered her voice. "That you're going to *kill* the Big Bad Wolf?"

"Oh my, no. I hear he's a bad boy. And apparently a bad boy is the complete opposite of a Prince Charming."

"And?" said Little Red.

"And I thought I might go on a date with him."

"Are you *crazy*? What if he decides to gobble you up?"

"Then Prince Charming is *bound* to rescue me." At the very mention of Prince Charming, I yawned. "I expect he's very reliable that way."

Little Red smiled.

"My disappointment amuses you?" I said.

"Not particularly. It's just that, if I'm to be spared digestion, and you don't want your Prince Charming, might you introduce him to me?"

"I'm afraid I can't do that."

"Why ever not?"

"I've already promised him to Cinderella."

"How greedy. Isn't one Prince Charming enough for her?"

I rolled my eyes. "More than enough, I should imagine. But if my Prince Charming falls for her, she needn't work her fingers to the bone while she waits for her own to show up."

"When is he supposed to do that?"

"In about a year. Give or take."

"That's not so long to wait. Not for happily ever after. If her Prince Charming is going spare, perhaps I can have him?"

"I don't see why not." I glanced down at Little Red's wooden shoes. "We'll have to get you a pair of glass slippers fit for a ball."

Little Red bounced a little on the spot and clapped her hands silently. "This is just getting better and better!" She handed me a few pages torn from *the book* – the ones she's permitted to read – and said I should bone up on her story. "It's only the last page that's been torn out of my copy," said she. "And now I know why."

And so it was that Little Red waved goodbye, and I went off down the path that lead to her grandmother's cottage.

It was a pretty little cottage with a thatched roof and hanging boxes filled with flowers, and a little red door with a welcome mat that said *No cold callers*.

Inside, the Big Bad Wolf had already gobbled up Little Red's grandmother, and now he was looking forward to having his main course: Little Red. But Little Red had other ideas, as did I. And mine involved the Big Bad Wolf taking me out on a date. "For the first time in my life, my fairest-in-the-land status is going to come in handy," whispered I, as I turned the door knob and went in. I found myself in a little hallway with a mirror. I stood before the mirror and waited for it to pronounce me the fairest in the land. "*Well*?" said I, expectantly.

"Well what?" replied the mirror.

I sighed and said, "Mirror, mirror on the wall, who's the fairest of them all?"

"Your stepmother the queen is the fairest. No question," said the mirror. Of that it sounded quite certain.

"Just my luck," said I. "A mirror with a sense of humour. No really, who is the fairest in the land?"

"Your stepmother is. And by a country mile."

"Are you *kidding* me?"

"Do I look like I'm kidding?"

"You *look* like a mirror."

"That's good to hear."

"Thanks for nothing," said I. "Is the big Bad Wolf here?"

"Of course he is. He's *supposed* to be here. What have you done with Little Red?"

"I don't appreciate your tone."

"You're in the wrong story. So I'll ask you again: what have you done with Little Red?"

"I've done her a big favour. She's in the woods. And thanks to me, she's looking forward to living happily ever after."

"Oh, but she can't be," said the mirror.

"Oh, but she is," said I. "Just as soon as her Prince Charming shows up."

"Can you read?"

"Of course I can read. How rude."

"Then you must know there is no Prince Charming for Little Red. There's only digestion. And indigestion for the Big Bad Wolf."

"That's where you're wrong. I'm going to provide Little Red with a Prince Charming all of her own."

"Yours?"

I shook my head. "I've promised mine to Cinderella, but I've promised Cinderella's to Little Red. Do try and keep up."

"It's quite the tangled web of Charmings you've weaved. So whose Prince Charming are *you* waiting for?"

"No one's. I've decided to date the Big Bad Wolf instead. I suppose he's waiting for me in Little Red's grandmother's bedroom?"

"You are exceptionally meddlesome."

"It has been said."

"He's in there, all right," said the mirror. "But he's not waiting for *you*. He's waiting for Little Red Riding Hood. Do you really think you're going to fool him by wearing her cloak and bonnet?"

"It matters not, for I intend to whip them off at the appropriate moment. I presume the bedroom's through there?" said I, heading in that direction.

You may have heard what they say about first impressions.

And if you haven't, they say they count. That was certainly true in the case of the Big Bad Wolf, who was lying on the bed wearing Little Red's grandmother's dress and bonnet, with the entire contents of her make-up box plastered on his face. I have never seen such red lips and rosy cheeks. As I watched the Big Bad Wolf paint the last of his toe nails, it occurred to me that he enjoyed dressing like a granny. I crept into the room and announced myself thus: "And I thought *I* had issues."

The Big Bad Wolf pulled the blankets up to his eyes and placed a copper ear trumpet to his ear. All the better to hear me with, I should imagine. "What did you say, dearie? Come closer where I can hear you." His voice sounded rather peculiar, and I supposed he was trying impersonate the old woman whose make-up and clothes he was wearing.

I folded my arms and said, "Just *look* at you."

He dropped the blanket from his face and sat up straighter. "Can you read?" he asked.

"Of course I can," said I, taking a step closer to the bed.

"Then you'd do well to stick to the script. That's right, come closer, so your old granny can get a better look at you."

I stood beside the bed and felt rather tiny next to the Big Bad Wolf. I was about to point out that he'd applied too much blusher when he raised a hairy finger and warned, "Stick to the script."

I sighed and decided to prove that I can actually read. "What large eyes you have, Granny."

"All the better to see you with, dearie."

“And what a large nose you have.”

“All the better to smell you with.”

“And what large lips you have.”

“All the better to kiss you with.”

I looked at the Big Bad Wolf's puckered lips, all smudged with purple lipstick. “No kissing. Not until you've learned how to apply your lipstick properly,” said I.

The Big Bad Wolf looked down his long nose at me, raised an eyebrow, and pulled out his well-thumbed copy of *the book* from under the covers. He flicked through its pages until he came upon the story we were in. The Big Bad Wolf read quietly to himself for a minute or two. He looked so studious, I thought it rude to interrupt him. At last he put down the book and peered closely at me. “Who are you?” he asked.

It was then that I whipped off Little Red's cloak and bonnet. “It is none other than I, the fairest in the land!”

“And who told you that?” said he.

“I am Snow White, and every reflective surface in the land tells me that – well, every reflective surface except that mirror out in the hallway. So what have got to say about that?”

“That I'm in agreement with that mirror out in the hallway.”

I decided I liked the Big Bad Wolf. “Your eyesight is first-rate. And you're nothing at all like Prince Charming,” I said.

The Big Bad Wolf narrowed his eyes. “You're in the wrong

fairy tale, *Snow White*."

"I know. I'm not stupid."

"I beg to differ."

"How rude."

"Really? Who else but a stupid person would come here… knowing they were going to be gobbled up?"

I smiled sweetly. "I didn't come here to be gobbled up, Mr Big Bad Wolf."

"You may call me Mr Big Bad."

"Too kind, I'm sure."

"So why did you come here?"

"I came because I heard you're a bad boy. And I thought it might be fun if you took me out on a date."

"A *date*?"

"Yes. Perhaps on a picnic. With sandwiches and cakes."

"You mean sandwiches with Snow White filling? Ditto the cake?"

I shook my head. "Cucumber sandwiches. And a Victoria sponge cake. It's my favourite."

"And what about your beau Prince Charming?"

"What about him? He's much too keen. Not to mention charming. I imagined you'd be neither, and you're actually worse than I imagined."

“I am worse. Much worse. And now I'm going to gobble you up.”

“No, you aren't.”

“And what makes you say that?”

I placed my hands on my hips, and said in my most commanding tone, “Because it is my intention to change you. That's why not.”

“Make me more charming, you mean?”

“No. Just more to my liking. So, from now on, you must think of yourself as my pet project. Understand?”

All of a sudden it went dark, and I imagined it must be a solar eclipse. Then I heard a muffled, “What have you done with my love? Where is Snow White?” *It's Prince Charming,* thought I. The Big Bad Wolf began to impersonate Little Red's grandmother's voice again, and as he spoke I could see Prince Charming, and then I couldn't see him, and then I could see him again and…

“You're in the wrong story,” the Big Bad Wolf informed Prince Charming.

“A tactical necessity,” Prince Charming informed the Big Bad Wolf. “I had to come.”

“Why? Are you stupid and meddlesome as well?”

“To the contrary: I am charming and gallant, and have come to rescue my one true love.”

“I haven't seen her,” said the Big Bad Wolf, yawning like he didn't have a care in this world.

I waved to Prince Charming from the Big Bad Wolf's stomach. "So, you haven't seen my one true love …" said he, drawing his sword.

"You had better not kill me," pointed out the Big Bad Wolf.

"And why ever not?" said Prince Charming, cutting a figure of eight from the air.

"Because you aren't even supposed to *be* in this story, and I still have to pursue the three little pigs. I expect you've heard of them?"

Prince Charming paced up and down, and thought about that for a while. He stopped pacing and said, "Ah, ha!" Then he reached into the Big Bad Wolf's stomach and pulled me out by the scruff of my dress. He threw me over his shoulder and made for the door. Which was quite gallant, I suppose. If you like that sort of thing.

"Just what do you think you're doing?" said I.

"I'm rescuing you, my petal."

"Who asked you? Put me down this instant!"

"No can do. You're coming with me."

"But where are we going?"

"To live happily ever after. Where else?"

"But I'm not ready! Big Bad Wolf, help! Oh, that reminds me, there's someone I want you to meet. And if you think I'm fair, just wait till you meet Cinderella!"

Thursday

My plan was afoot. That's to say, everything was arranged. I'd told Prince Charming to meet me and my friend Cinderella at the lake, at the most romantic spot you can imagine. I'd discussed my plan with the dwarves, and Meddlesome thought it quite the best plan he'd heard in ages. Not Particularly Hopeful and Insecure said they had their doubts about it, while Awkward hopped around nibbling on a toe nail until he tripped over and fell in a heap on the carpet.

My favourite songbirds – the ones that sing while I do the housework – were to hide in the trees and serenade Prince Charming and Cinders during their date. What's more, Meddlesome had agreed to hide below some lilies on the lake's surface, and proclaim Cinders the new fairest in the land. I had told Prince Charming I would meet him there with Cinders, but I planned to hide in a hollowed-out tree close by.

I met Cinders early and made sure everything was in place. The picnic looked scrummy, and was laid out inside the tumbling branches of a weeping willow tree. Up in the tree's branches, my songbirds rehearsed and sounded enchanting. Just beyond the willow tree the sun glistened on the lake, and upon the lake's surface floated some pink lilies. And submerged below the lilies, with a bamboo cane for breath, Meddlesome rehearsed his line. I leaned over the water and studied my reflection in the water beside the lilies. “Let's rehearse one more time, Meddlesome,” said I.

“Want to cue me in?” said he, through his bamboo cane.

"Right you are. Lilies, lilies of the lake, who has by far the sweetest face?"

"You do," said Meddlesome.

"You do, *Cinderella*. Make sure you mention her by name. It's very important." I heard Cinders behind me. "Did someone call me?"

I turned to see Cinders making her way into the little clearing. "Oh, dear," I said.

"Something the matter?" asked Cinders.

"Whatever are you wearing?"

"Don't you like it? It belongs to one of my sisters. I borrowed it, and must return it before six, otherwise she'll discover it missing and have my guts for garters." I shuddered. For in a fairytale land such as this one, when someone has your guts for garters, they make underwear out of your guts. "The dress is designer, you know," said Cinders. "A Panocci. From his spring collection."

I nodded mournfully. "That's why it looks as though a snot dragon has sneezed P's all over it."

"And I have a Panocci handbag to match," said she, pointing out the big green *P* on each side. "What's the matter? Don't you think Prince Charming will like my ensemble?"

I shook my head. "He'll think it vulgar. He imagines the fairest in the land has simpler tastes. And just *think* of all the charitable deeds that might have been done with the money that ensemble cost."

"Oh, dear. Whatever is to be done?" said she.

From below the lilies, Meddlesome made a suggestion through his bamboo cane. “I know of a tailor not far from here. His name is Rumpelstiltskin.”

“I've heard of him,” said I. “He has a loom, and he uses it to weave gold from straw.”

“Yes,” said Meddlesome. “But he also makes clothes on the side to make ends meet. I hear he's very talented, and that he doesn't charge an arm and a leg.” This was music to my ears, as in an enchanted land such as this, an arm and a leg wouldn't just mean expensive, it would mean an actual arm and a leg.

Cinders looked worried. “I'd prefer to keep my arms and legs if possible, Snow,” said she.

“And keep them you shall.” I stuck two fingers in my mouth and whistled for Barry.

Barry trotted into the clearing as though he'd been waiting to do so. “Someone need a ride?”

I leapt onto his back and Cinders climbed on behind me. “We need to get to Rumpelstiltskin's, pronto. Thank you, Barry.”

Barry the boar kicked up some dirt with his back hooves but remained on the spot. “You sure that's wise? Only, Rumpelstiltskin has a bad reputation.”

“How so?”

“Word is he expects the earth in payment for his services.”

“Not according to Meddlesome. Anyway, we'll cross that bridge when we come to it. Cinders must have a new dress.”

"What's wrong with the one she has on?"

"Have you no taste?"

"I like to think so. It's a Panocci, isn't it?"

"Exactly."

"The bag alone must have cost a small fortune," said Barry.

"*Exactly*. Which is why you must take us to Rumpelstiltskin *now*."

"Alright, but I hear he's a wicked little imp."

I yawned. "Maybe so, but if he becomes troublesome, then my Prince Charming will appear and save me. We'd better make sure it doesn't come to that."

"*Your* Prince Charming?" said Cinders. "Don't you mean *my* Prince Charming?" I stood corrected. Or more accurately, I sat corrected.

Not long after, we came upon a little tower with a single room at its top, from which came the sound of laughter. If I'm honest, the laughter didn't sound particularly good-natured. Indeed, so wicked and mocking was it, that it sent shivers down my spine.

"His laughter is just too horrible," said Cinders.

I climbed off Barry and looked up at the window. "I'll have to climb up there and see what has so amused him."

"Do you think that wise?" asked Cinders.

"Do you still want my Prince Charming to fall in love with

you?"

"Yes. Of course."

"Then I have no choice." Cinders climbed off Barry and offered me a leg-up. Barry began to trot off. "Where are you going?" I asked.

"To get Prince Charming. Something tells me you're going to need rescuing."

"You'll do no such thing. It's important *we* handle this. Otherwise he'll start to ask questions."

I clung to the green vines that grew all over the tower and made my way up to its top. It was a warm day and the window was wide open. I peered over the top of its frame, into a small room with a single chair and loom. Upon the loom was thread of the brightest gold. Rumpelstiltskin was dancing in circles around it – well, I say dancing, but he looked more like someone being savaged by a swarm of bees. As he danced, he laughed his horrid laugh. I was about to enquire what had so amused him, when I heard the sound of a toilet being flushed. A little door opened and a young woman, known in her story as the miller's daughter, stooped to get through it. The miller's daughter had long brown hair that curled at the bottom, and big brown eyes all awash with tears. "I'll give you anything you ask for!" said she. "Anything but my baby! I can get you all the jewels and money you desire!"

Rumpel danced about his loom and replied, "That's only because the king married you! If I hadn't spun all that straw into gold, he was going to kill you instead." Rumpel stopped dancing and took three short steps to the miller's daughter, whose tiny waist he barely reached. "You made me a promise," he growled. "You promised that in return for spinning the straw into gold, I could have your first-born child. And now you must be off and fetch the little tyke."

"I have forgotten nothing," said the miller's daughter, sobbing.

It was then that I climbed through the window and made myself known. "Talk about grim," said I. "Whatever has a person to do to get a break in this land?" Rumpel and the miller's daughter looked at me in a way to which I have grown accustomed: like I didn't belong in their story. And to be fair, they had a point. Rumpel was about to say something, but I held up a palm and silenced him. "Don't bother. I know. I've heard it all before. I'm not supposed to be here."

"Well, you aren't, and…" I silenced Rumpel by raising my other palm, and with both palms raised, I paused to see if he wanted to play pat-a-cake. The expression on his face led me to believe he did not.

The miller's daughter wiped away her tears with her sleeve. "I recognise you from your illustrations. You're *Snow White,* the fairest in the land," said she.

"Well, yes and no," I replied.

Rumpel narrowed his left eye and peered up at me. "What do you mean, yes *and* no? Either you're Snow White or you aren't."

"It is true that I am she. But even this poor woman, who has never even been given a name, and is known only as the miller's daughter, is fairer than I."

"I think you'll find that I do have a name," said the miller's daughter.

"What is it?" I asked.

The miller's daughter thought for a moment, and then began to sob quietly to herself. Rumpel folded his arms. "Now look what you've done. You've upset her."

"Oh, that's rich. Coming from you. How could you even *think* of taking her baby away from her?" I gave the miller's daughter a hanky so she could blow her nose. "At least you have initials," said I.

My words must have comforted her, for she perked up a little and said, "I do? What are they?"

"T.M.D."

"T.M.D? What do they stand for?"

"The Miller's Daughter. What else?" She began to cry again, so I added, "By the powers invested in me to make *teensy weensy* changes to stories, I hereby take those initials and christen you Thelma Mavis Doodlebug."

"Thank you," said Thelma, blowing her nose again.

"It's the least I can do."

Thelma looked down at Rumpelstiltskin and grimaced. "While you're here, Snow White, might you make another *teensy weensy* change to my story?"

"Call me Snow. All my friends do." I too cast my gaze down at Rumpelstiltskin, and beheld his horrid little face. "I don't see why not," said I.

Rumpel didn't much like being tied up with thread from his own loom, not even when I explained just how lucky he was compared to what had happened to the witch in Gretel's story. Indeed, so appalling was the din he made that I was forced to fill his mouth with golden thread. The very last thing Rumpel said before he was silenced completely was, "Just what are you doing here anyway!" His question was a timely reminder. I looked again at the loom, and down at the tied-up Rumpelstiltskin. "Oh dear," said I.

"What's the matter?" asked Thelma.

"How is Rumpel to make Cinders a new dress?" Rumpel smiled and, despite being cocooned in his own gold thread, and his cheeks BULGING with thread, he somehow managed to look rather pleased with himself.

"You can have *my* dress if you wish," said Thelma.

Thelma's dress was perfect! Cream-coloured and made from silk, and although fit for a queen, it was unfussy and tasteful. "It's perfect!" said I.

"But what am I to wear home?" asked Thelma.

"Have a look out of the window. Cinders is waiting below in one of her sister's dresses. You can swap." As Thelma Mavis Doodlebug moved towards the window, I apologised to her.

"By why are you apologising?" she asked.

"It's a Panocci original."

Thelma Doodlebug was clearly a young woman of taste, for she sighed with resignation and said that as soon as she got home, she'd have it torn up and made into nappies. I spared a thought for Cinders's guts, for her sisters would surely have them for garters now. But as Little Red is to point out later on in this diary, you can't make an omelette without breaking some eggs.

When Cinders and I returned to the lake, I told her to lie down on the blanket and prop her head in her palm. "How's this?" she asked, assuming that very pose.

"It's perfect. You look as pretty as a picture."

"Do you think Prince Charming will find me so?"

"He's not completely blind. How could he not?" I stepped over Cinders and opened a secret door in the trunk of the willow tree. I climbed in, and placed my eye against a little peep hole. Arranged thus, I saw Prince Charming arrive on his white stallion. "What do you think of him?" I whispered through the hole.

"I think him divine!"

"If you like that sort of thing."

"Tall, dark and handsome. And a prince! What's not to like?"

The prince climbed off his horse not ten feet from the weeping willow tree. Its branches were so plentiful, however, that Cinders was completely hidden from view. Prince Charming placed his hands on his hips and cast his gaze over the lake. "I presume this is the correct location," he murmured.

"Say something," I whispered to Cinders.

"Like what?"

"Something like *Here I am! Your princess! And I'm quite ready to live happily ever after!*"

"But I'm not."

"Of *course* you're ready to live happily ever after."

"That isn't what I meant. I'm not *his* princess. You are."

"Not any more. I've given him to you."

"But what if he isn't yours to give?"

"If not mine then whose?"

The prince was about to climb back onto his horse when Meddlesome spoke up from below the lilies. Through his bamboo cane he said, "Where do you think you're going?"

The prince spun about and drew his sword. "Show yourself!" said he. He sounded so gallant that Cinders swooned, and her head fell off her palm and onto the blanket. She lay so still that I imagined her unconscious, then she sighed and placed her head back on her palm. The prince cut a figure of eight from the air with his sword (I've since learned that Prince Charmings are only able to count to eight). "Who are you?" he asked the invisible owner of the voice. "Show yourself this instant! Or forever hold your tongue."

"Hold my tongue? Then how would I speak?" replied Meddlesome from below the lilies.

Prince Charming rolled his eyes. "*Hold your tongue* is an expression. It means to remain silent."

"For how long?" asked Meddlesome.

"I think you'll find the clue in the word *forever*."

"Forever is a long time to remain silent."

"I suspect not so in your case."

"But I need to tell you something, something you're going to find of interest," said Meddlesome.

Prince Charming walked to the edge of the enchanted lake and gazed down at the lily pad. He slid his sword back inside its scabbard. "What possible information could a floating *plant* have that I might find of interest?"

"Only the name of the fairest in the land," said Meddlesome.

The prince placed his hands on his hips and chuckled quietly to himself. "I already know her name. In fact, I've come here to picnic with her."

"You think you know her name but you do not. The truth is you've never even met her," said Meddlesome.

"It's lucky for you you're a floating plant, otherwise…"

"Otherwise what?"

"Otherwise I would challenge you to a duel for casting doubts upon the beauty of my one true love. Let's face it, only a floating plant of questionable intelligence would *not* think Snow White the fairest in the land."

"She might have been, once upon a time. But now there is a new fairest in the land."

"*What* was that?" asked the prince.

"Her name is Cinderella."

"I suspected as much," spat the prince. "And now my suspicions have been proved correct."

"Really?" said Meddlesome. "You suspected that Cinderella was the fairest in the land?"

"No. Don't be ridiculous. I suspected you to be a moronic floater. It is *that* suspicion that has been proved correct."

"Have you ever met Cinderella?"

"I have no need to, for I have met her sisters. And they tell me she is quite the *opposite* of the fairest in the land."

"Is that what they say?"

"That and more."

"More?"

"Yes. Much more. They say that Cinderella's face resembles the face of a constipated warthog."

"Is that what they say?"

"They do. And that her skin is as coarse as a crocodile's. That her eyes – and she has three of them, mind – are as green and putrid as a snot dragon's."

"Is that *all* her sisters say about her?"

"Not all, no. They say her breath smells like a rabid dog's, and that the rest of her smells worse still."

"Is... ah, is that *all* they say?"

"No. They say that when she walks she shuffles like a zombie, and that when she sneezes she sneezes acid that could burn a hole through steel."

"Her sisters have not painted a very pretty picture," said Meddlesome.

"Maybe not. But it's a true picture. Enough of this talking to a floating plant of very little intellect. I have arranged to meet the fairest in the land at this very spot." Bubbles came to the surface about the lilies, a sign that Meddlesome was about to speak. At their appearance, Prince Charming held up a palm. "Say nothing, floating plant. Unless it is to tell me where I might find my one true love."

"She awaits you inside the weeping willow tree yonder."

Prince Charming turned towards the weeping willow, beyond whose falling branches of white blossom Cinders swooned, her head falling out of her palm and onto the blanket again. "Pick it up!" whispered I.

Cinders sighed. "Pick what up?"

"Your head! Otherwise the prince might think you lazy. Or worse still, drunk!"

But it was too late. Prince Charming brushed aside the willow's branches and beheld Cinders. "What is this?" said he, moving swiftly to her aid. "A fair maiden has fallen foul of some dreadful sleeping sickness!" Prince Charming lifted Cinders into a sitting position, removed his hat, and began to fan her.

Cinders opened her eyes and beheld her prince. That's to say, *my* prince. "Oh, Charming!" said she, fluttering her eyelids.

Don't flutter, I thought. *Prince Charming isn't so soppy as to fall for fluttering.*

"Oh, how your eyelids flutter, fair maiden," said he, falling for their flutter. "And what beautiful eyes are revealed... hidden... revealed... hidden... revealed." Cinders parted her cupid-bow lips. "Do you really think my eyes beautiful?"

"I do," swooned *my* prince.

"You are very kind," said Cinders, "but are you not already betrothed to another?"

"To another what?"

"To another *girl*. The fairest in the land, no less."

"The fairest in the what land, my love?"

"*This* land."

"Oh, her." The prince brushed his hand past his nose as though shooing away a fly – a fly called Snow White. Inside the trunk of the weeping willow, my own hands balled into fists.

Cinders fluttered her eyelids again. "Do you really prefer me to Snow White, then? After all, she is far more beautiful than I. Is she not?" said Cinders, fishing for a compliment.

Prince Charming shook his head. "No, she is not. The fact is," said he, solemnly, "that she is so pale that she can be seen from space most nights."

"That isn't very charming," Cinders pointed out, quite correctly.

"They are her own words, not mine. I read them in her diary," said the prince.

"You've been reading her diary?" said a shocked Cinderella.

You've been reading my diary? thought an angry Snow White.

Prince Charming nodded. "I thought her diary might contain clues on how to make her less… peculiar."

"And did it?"

"It did not."

"And what conclusions have you reached?"

"That she's meddlesome, insecure and not particularly hopeful about living happily ever after. But enough about her. You have stolen my heart, and yet I do not even know your name."

"I am Cinderella."

"But you can't be."

"Yet I am."

"No, really. Tell me your name!"

At that moment, the confusion was shattered by the sound of an alarm clock. Cinders jumped up and pulled the ringing clock from her pocket. "Oh, my! Is that the time? I must prepare tea for my sisters, otherwise they will have my guts for garters!"

"You cannot be thinking of leaving now, my love."

"But I must! For I need my guts."

"But I have only just found you!"

With that, Cinders was gone. And a faster runner I have never seen. Prince Charming stood up, then he leaned down and picked something up. It was one of her slippers.

Friday

When I woke up this morning, it occurred to me that things in the land had become a little tangled. My own Prince Charming had fallen for Cinderella, and had since been seen wandering forlornly with her slipper, mumbling about how he must find her. Meanwhile, Little Red Riding Hood's heart was set on Cinderella's original Prince Charming (when he finally shows up in a year and a bit), and Rumpelstiltskin was tied up in his tower, but for how long? He must have spat out the gold thread, because he had been heard shouting about how he's going to make me pay for my meddling – and we know how harsh he can be when it comes to payment. The Big Bad Wolf had been denied his Little Red supper, and he too was out for revenge. I sighed and thought, *at least Hansel and Gretel are happy.*

The dwarves had left for work, and I was about to begin my housework when someone knocked on the door. It was a messenger sent by my stepmother. He handed me a note that read: *You are invited to a cider tasting at the palace today at 12pm*. The invitation reminded me of my most pressing problem: the evil stepmother who is determined to poison me. I say the most pressing problem, because in my story she actually succeeds. And the idea of being poisoned with a sleeping sickness and then waking up to find that two-timing prince *kissing* me was worse than ever. I needed to come up with a plan to stop her. I paced up and down for a time. Then I sat on Not Particularly Hopeful's chair, and did not feel particularly hopeful about finding a solution. So I skipped across to Awkward's chair and fell straight off onto the carpet. Red-faced, I sat on Insecure's chair and felt that any solution would be beyond my feeble little mind. I was quite determined to stop my meddling when I sat on Meddlesome's chair. But it was upon that very chair that the solution came to me! I jumped up, went into my room and stood before my mirror. I placed my hands on my hips and listened to its pronouncement. “Welcome back,” it said. “You are still, and without any shadow of a doubt, the fairest in the land.”

“You are so predictable,” I replied.

“Then why did you ask?” said the mirror.

“Ask? Did you see my lips move?”

“Well, no, but–”

“Well but nothing. And that's just the kind of mirror talk that's got me into so much trouble with my stepmother.” The mirror made no reply, and I supposed that had it shoulders, it would have shrugged them. I tried Cinderella's trick, and fluttered my eyelids. “Mirror, mirror on the wall, if I take you to see my evil stepmother, would you tell her *she* is the fairest in the land?”

“Go off message, you mean? No can do.”

“Would that be the opinion of all the mirrors in the land?”

“It would.”

“That's where you're wrong! I know of a mirror that's of the opinion that my stepmother is the fairest in the land. It belongs to Little Red's grandmother – or it did until the Big Bad Wolf ate her. And I don't suppose she really needs a mirror now that she's been digested.”

“What are getting at?” asked the mirror.

“It seems to me that all I have to do is swap Little Red's grandmother's mirror with my evil stepmother's mirror.”

“And what will that achieve?”

I didn't much like the tone of my mirror's voice. I placed my hands on my hips. “When Little Red's grandmother's mirror tells my stepmother that *she* is the fairest in the land, and not I, she will no longer want to poison me.”

“That's supposing she doesn't find you as annoying as ever. Which is supposing a lot.”

“She might,” said I, “but not *so* annoying that her every waking moment is spent trying to poison me.”

“I have known you a long time,” said the mirror, “and speaking from experience, I wouldn't be so sure.”

I'd had quite enough aggravation from a reflective surface for one morning, and set off to find Little Red. I wanted to ask her if I could borrow her grandmother's mirror, indefinitely.

It was a nice day, so I decided that rather than whistle for Barry, I would look for Little Red under my own steam (that's to say, I would walk perfectly normally, not impersonate a train). And so off I went in the general direction of her fairytale story, and her grandmother's cottage, and the mirror I sought therein. I hadn't gone far when I came upon a pile of straw that had once been a house. A set of trotter prints led away from it, and close to these I discovered the paw prints of a large wolf. *Oh my*, thought I. *I hope the little pig got away*. I followed the trotter and wolf prints, and soon came upon an enormous pile of sticks. It too had been a house once, before someone had knocked it down. The pig prints went through where once a front door might have been, and so too did the wolf's. I feared the worst for the poor pig, who must have imagined itself safe inside its house of sticks. But then I spotted more trotter prints! It appeared that *two* little pigs had been chased into the woods by one wolf. *Oh my*, thought I. *I hope the two little pigs got away*. I followed the prints, and not long after came upon a pile of bricks that had once been a house. And beside the pile of bricks was a crane with a wrecking ball attached. I'm no Sherlock Holmes, but a pattern was emerging. I was about to look for the prints of two little pigs and a wolf, when I heard Little Red's voice above me. "The Big Bad Wolf has taken them," said she, mournfully. I looked up and saw Little Red sitting on a branch. She was holding her own copy of *the book*.

"The Big Bad Wolf has them?" said I. "The very same Big Bad Wolf who wanted to gobble you up?"

"The very same," said she.

"The very same Big Bad Wolf who I wanted to take me on a date?"

"That would be him, yes."

"And he has *both* little pigs?"

Little Red shook her head. "I'm afraid he has all three of them."

"*Three*? Are you sure?"

Little Red tapped *the book* with her fingers. "It even says as much in their story."

“What's their story called?”

“The *Three Little Pigs*.”

“I see. And the story doesn't end well for them?”

“It did end well, once upon a time. The three little pigs were supposed to be safe inside their house of brick.” Little Red opened the book and read the following: “And the wolf came upon the house of bricks and said, *By the hair on my chinny-chin-chin, I'll huff and I'll puff and I'll blow your house in!*” Little Red stopped reading. She peered down at me and said, “According to the story, the wolf's huff and puff wasn't strong enough to knock this house down.”

I looked at the crane and wrecking ball. “And there's no mention of the wolf using a wrecking ball?”

Little Red closed the book. “None whatsoever. And as I said, the three little pigs were supposed to be safe inside there.”

“So what changed?”

Little Red shuffled a little on her branch, and made herself more comfortable. “I watched the Big Bad Wolf erect his crane and wrecking ball in secret. And as he did so, I heard him say the following to himself, 'What is good for the goose, is also good for the gander.'” Little Red pointed a finger at me. “I think *you* are the goose he was talking about.”

“*I'm* the goose?” said I, looking over my shoulder and half expecting to see a goose. “What does that mean?”

“That the Big Bad Wolf is of the opinion that if *you* can change stories willy-nilly, then so can *he*.”

"Willy-*nilly*? I take exception to that. I haven't changed a single story willy-nilly. I've considered all my changes very carefully."

"That's not the way the Big Bad Wolf sees it."

"So what's to become of the three little pigs now?"

"The Big Bad Wolf is going to have them for supper."

"All of them?"

"Yes. As he carried the little pigs off, he explained to them how erecting this crane had left him famished."

"It's just too horrible! And it's all my fault."

Little Red nodded. "Look on the bright side: at least you saved me. And you know what they say: you can't make an omelette without breaking some eggs."

"You don't suppose that the Big Bad Wolf will change his mind, and make an omelette for his supper instead?" said I, grasping at straws.

"I'm afraid not. His heart is set on sausages. Of the pork variety."

"I won't allow it!" I looked up at Little Red, and she was pointing somewhere. "I somehow thought you wouldn't allow it," said she. "You should know that he's taken the little pigs to my grandmother's cottage. And it's that way."

"How very convenient," said I.

"It is?"

“Yes. And it reminds me: would you have any objections to my taking your grandmother's mirror?”

“Her mirror?”

“The one in the hallway of her cottage.”

“You have saved my bacon. *And* promised me Cinderella's Prince Charming. So by all means take it. But what do you want with that old mirror?”

“It is the only one that does not think me the fairest in the land. In fact, it's very rude about my appearance every time I look in it. And that's why I must have it.”

“And I thought *I* had issues,” said Little Red, swinging her legs.

“It seems that everyone has them,” said I. Little Red agreed, and I walked off in the direction of her grandmother's cottage.

I approached the cottage with caution, and tiptoed up to the kitchen window. Inside, the three little pigs were sitting at a table. They might have been waiting for their mother to serve them supper, but for these clues to the contrary: an apple had been stuffed in each of their mouths, they were tied up with string, and wrapped in baking foil. I thought, *What does a little pig have to do to get a break in this land*?

The front door to the cottage was open, and I crept into the hallway. As I tiptoed past the mirror I'd come to find, it said, “You're even uglier than I remember. And stupider.”

“I am not stupider,” whispered I.

“You are stupider. Case in point: the last time you were here you weren't tiptoeing about for no reason like a stupider person."

"But I have a reason. I'm on my way to rescue the little pigs."

"And is that the only reason you've come back?"

"Now you mention it, no it isn't. I've come for you."

"I see. So now you've added *thief* to your list of issues. Tut, tut, tut."

"How *dare* you tut me thrice! Little Red said I can have you."

"Why would she?" said the mirror.

"As a thank-you, for saving her from the Big Bad Wolf. What have you to say to that?"

"That your meddling has placed the three little pigs in grave danger."

"Precisely. And it's my intention to rescue them. Why did you *think* I was tiptoeing towards the kitchen?"

"I imagined that one so plump must tiptoe towards a lot of kitchens."

The mirror's observation was one I could not argue with. So instead I nodded and said, "I'm going to save the three little pigs now."

"Then you'd better get a move on, the Big Bad Wolf is due back any minute."

I stood straight and spoke up. “You mean to tell me the wolf isn't even here?”

“That's right. He's gone to market to get herbs and stuffing.”

“You might have told me that earlier. There's obviously no time to lose, then.” I grabbed the mirror and ran to the kitchen with it under my arm. I removed the apples from their piggy mouths, and all three said how they'd much prefer being rescued to being digested. They said they simply couldn't understand it, that according to *the book* they were supposed to be safe inside their house of brick. I told them that I *might* have had something to do with their story being changed. And from under my arm, the mirror piped up and said, “That's what's known as an understatement.” It also said that they should take a long hard look at me, and when they asked the mirror why they should do so, the mirror said so that they could avoid me in future. As the three little pigs scampered into the woods, the mirror said that I was by far the most repulsive creature ever to be reflected in its glass. “Where are you taking me?” it added peevishly.

I'm going to take you somewhere where your opinion of me might actually be useful.”

“And where might that be?”

“My stepmother's palace.”

The Found Diary of Orange Orange

The very next morning, I set out on foot with the mirror under my arm. It was wrapped in a black cloth and, covered thus, the mirrors of the land have much in common with parrots in covered cages: they too stop chattering and remain silent when hidden. I had not gone far when I came upon a little girl in a blue dress. She was sitting in the shade of a tree and eating from a bowl with a wooden spoon. I went straight over to her and said, "That smells nice. What is it?"

"Curds and whey," said she, licking her spoon.

"What does it taste like?"

The little girl scooped up another mouthful of curds and whey and began to eat it. "It tastes… cheesy," said she, thoughtfully.

"I like cheese. What's your name?"

"Little Miss Muffet. And you are?"

"Snow White."

"The fairest in the land?" she murmured between swallows.

I shook my head, put down the mirror, and folded my arms. "As tasty as that dish doubtless is, it's obviously done nothing for your eyesight. I suggest you add carrot to it in the future."

She wrinkled up her nose and said, "Add carrots to *cheese*?"

"Yes."

"And make what, exactly?"

"I'm rather partial to cake myself."

"Make *cheese* cake?" said she, wincing. "Sounds horrible. What have you got there?" she asked, pointing to the mirror wrapped in a cloth under my arm.

"It's a mirror. Not just any mirror, but the only mirror in the land that doesn't think me the fairest of them all."

"I expect you're off to smash it, then."

"Goodness gracious me, no. I'm going to give it to my evil stepmother as a present."

Little Miss Muffet nodded, then lowered her voice and said, "I've heard about you, you know, Snow."

"About me? What have you heard?"

Little Miss Muffet looked left and right, checking that we were alone. "Well," said she, "I have heard through the grapevine that you've been... how can I put this? Rather meddlesome."

"I cannot deny it. But I have only tried to do right by others," said I, proudly.

Little Miss Muffet dropped her voice to a whisper. "That's

not all I've heard about you through the grapevine."

"It isn't?"

"No. According to the grapevine, you've made enemies of the Big Bad Wolf *and* Rumpelstiltskin."

I nodded. "But you know what they say: you can't make an omelette without breaking some eggs."

"I believe they do say that, yes. Aren't you worried about being alone? Out here in the woods, I mean."

"Well, I wasn't…" I felt a shiver run down my spine, then heard it land with a crunch upon the dry leaves and scurry off into the undergrowth.

"Perhaps you should consider a disguise," said Little Miss Muffet helpfully.

"I think perhaps you're right," said I. "Any ideas?"

She put down her bowl and pointed at her face with both of her forefingers.

"You're offering me your *face*?" said I.

"You must have noticed it."

"Noticed it? I've spent the last few minutes talking to it."

"Not my face. My tan."

"Oh. Yes. Have you never thought of spending more time in the shade? Only, sunshine can be horrid to the skin."

"It's fake."

"The sun's fake?"

"My tan's fake."

"Really? How's that possible?"

Little Miss Muffet reached into her pocket and pulled out a small tube. "Thanks to the powerful magic inside here."

"Whatever is it?"

"It's called fake tan, and it comes from a land called *Essex*."

"Essex? I don't believe I've heard of it."

"They absolutely swear by it there," she said, handing it up to me.

I looked closely at the tube, and read the warning printed on its side: *For medium to dark skin only.*

Little Miss Muffet observed the expression on my face. "What's the matter?" she asked.

"I think you'll find the clue to the matter is in my name. I'm so pale that I can be seen from space most nights."

She nodded as though she'd read my first diary. "All the better to disguise yourself with, then," she pointed out.

"I suppose drastic times call for drastic measures," said I, unscrewing the lid. "How should I apply it?"

"Liberally," said she.

"Liberally?" said I.

"Use the whole tube."

“If you think it best.” With the contents of the tube relocated to my face, I pulled the cover from the mirror with a flourish, and picked it up. “Oh, my,” said I, gazing at my reflection. I turned my head this way and that, and that way and this, but it mattered not how I turned my head; the result was the same: I was orange. So orange, in fact, that I looked nothing like my former self – a point reinforced by the mirror, which enquired, “Who are you? And what have you done with Snow White?”

I was about to explain that it was I, when Little Miss Muffet cleared her throat as though it contained an obstruction of considerable size. I looked down at her to see if she needed me to perform the Heimlich manoeuvre. If you've never heard of the Heimlich manoeuvre, it involves grabbing a person from behind and squeezing them until their blockage pops out. But far from needing this manoeuvre, her eyes were narrowed and she looked rather confident. She pressed a finger to her lips, and either she had something in her eye or she was winking and trying to tell me something.

“Oh!” said I, as the penny dropped. *She thinks it a good idea to keep my true identity a secret from the mirror. I've made so many enemies of late that I quite agree.*

“Answer my question. Who are you and what have you done with Snow White?” asked the mirror again.

“Isn't it obvious who I am?” said I, playing for time. “If not Snow White, then I can only be…” I looked at my reflection and hoped for some inspiration. Only one word came to mind, so I thought it best to say it twice. “…Orange Orange.”

“Orange Orange? I've never heard of you,” said the mirror.

“She's a new character,” said Little Miss Muffet helpfully.

"Where *exactly* did you come from?" the mirror asked me suspiciously.

"From inside here," said I, holding up the emptied tube of fake tan.

"And where's Snow White?"

"She's inside the tube," said Little Miss Muffet. "Orange Orange is Snow White's cousin, and…"

"And?" pressed the mirror.

"And they're on an exchange programme," said Little Miss Muffet.

"Really?" said the mirror.

"Yes, spending time inside this tube has been at the top of Snow White's bucket list for years," said I.

"I always did think her peculiar. What is she doing in there?" asked the mirror.

"Very little, I should imagine," said I. I put down the mirror and covered it again, thereby rendering it deaf and silent. "Thank you for being such a help, Little Miss Muffet."

"That's quite alright."

"Is there anything I might do for you in return?"

"Actually, now you ask… I'm rather worried."

"You *are*?"

"You sound surprised, Snow. I mean, Orange."

"If I sound surprised it's only because, in all my wanderings, I don't think I've ever come across a more confident character. What is it? Whatever is the matter?"

"Well, the thing is, I've been sitting here and eating curds and whey for a long time…"

"How long, exactly?"

"For as long as I can remember."

"Oh. And?"

"And I have a horrible feeling something's going to happen. Something horrid."

"Like what?"

Little Miss Muffet shrugged, and her gaze fell to *the book* in my pocket. "I know it's against the rules to enquire about how one's own story ends, but…"

I looked left and right to check that nobody was around, then pulled *the book* from my pocket. "Rules schmules. It's not as though I haven't done this before," said I, flicking through its pages until I found Little Miss Muffet's nursery rhyme.

"That's what I'd heard. I wouldn't have dreamt of asking you otherwise," said she, hugging her knees to her chest.

"Here it is," said I, and I started to read her nursery rhyme to myself. It only had one verse, and while I read it she waited patiently. I closed the book and put it back in my pocket. "What... ah, what's the worst thing you can imagine?" I asked.

Little Miss Muffet shuddered so hard that she rustled the

leaves of the tree against which she was sitting. Her eyes opened wide and she said, “Please. *Please*. Tell me it's not a spider.”

“Alright. It's not a spider,” said I, looking up into the tree and trying to spot the spider that planned to come and sit down beside her. Little Miss Muffet gulped. “It *is* a spider, isn't it?”

Was a spider, thought I, reaching up for the closest branch and pulling myself up.

Two branches higher up, I came face to face with the spider in question. It stretched four of its eight legs and said, “Get out of my tree. You're in my way.”

“What are you going to do?” I asked.

“Climb down and sit beside her. What else?”

“You can't.”

“Why not?”

“Because you'll frighten her.”

“So you *can* read. I'm surprised.”

“How rude.”

“Who are you? And what are you doing on this branch?”

“Don't you recognise me? I'm none other than Sn-ot… Orange Orange.”

“Snot Orange Orange? What a ridiculous name. It suits you.”

“It's *just* Orange Orange.”

From below, Little Miss Muffet called up, “What's going on? Who are you talking to?”

“No one,” replied I, chirpily.

“*No* one?” said she, suspiciously.

“Just to myself.”

“Do you climb up trees and talk to yourself often?”

“Yes.”

“But why?”

“On account of my many issues.”

“Oh, right. I've heard about your issues.”

“Have you? From who?”

“The grapevine.”

“And what else did the grapevine say about me?”

“That you're insecure, meddlesome, inconsolable, awkward, and not particularly hopeful about living happily ever after with Prince Charming.”

“The grapevine is awfully well informed,” said I.

“Well, it *is* the grapevine.”

The spider stretched its other four legs and said, “I'm sorry to interrupt your little tête-a-tête, but you need to go away so I can climb down and get on with my job.”

“If you ask me, you have a horrid job.”

“Nobody asked you.”

“I think you should find another job.”

The spider sighed. “I have thought about it. After all, it's not as though the prospects for promotion are good in this line of work. All I do is drop down and sit beside her.” The spider checked the ends of two of its legs, as though it had fingernails and wanted to check them for dirt, then continued, “It's not like she's even going to hang around for a chat.”

“That's because Little Miss Muffet is *petrified* of spiders.”

“And how does she think that makes me feel?”

“I don't suppose she'll be thinking much about your feelings, not while she's running away and screaming.”

“Rub it in, why don't you? The last girl I had a crush on ran in front of a herd of charging elephants. I was only chasing her because I wanted to tell her how beautiful she was.”

“I'm very sorry to hear that.”

“You should be. It wasn't exactly the crush I had in mind.”

“Are you *sure* you're not talking to a spider up there?” asked Little Miss Muffet.

“Quite sure. I'll be down presently,” said I, turning my attention back to the spider. “Look,” I told it, “I'm on my way to visit the queen.”

“No you're not. You're sitting in my tree.”

“I will be presently. How about this? I'll hide you under that blanket down there."

"What's under it?"

"A gift for the queen. A mirror. When we arrive at the palace, I'll set you free. It's a big palace and you'll find lots of job opportunities there."

The spider shook its head.

"Do you have a better idea?"

"Maybe… just maybe."

"Maybe what? Spit it out, spider."

"If truth be told," said it, bouncing a little on its web, "I've been sitting above Little Miss Muffet in this tree for as long as I can remember, and…"

"And?"

"I've grown rather fond of her."

I shook my head. "I'm very sorry, but if you want me to arrange a date for you with Little Miss Muffet, I think it quite out of the question."

"Why?"

"I should have thought it obvious."

"Not to me."

"I'm no expert in dating, trust me, but even I can see it's not possible to date someone while they're running away and screaming."

“Maybe if you introduced me, she wouldn't run away.”

“Introduce you?”

“Yes. As a long-lost relative.”

“A long-lost relative with eight legs who just *happened* to be up in this tree?”

“Stranger things have happened.”

“True. But not a whole lot stranger, if I'm honest.”

I have to admit, I had my doubts at first. But once I'd explained to Little Miss Muffet that the spider was an eight-legged uncle of mine, and that he'd keep his distance for as long as she wanted, she agreed to meet him. I said my goodbyes to both and, once a good distance away, I turned to see that all was well. And indeed it was. The spider must have told Little Miss Muffet a very funny joke, for she was laughing so much she had to wipe the tears from her eyes. I got the impression that the spider could be quite the little charmer. And so it was that I continued my journey to my evil stepmother's palace disguised as Orange Orange, the mirror tucked firmly under my arm.

A little later that day…

As I said in my previous diary, my evil stepmother's palace is very large and her butler very small – about the same height as a miniature poodle. I knocked on the door for what felt like an age before he finally opened it. "Yes?" said he, gazing up at me like I was a complete stranger.

"I have come with a gift for the queen," said I, and indicated the covered mirror with a pointed finger.

"Is her Royal Highness expecting you?"

"Not as such, but she's going to love her present," said I, attempting to brush past him. In this he expertly thwarted my every attempt, and pretty soon it began to feel as though we were out on a date, dancing. I stopped trying and, after he'd complimented me on my ballroom skills, he said, "Wait here while I go and see if the queen's available. Whom shall I say is calling?"

"Orange Orange."

"Orange Orange? I've read *the book* many times, and I've never heard of you."

"I've never come across you in *the book* either. But that's hardly the point."

"What is the point, Miss?"

"Beats me. Look, I'm Snow White's cousin."

"Snow *White's* cousin?"

"That's right. We're on an exchange programme."

At the very mention of Snow White, the butler grimaced and shuddered. "You'd better come in then," said he, stepping aside.

The butler lead me through the palace and out the other side to an apple orchard in the garden. It was there I came upon my stepmother picking apples and placing them in a basket. The butler cleared his throat to get her attention and said, "You have a visitor, Your Highness… may I present Orange Orange."

My stepmother turned and beheld me. For a moment, I imagined she could see through my orange deception, but then she almost smiled and said, "Have we met?"

I curtseyed and said, "No, Your Highness."

"You look familiar."

"I am Snow White's cousin."

"I've never knew she had a cousin."

"I'm a new character."

"I see. And what have you got there?"

"It's a gift for you."

"For me? You shouldn't have," said she, extending a hand. I removed the cover from the mirror and handed it to her. The mirror, that is. Not the cover. The cover I handed to the butler (well, I say handed, but it covered him completely). As she held it up and looked into it, I said, "Its opinions are the most up-to-date in all the land, Your Majesty."

"The most up-to-date in all the land, you say?"

"I do say. Maybe you have a question you'd like to ask it?"

My stepmother tossed her head so that her pretty black curls fell about her face. "Mirror, mirror, soon to be on my wall, who is the fairest of them all?"

"You are," replied the mirror.

"*Me*? But what about Snow White?"

To this, the mirror produced a strangulated mew, like it was about to projectile-vomit all over the orchard. Then, through gasps, it said, "What about Snow White?"

"Is *she* not considered the fairest in the land?"

"By *whom,* Your Majesty? The no-eyed, no-brained toad that sells curds and whey at the enchanted pond?"

I must admit that on this point, I found myself nodding in agreement with the mirror.

My stepmother looked at me and said, "Where is she? Where is Snow White?" Her eyes narrowed. "Has she left the land?"

"No. How could she? It's not possible to leave it."

"She's lying. They're on an exchange programme," said the mirror helpfully.

"So where *is* Snow White?"

"She's inside the empty tube that Orange Orange has hidden inside her pocket, Your Highness."

"Give it to me," said she, snapping her fingers at me.

"Give what to you, Your Highness?"

"You know very well. The tube! The tube in your pocket."

"What? *This* tube?" said I, taking it from my pocket and handing it to her.

My stepmother snatched it from my grasp and held it before the mirror. "Snow White is inside of *here*? Are you sure?"

"Orange Orange told me so herself," said the mirror. My stepmother examined the empty tube of fake tan closely. "The land inside it must be very *small.* Smaller even than Lilliput. What's she doing in there?"

"Very little, I should imagine," said the mirror, repeating what I'd told it in the woods.

"What are you going to do?" said I, clasping my cheeks in mock horror.

My evil stepmother chose to answer my question with actions rather than words. She dropped the tube upon the ground, and giggled as she stamped it into oblivion.

Tuesday

This morning, when I sat before my mirror and asked it, "Mirror, mirror on the wall, who is the fairest of them all?" and it replied "Not you, that's for sure," it felt as though a great weight had been lifted from my shoulders – so much so that I felt able to shrug properly for the first time in ages. "Something wrong with your shoulders?" asked my mirror.

"Why do you ask?" said I.

"They appear to be trying to swallow your head. Maybe they're confusing it with an actual orange. Easily done, I suppose."

"I suppose," said I, standing up.

I was determined that nothing would ruin my good spirits. Emboldened thus, I went out onto the porch, handed each dwarf his pick-axe and lunch box, and waved them off to work. Earlier during breakfast, they'd looked terribly downcast, and had spoken hardly a word to Snow White's cousin and replacement, Orange Orange. Not Particularly Hopeful said he'd *never* been particularly hopeful about Snow White outwitting her stepmother forever. Meddlesome raised a glass of milk by way of a toast, and said he was bursting with pride for Snow. "Some might call it meddling," said he, "but she only ever tried to help others." Awkward blew his nose into his hanky, and then rubbed snot into his eyes as he wiped away his tears. Blinking thus, he stumbled over a footstool and landed in a heap, sobbing. Insecure had been almost as inconsolable as Inconsolable, who had curled up into a wet little ball of misery. But, for the time being at least, I was resolved to follow Little Miss Muffet's advice and tell no one of my orange deception – except for the little lamb who skips past my cottage every morning. For the little lamb is famous throughout the land for keeping secrets.

Outside on the porch, I looked to my right and fully expected to see the little fellow hop, skip and jump out of the forest. Not a peep. “How strange,” said I to myself, “I have never known the little lamb to be late. He's just not written that way. Always on the move and quite unable to slow down.” There was much that I wanted to tell the clever little fellow: for instance, how I'd used my disguise to outwit my evil stepmother, and how she believed me crushed underfoot in her apple orchard. And how, now that she no longer needed apples to poison me, her orchard was being replaced by a croquet lawn. I was keen to tell the little lamb that news of my demise had been spread by the grapevine throughout the land (for once it seemed that the grapevine had got its facts wrong). *Maybe the grapevine isn't so reliable after all?* I thought. I was desperate to tell the little lamb that my Prince Charming wasn't so charming after all. About how easily he'd fallen for Cinderella's fluttering eyelids, and how he'd read my diary and thought me peculiar. It was then that I heard a rustling in the undergrowth, and hoped to see the little lamb pop out of it. But alas, it wasn't the little lamb, but Barry the boar. So downcast was Barry that he didn't even notice me.

“Whatever is the matter?” said I.

At the sound of my voice, Barry practically jumped out of his skin. “*Snow*?” said he, expectantly. But when he beheld my orangeness, his snout fell into the dirt.

“Barry? What's the matter?”

“For one happy moment, I thought you were Snow White.

But how could you be?"

"But I–" I bit my lip.

"Poor, *poor* Snow. Her evil stepmother finally got the better of her."

"But I–" I bit both my lips.

Barry gazed up at me. "You must be Orange Orange. I heard about you through the grapevine. Although the grapevine never mentioned that your mouth tries to swallow itself whenever you speak."

I unfurled my lips. "I had no idea you cared so much for Snow White, Barry."

"Being a new character, I don't suppose you know much about anything. Not even where I'm going."

"Where are you going?"

"To Snow's funeral."

"Her funeral?"

"That's right. They're burying the tube she was in when... well, when she had her *accident*…"

"You must be the only person who's going. Thank you, Barry."

Barry shook his head. "Shows how much you know. Why are you thanking me, anyway?"

"Snow *was* my cousin. And I'm going with you," said I, climbing onto Barry's back.

In a clearing, not far from the enchanted lake, we came upon a gathering of people. Just about everyone I'd ever met was there. Even the dwarves had taken the morning off work, and the dwarves *never* took time off. Little Red stood beside them looking downcast under her bonnet, and next to her stood Cinderella with my Prince Charming. They held hands as though they were on a date. Cinders was crying, and every time my prince leaned in close to offer a comforting word, she fluttered her eyelids and splashed him with her tears. Thelma Mavis Doodlebug was there with her baby, its poop-filled nappy made from the Panocci dress that Cinders had swapped with her. You may remember that the dress had belonged to one of Cinderella's sisters, and how Cinders had borrowed it to meet my Prince Charming. She hadn't been able to return it, and that explained why her sisters had turned up wearing her guts for garters.

Even though she knew about my Orange deception, Little Miss Muffet had come along with her new best friend the spider. The trees were filled with the songbirds who helped me with my chores every morning, and although such a thing should not be possible, their chirping sounded miserable. Hansel was there with Gretel, and poor Gretel's eyes were puffy from crying. Of all people, the Big Bad Wolf was there, and he alone was smiling. As far as I could tell, the only people who weren't there were Rumpelstiltskin and the little lamb who hops past by my cottage. Rumpelstiltskin made sense, but what had become of the little lamb?

They had all gathered around a hole in the ground (well, I say a hole, but it was more of a scraping just large enough for a squashed tube of fake tan). Out of the woods came a skunk harnessed to a tiny carriage, and upon the carriage, wearing a top hat and holding the reins, was my evil stepmother's butler. Walking behind, towering above the carriage, was none other than my evil stepmother. She was dressed in black with a black veil, sobbing and clutching a hanky to her veiled nose. I looked at the gathering, and hoped to see scorn and disbelief upon their faces. But Cinderella alone amongst them had the look of someone who wanted to bop a fake mourner on her nose. The butler climbed down off the tiny carriage, and placed the squashed tube (and I have never seen anything flatter) upon the backs of four baby mice. They were the pallbearers and they bore the pall (or in this case the flattened tube) about half a foot to its final resting place. They dropped it in, spun about, and used their back paws to kick dirt all over it. My evil stepmother, apparently overcome with grief, collapsed to her knees and placed an apple upon the little mound of dirt. I realised my hands had balled into fists, and the sight of that apple, doubtless the first from her orchard that hadn't been poisoned, was too much to bear!

I stepped forward, picked it up, and was about to bite into it when my stepmother wrestled me to the ground. "Don't eat it, Orange!" said she. "It is the last apple from my orchard and it is poisoned!" A sigh rose from the crowd as she helped me to my feet.

"*Poisoned*?" said I, making my point like a lawyer in court room. "But why ever are the apples in your orchard poisoned?"

"To kill slugs and termites," said she, checking her black nail polish for imaginary blemishes. "Why else?"

I placed my hands on my hips. "To poison slugs, was it?"

"Yes, that's right. And termites."

"So you haven't been trying to poison *Snow White* with

apple-based dishes for years?"

"How could you say such a thing?" She pressed her hanky to her veiled face and blew her nose (into her veil). As she sobbed, she mumbled something about how Snow had always been her favourite stepdaughter.

"Snow was your only stepdaughter," I pointed out.

"And so beautiful!" sobbed my stepmother.

I had a hunch and, stepping up on tiptoes, I pulled her veil from her face to reveal a smile that not only covered it but overflowed from its edges. "Something amuses you?" said I.

Her smile vanished so fast that it practically pulled her face inside out. "Beauty can be such a curse," said she, pulling out a compact and gazing into it. "Compact, compact in my hand, who is the fairest in the land?"

"You are," said the compact. She snapped it closed.

"Happy now?" said I.

She turned her gaze upon me. "Count your blessings," said she.

"My blessings?"

"Yes. That you resemble a mutated orange."

Later that day…

Later that day, I returned to my cottage only to find a note stuck to the door with a dagger. It read: *I have the little lamb that hops, skips and jumps past your cottage every morning.*

"And!?" said I.

And, the note went on, *unless you bring me Thelma Mavis Doodlebug's first-born child, I'm going to make a hotpot for my supper. I presume you get my meaning?*"

"I do!"

Good, said the note. It was signed *Rumpelstiltskin*.

I tore it from the door. "But why have you chosen me to bring the baby?"

PS, said the note. *Because as Snow White's closest relative, you're answerable for her crimes*."

"What crimes?"

Her meddling!

"What a conundrum!" exclaimed I. If you're wondering what a conundrum is, it's like a problem with knobs on. I reasoned that I could hardly let that horrid little imp make a hotpot out of the little lamb, no matter how tasty. And neither could I take him Thelma Mavis Doodlebug's baby. I sat down on the porch and placed my head in my palms. *If only the little lamb were here, he'd know what to do*, thought I.

It was then that a little hedgehog walked from the undergrowth and said, “You know what *They* say, don't you?”

“Yes, that you can't make an omelette without breaking some eggs. But how is that useful in this situation?”

“It isn't,” said the little hedgehog, scratching its ear.

“Then why bring it up?”

“Because that's not the only thing They say.”

“It isn't? What else do They say?”

“Lots of things. In fact, there's nothing They don't know.”

“You mean, They might have the answer to my conundrum?”

“Of course They will.”

I stood up. “Any idea where I might find They? I mean, Them?”

“Not exactly. All I know about They is that They live in the Forest of All Knowledge.”

“And is it far?”

“Not as the crow flies, no.”

“What about as the Orange rolls?”

“The Orange would do well to hitch a ride on the crow.”

I gazed up at the sky and placed a hand over my eyes to shield them from the sun. “I haven't seen the crow in ages.”

"Maybe so, but he's easy to summon. All you need to do is trot up and down on the spot, flap your arms so that your elbows knock against your sides, and squawk like a two-headed chicken."

"And why will that summon the crow?"

"Beats me. It's a conundrum. If you find Them you can ask Them."

"I will. And thank you, little hedgehog," said I, trotting up and down on the spot, flapping my arms and squawking like a two-headed chicken.

"Only too pleased to help," said he, continuing on his journey.

I was engaged in summoning the crow thus, when I heard Barry the boar 'whistling.' Barry trotted from the undergrowth, and when he saw me, he stopped *dead* in his tracks and said, "Have you ever considered therapy, Orange?"

Already a little out of breath, I said, "You are mistaken, Barry, for I am not bonkers."

"Having issues is nothing to be ashamed of. They obviously run in the family."

"Whatever do you mean?" said I, trotting and flapping on the spot for all I was worth.

"That your cousin Snow had her fair share of issues, too."

I added a nod to my trot and flap. "You're not wrong there, Barry. But you really are mistaken, for I am engaged in summoning the crow."

“That's not how you summon the crow,” said Barry.

“I think you'll find that it is…”

“I think you'll find that's how you summon the men in white coats.”

I was about to argue the point when two men in white coats emerged from the forest, one holding a syringe and the other a straitjacket. “Somebody summon us?” said the one with the syringe.

“No. It's a false alarm,” said Barry. “She's trying to summon the crow.”

“Oh,” said the man with the straitjacket. “You must have met the little hedgehog.”

I stopped nodding, trotting and flapping and stood quite still. “He was here just a minute ago,” said I, craning my neck in the direction he'd gone.

“That little hedgehog is quite the practical joker,” said the man with the straitjacket.

“Was he also lying about They?” I asked.

“What about They?” said Barry.

“The little hedgehog said that They live in the Forest of All Knowledge. And that They have the answers to any conundrum.”

“If you have a conundrum, you'd better jump on, Orange, and I'll take you to see Them.”

The Forest of All Knowledge was full of whispering trees,

and no matter how hard I tried to listen, it was impossible to hear what they were saying. We came upon They fishing in a little brook. As it turned out, They was a groundhog called Frank.

Frank cast his fishing line and said, "I knew you were coming. There's actually not a lot I don't know about anything."

I climbed off Barry and said, "Where are the others?"

"There are no others. I am They," said Frank, twirling his whiskers.

"What? *All* of them?"

"Every single one."

"But you *can't* be They," said I.

"And why not?"

"I should have thought that obvious. *They* is plural. It means *more* than one."

"Think about it," said Frank. "If I called myself I, then people would sound like English gentlemen every time they quoted me. For example, *I say, you can't make an omelette without breaking some eggs*. Or, *I say, good things come to those who wait*. Or, *I say, you should never count your chickens before they're hatched.* Need I go on?"

I sat down on a tree trunk beside Frank and scratched my head. "I do see your point."

"Good. I presume you haven't just come to point out that I'm singular?"

"Indeed, I have not. Something terrible has happened, and it has given me a conundrum. I was hoping you might be able to solve it." I explained to Frank how Rumpelstiltskin had kidnapped the little lamb, and how he was going to turn him into a hotpot unless I brought him Thelma's baby. Once I'd explained all, Frank said, "You know what They say, don't you?"

"What do you say?"

"That you can lead a horse to water but you can't make it drink."

"Is that useful?"

"Not particularly. But luckily for you, I'm only just getting warmed up."

"Pleased to hear it."

"You've met the little hedgehog, also known as Mr Wind-Up?"

"Indeed I have. He wound me up so much that he had me summon the men in white coats. It's a good thing Barry was there, or they would have locked me away somewhere horrid. What of the little hedgehog?"

"He's the answer to your conundrum," said Frank thoughtfully.

"I hope you're going to explain *how*."

"Alright. You're going to give the little hedgehog to Rumpelstiltskin."

"Why? Does Rumpel want him?"

"Of course not. That's why you must tell Rumpelstiltskin that the little hedgehog is Thelma's baby."

I sighed and shook my head. "He looks *nothing* like her baby. For starters, he's a lot more prickly."

"That's because he's a little hedgehog."

"Good to see you're coming round to my way of thinking."

"That's why you must ask Cinderella's fairy godmother for help."

I sat down on the ground, crossed my legs, and rested my heavy head in my palms. "I came here today thinking you were going to help *unravel* the confusion, but you seem intent only on adding more knots."

"I need you to bear with me, Orange."

"I'll try. But only if you jump to the part of your plan that's in some way helpful."

And that's precisely what Frank did when he said, "Cinderella's fairy godmother can cast a spell upon the little hedgehog, and make it the spitting image of Thelma's baby – at least until the clock strikes twelve. But that should give you plenty of time to exchange him for the little lamb."

"Oh! I see. And when the clock strikes twelve, I suppose the little hedgehog is going to turn into a pumpkin," said I, making what I considered to be quite a funny joke.

Apparently *They* have no sense of humour, for They (or to use Their correct name, Frank) shook his head and said, "No. When the clock strikes twelve, the little hedgehog will turn back into a little hedgehog."

"But why would the little hedgehog agree?"

"Because he'll grasp any opportunity to wind up Rumpelstiltskin. He isn't known as Mr Wind-Up for nothing. What's the matter?"

I considered my words very carefully and said, "The thing is, Frank…"

"There's a thing?"

"Indeed there is."

"Well, if there's a thing, you'd better tell me what it is."

"The thing is this: my cousin Snow *might* have upset Cinderella's fairy godmother. And, in a land such as this, a person's deeds are inherited by their closest relative. And that would be me."

"And what *might* your cousin Snow have done to upset her?"

"You obviously haven't spoken to the grapevine recently."

Frank shook his head. "Not since I heard through him that you should take everything They say with a pinch of salt. So? What has your cousin done?"

"She arranged for Cinderella to go on a date with *her* Prince Charming – Snow's Prince Charming, that is. And they really hit it off."

"And?"

"And that means that the whole thing with her turning a pumpkin into a carriage must be off now. I believe it was to be her fairy godmother's big moment."

Frank began to reel his fishing line in. "Don't worry," said he. "Before I fell out with the grapevine, I heard through him that Cinderella's fairy godmother is not one to hold a grudge."

"Oh, that's marvellous news!" said I, standing up. "However can I thank you, Frank?"

"Think nothing of it, for you know what They say."

"What do you say?"

"That kindness brings its own rewards."

"Can't say I've seen much evidence of that," murmured I, as I climbed back onto Barry's back.

Later that day …

I knew I had no time to lose, for if Rumpelstiltskin intended to turn the little lamb into a hotpot for his supper, he would start his cooking preparations early. I hightailed it over to Cinderella fairy godmother's place (or, more accurately, Barry hightailed it while I clung to his tusks for dear life). We came upon the fairy godmother sweeping her front porch. I say sweeping, but, in truth, her broom was doing all the work while she waved her wand about as though conducting an orchestra. Barry was panting when I climbed off him and said, "Thank goodness you're here, for I need your help!"

Cinderella's fairy godmother, who, from now on, I shall refer to as CFG as a labour-saving measure, rested her ample hands on her ample hips and said, "Do you now?"

"Yes, I do."

Rather than enquire what had vexed me so, she simply said, "Follow me, young lady." CFG moved her ample self off her porch, and headed around the back of her house and into her back yard. Once there, we came upon something large covered in a sheet. She removed the sheet to reveal the biggest pumpkin you've never seen.

"My, what a large pumpkin," said I. "It's easily as big as a..." I closed my mouth.

"You were saying?" said she, folding her arms and tapping her wand against her chin.

"It's easily as big as… well, as..."

"A carriage?"

I nodded.

"Do you have any idea how long it took me to grow this pumpkin?"

"A while, I suppose."

"For*ever*. And now, thanks to your meddling cousin introducing Cinderella to the *wrong* Prince Charming, I've absolutely no use for it." CFG frowned and, if truth be told, fairy godmothers are particularly difficult to make frown. And making one as grumpy as this was unheard of.

I cleared my throat and said, "If Snow were here, I imagine she would say how sorry she is for introducing Cinders to her Prince Charming. She might also say, were she here, that she only had Cinderella's best interests at heart."

"*Would* she now."

"Yes, she would. And that she acted out of good intentions."

"Well, you know what *They* say about good intentions, don't you?"

I shook my head. "I just saw Frank, and he didn't mention anything about that."

"Well, I'll mention it for him. They say that the road to hell is paved with good intentions."

"But whatever does that mean?"

"That meddling doesn't always turn out for the best. Which reminds me, why have you come to see me?"

"I need your help."

"That much I had gathered. This would be your opportunity to elaborate."

"Elaborate?"

"Tell me what has you so agitated, young lady."

"It's Rumpelstiltskin…"

"What about him?"

"He's kidnapped the little lamb that hops, skips and jumps past my cottage. And unless I take him the baby that Thelma Mavis Doodlebug promised him, he's going to turn the little lamb into a hotpot for his supper."

"Oh."

"I know."

"And what might I do about that?"

"*They* said you might turn the little hedgehog into a duplicate of Thelma's baby. And that I might exchange him for the little lamb."

"Is that what Frank said?"

"It is."

"I suppose They know best." CFG waved her magic wand and the little hedgehog appeared at her feet. "Fairy godmother," said it, doffing a top hat. "What can I do you for?" CFG pointed her wand at me, and the little hedgehog turned to face me.

"You look surprised to see me," said I.

"I am."

"And why is that?"

"I thought you'd be spending quality time with the men in white coats."

"Quality time? I think not. Thankfully, Barry explained to them that *you* were responsible for my on-the-spot trotting, arm-flapping and squawking like a two-headed chicken."

"Ah, well. Glad you see the funny side."

"Do I *look* like I see the funny side?"

The little hedgehog shrugged, placed his top hat back upon his head, and looking back and forth between CFG and myself, asked again what he could do us for.

"Rumpelstiltskin has the little lamb that hops, skips and jumps past Orange's cottage," said CFG.

"So?" said the little hedgehog.

"So this," said I. "He's planning on turning him into a hotpot."

The little hedgehog's reaction could be considered insensitive, for it leapt into the air, clicked its heels and said, "I *love* hotpot. *Please* tell me Rumpel has invited us all for supper?"

"No. He has not," said I, making fists and planting them firmly on my hips.

"What then?" asked the little hedgehog.

CFG extended her magic wand towards me and said, "Need you ask?"

The little hedgehog shook his head. "Meddling runs in the family, does it, Orange?"

"I prefer to call it having good intentions."

The little hedgehog scratched itself. "The road to hell is paved with good intentions," said he.

"I have been made aware of that possibility, yes."

"Then I suggest you let Rumpel enjoy his hotpot."

"I'll do nothing of the sort. You're going to help me save the little lamb *and* Thelma's baby."

"And why would I do that? What's in it for me?"

"An opportunity for the wind-up of the century," said CFG, waving her wand and turning the little hedgehog into a duplicate of Thelma's baby.

Not only was the little hedgehog the spitting image of Thelma's baby, but he was nestled in a lovely pram. Upon his little head was a bonnet, and in his mouth a dummy, which he spat out. "Ga! Ga!" he said, urgently.

"What's that?" I asked.

"GA! GA!"

"Saying the same thing, only in capitals, leaves me none the wiser, little man-hog."

"GA! GA! GA!"

"Similarly, neither does saying it thrice." I looked at CGF, who said that she *supposed* he'd need a larger vocabulary if he was to wind up Rumpelstiltskin. With that she waved her wand and "GA! GA!" became a string of words that have no place in a young woman's diary. So I have found no place for them.

Once the little hedgehog had calmed down, he asked for his dummy back. Not something I'd expected. I picked it up and handed it to him, one eyebrow raised. "It's comforting," said he, snatching it away. CFG pointed out that the time for supper was fast approaching and, with that, she waved her magic wand and transported the little man-hog and myself to Rumpel's tower.

As described in my previous diary, Rumpel's tower is tall and thin, and has vines growing all over it. At its top is a single room with a single window, out of which wafted the aroma of cooking. I gazed up at the window, and was relieved to see the little lamb appear… then disappear… then appear… then disappear… "Thank goodness we're not too late," said I.

The little man-hog removed the dummy from its mouth and said, "More's the pity. I'm famished." I snatched away his dummy and, before he had time to elaborate, I shoved it back into his mouth.

The tower contained a great many steps – one hundred and eighty-six, to be precise. All of these I had to navigate backwards while pulling the pram. Once at the top, I

knocked upon the door. The door had a great many locks, and while Rumpel turned a great many keys, I pulled the little man-hog from the pram and cradled it to my breast. I removed the dummy from its mouth and it said, "Like I told you downstairs, I'm hungry."
"Don't push it," said I. The door opened to reveal the horrid little imp and, beyond him, the little lamb jumping about at the window. I barely recognised the little lamb, for all his lovely wool had been plucked out. "How *dare* you pluck the little lamb that hops, skips and jumps past my cottage!"

"I do dare. Did you expected me to cook a woolly hotpot?" I gazed down at Rumpel, who was wearing a Panocci apron with the letter P all over it. He rose up on tiptoes and peered closely at the 'baby' in my arms. "You did it… you have brought what was promised me… what is rightfully mine. Now hand it over," said he, extending his grubby little hands.

"Don't do it, Orange!" cried the little lamb.

"But I must, otherwise he's going to turn you into a hotpot."

"A common fate for little lambs such as I," said the little lamb, philosophically.

"But you deserve better, my little friend."

"*Friend?*" bounced the little lamb. "But we've only just met. We haven't even been formally introduced." I folded my arms and looked down at Rumpel, who said, "Well, *excuse me* if not in the habit of introducing visitors to my dinner."

"He's not your dinner," said I, handing the little man-hog down to him.

"You can't!" bounced the little lamb. "Snow would never

approve!"

"It's done," said Rumpel. He held the little man-hog aloft, danced about his lome and added, "It would be a terrible shame to let all my herbs and stuffing go to waste!"

"We'd best be going," said I to the little lamb. The little lamb barely bounced past me, and refused to say even a single word as we descended the tower's many steps. Once we reached the bottom, I caught him mid-bounce and, holding him stationary with arms outstretched, I whispered, "Fear not! For I have not given Rumpel Thelma's baby!"

At first, the little lamb, who was not accustomed to being stationary while airborne, opened his eyes wide and looked towards the ground. He swallowed hard and said, "But I saw you."

"You only think you did. What I actually gave him was the little hedgehog, also known as Mr Wind-Up."

"How's that possible?" asked the little lamb, eyeing the ground.

"Thanks in no small part to Cinders's fairy godmother. Need I say more?" Had the little lamb features, I imagined he would have arranged them into a smile.

The next morning…

The next morning, I awoke with the feeling that all was well in the land. Yes, I was deluded, but They say ignorance is bliss. And having met Frank, I felt inclined to agree with him. However, my blissful ignorance was not to last long, for the grapevine slithered through my bedroom window and said, “I've come to do a background check.”

“On whom?”

“On you, Orange Orange.” In case you haven't heard much through the grapevine recently, he sounded much like a policeman conducting an interview with a criminal.

I sat up in bed, yawned and said, “A background check? On I? Whatever for?”

The grapevine sprouted a tentacle, and it hovered close to my face.

“Take a picture, why don't you?” said I to it.

“I like to get my facts straight before I spread them about.”

“*And?*” said I as the tentacle touched the tip of my nose, making me go boss-eyed.

“And I've never heard of you, Orange Orange.”

“That's because I'm a new character.”

“That's what I heard.”

“Through your*self*,” said I, stifling a chuckle.

“No. And therein lies the problem.”

“So who did you hear it through?”

“Little Miss Muffet.”

“Lovely girl. Crazy for curds and whey.”

“Quite so. She keeps the no-eyed, no-brained toad who sells curds and whey at the enchanted pond in business.”

“Does she now.”

“Yes. And if anybody asks, you can tell them you heard it through me.”

“Alright. Look, if Little Miss Muffet says I'm a new character, then her word ought to be enough.”

“Her word might have been enough, once upon a time, but...”

“But what?”

“She's been acting strangely lately.”

“How so?”

“For starters, she hasn't been spending all her days eating curds and whey.”

“A lifestyle improvement, if you ask me.”

“That isn't all. She's also spending more and more time away from her tree, and has become quite inseparable from the spider that was *supposed* to drop down and sit beside her.”

“They're friends now. What's wrong with that?”

“Spiders aren't supposed to have friends.”

“Oh, that's grim, even by the standard of the land.” I pushed the tentacle away. “I hope you're satisfied that I am who I say I am. I have chores to attend to now.”

“I suppose I'll have to be for the time being. But I'll be keeping an eye on you, Orange. Something about you smells fishy.”

I stifled a burp. “That would be the clams I had for supper. Oh! While you're here, I don't suppose you have any news of the woodcutter?”

“Woodcutter?”

“Yes, the one who was supposed to kill Snow but decided to let her go.”

“What's it to you?”

“I wanted to explain one or two things to him on Snow's behalf.”

“Regarding the woodcutter, the news is not good,” said the grapevine.

“Is the poor fellow alright?”

The tentacle that had hitherto been trying to peer up my left nostril pulled back and shook itself. “He's very worried about his son, Edward.”

“Has something happened to Edward?”

“As a punishment for not killing Snow White, the queen has taken Edward to be her slave, and is quite determined to work the poor boy to death."

"Is that in *the book*?"

"Of course not, but all sorts of strange changes have been taking place throughout the land of late. Due in no small way to that meddling cousin of yours."

I felt in some small way responsible for poor Edward's fate. After all, it had been entirely my fault. If only I'd accepted my own fate, been philosophical about it, and allowed the woodcutter to kill me, then his son Edward would have been spared his terrible fate. My conscience was eased a little when I remembered that letting me go had been written in *the book*. So whoever wrote *the book* ought to shoulder at least *some* of the blame.

During breakfast with the dwarves, I discussed my plan to rescue Edward. Not Particularly Hopeful said I should stop my meddling ways, for no good would ever come of them. At which Inconsolable burst into tears and pointed out that it had been Snow who had meddled so, not her cousin Orange. At which point, Meddlesome banged his fist upon the table and told Not Particularly Hopeful that *plenty* of good had come of Snow's meddling ways. Insecure said that it didn't matter either way, because I'd make a mess of whatever I decided to do. Awkward remained perfectly composed and perfectly still, surprising everyone present. After Not Particularly Hopeful had checked Awkward for a pulse, and had been surprised to find he still had one, I left. My destination? The front porch, where I whistled for Barry.

"Where can I take you, Orange?" said he.

"Snow's stepmother's palace."

"You sure that's such a good idea?"

"I have no choice, Barry. For it is there that I will find Edward."

"Edward?"

"The woodcutter's son. Thanks to Snow *and* the writer of *the book* for allowing his father to release her, poor Edward has been enslaved by the queen. And she is quite determined to work the poor boy to death."

"So what are you going to do?"

"I'm going to save him."

Barry produced a little squeal that sounded very much like a stifled sob.

"Whatever is the matter?" I asked.

"It's just you remind me of your cousin, Snow." Barry 'whistled,' kicked up some dirt with his hind legs, and we set off for my stepmother's palace.

After the debacle at the funeral, I felt certain I would not be welcome, so I told Barry to drop me off at the end of the drive and made my way on foot towards the palace through its beautiful grounds. I came upon a gardener, hard at work digging a hole. The man was toiling dreadfully, and I had no wish to startle him. I crept up and from behind a bush I whispered, "Would you, perchance, be the woodcutter's son, Edward?"

The gardener, who looked nothing like the woodcutter due to his bald head and pug-like face, wiped the sweat from his brow and said, "I thought I'd uprooted all the talking hedges." He climbed out of the hole and rubbed a crick in his neck. "It's a good thing you spoke to me and not the queen. She'd have had what's left of me for garters," said he, poised to drive his shovel into the bush's roots.

"Don't!" exclaimed I.

"Why not?"

"For you are mistaken. I am not a whispering bush."

"I know, you're a talking hedge. It's all the same to me."

"I am neither hedge nor bush," said I, poking my head above the hedge/bush. At the sight of me, the gardener stumbled back and fell in his hole, disappearing from sight. From the hole there came a low groan, like the sound of a gardener in pain. This was reassuring, as it seemed to me entirely appropriate. I tiptoed out from behind the hedge/bush and peered down at him. "I imagine you mistook me for an orange troll. Take heart, for it bodes well for your eyesight."

The gardener shook his shiny, pug-like head. "I thought you a mutant orange, something hideous that escaped from the orchard."

"That makes sense also. Need a hand?" I crouched down and extended mine into his hole.

"No, thank you," said he.

"So?" I pressed.

"So what?"

"Are you Edward, the woodcutter's son?"

At the mention of Edward's name, the gardener shuddered. “I'm not him. And every day I thank my lucky stars that I'm not.”

“So Edward hasn't been having the best of times, then?”

“You think I was toiling hard?”

I nodded heartily.

“This enormous hole? Nothing. A mere trifle when compared to what the queen makes Edward do every day.”

“Bad, then?”

“I'll say. She won't be satisfied until she's worked him to death.”

I cast my gaze about the beautiful gardens. “Then I must find him as soon as possible.”

“What good will that do?”

“I'm going to rescue him. Where is he?”

The gardener pulled a pocket watch from his waistcoat and observed its hands. “Twelve o'clock,” said he. “He'll be starting his afternoon session on the electricity wheel.”

“The electricity wheel?”

“Biggest wheel you've never seen. Provides electricity for the whole palace. Before Edward arrived, it was turned by eight oxen.”

I jumped up. “Where is it? You must point me in the general direction of the wheel! For I fear there may be no time to lose."

"It's that way," said the gardener, pointing.

Like his eyesight, the gardener's sense of direction was first-rate, and it was not long before I came upon the enormous wheel. It lay flat, close to the ground, and was easily the circumference of a house. I made my way around it and came upon a bare-chested young man, drenched in sweat and grasping a wooded handle. "Excuse me?" said I. "Are you Edward, the woodcutter's son?"

The young man paused mid-toil, and gazed at me over his bare shoulder. His hair was of the brightest gold, his eyes of the deepest blue, and his dimpled jaw of the squarest kind. What's more, his cheekbones were high and chiselled as though from marble, and... and… and that's when I passed out. From hunger, you understand. When I came round, I beheld the face as just described looming over me. "Do not attempt to speak, for you have suffered a nasty fall. You must drink some water," said he, pulling a canteen from his belt. He placed it to my lips and smiled. I must have been absolutely *famished,* for I passed out again. He splashed water on my face, and when my eyelids fluttered open he said, "Who are you? And what has brought you here?"

I cast my gaze over his sinewy torso, doubtless made so by all the toil he'd been forced to endure thanks to my wilful selfishness, and all I could think to do was apologise. "I am truly, *truly…*"

"Truly who?"

I shook my head and murmured, "Orange."

"Truly Orange. Your name is an apt one, but you shouldn't

be here. Don't you know that no one is permitted to speak with me?"

I was about to explain the confusion over my name, but he smiled again and I passed out again. When I came round for the second time, he asked if I had an underlying medical condition. I shook my head and requested that he not smile. "At least, not until I've had something to eat," said I, sitting up.

"It was from hunger that you fainted, then?"

"What else?"

"A problem easily rectified with my sandwich," said he, opening his lunch box and taking out the smallest sandwich I had never seen.

I beheld it and wondered if a single slice of bread, with nothing on it, could reasonably be described as a sandwich. "Is that *all* you have to sustain you?" said I.

"It is. But I will gladly give it to you, for it's clear that your need is greater."

I gazed at the enormous wheel that he had to turn, and then at the tiny 'sandwich' that must sustain him. "*You* must eat it."

"I have no need of it, for I was permitted a similar meal only last week," said he.

"Last week? What has a woodcutter's son to do to get a break in this land?" I looked away from his face in case he should smile, and then decided to take Prince Charming's advice and get a grip for once in my life. So, and despite my famishment, I stood, brushed myself down and asked him politely again if he would refrain from smiling.

“But why?”

“Apparently it makes me *very* hungry when you do.”

“My smile makes you hungry, Truly?”

I thanked my lucky stars that I was orange, for it prevented me going red.

“You have turned the colour of sunset,” said he, covering his mouth to hide his smile. “Despite my ridiculous hue, you're coming with me,” said I.

“I cannot. I have been enslaved by the queen and cannot leave here.”

“Haven't you heard?”

Edward shook his head. “The grapevine has not passed through here in sometime.”

“I see. Well, I've been making some small changes to stories, and–”

“You? I heard it was Snow White that has done so.”

“Yes,” said I, brushing myself down needlessly and purposefully and looking away from the object of my desire. Did I just say *desire*? I meant famishment. “I'm Snow's cousin, and I share her determination to make changes where changes are required.”

“Required by who?”

“By anyone who can't seem to get a break in this land.”

“With the exception of the queen, that could be just about anyone.”

“Tell me about it. Which is why my cousin Snow and I have had our work cut out for us.”

“And you imagine that I require your assistance?”

I looked at his forehead, it being the least hunger-inducing thing about him, and murmured softly, “I do.”

“You do?”

“I *do* think you need my assistance. And that is why you are coming with me, away from this dreadful place.”

“Truly, is that your heart's desire?”

“It is.”

“Then we'd best get going, for I am due a flogging any minute.”

We had not gone far when came upon a pretty spot where Edward suggested we had lunch. “Lunch?” said I.

“You said yourself how famished you are. And I still have my sandwich,” said he, producing his lunch box and removing the lid.

I gazed down at our intended meal and said, “Are you sure that's a sandwich? Only, does not a sandwich require *two* slices of bread, and something between them?”

Edward looked at his sandwich and sighed. “Truly, it requires a little imagination to make it a sandwich.”

I sighed too and stumbled slightly. Edward reached out a hand and steadied me. We sat upon the ground, surrounded by bluebells, and Edward divided the sandwich that required a little imagination to make it so in two. I say in two, but he gave me the lion's share, and the piece he kept for himself could hardly be described as a piece. It was a morsel. As I nibbled upon my larger morsel, I felt his gaze upon me. "Why do you watch me so?" said I. "Am I not hideous to gaze upon? I wouldn't for all the land want to put you off your sandwich."

Edward shook his head. "That is not possible."

"You are too kind. For I resemble a mutated orange at the best of times," said I, getting the obvious comparison out of the way.

"I believe it important to see beyond colour…"

"Beyond?"

"Yes. To the person within."

"To... to... to… the person within? *Please*. You must refrain from doing so in my case. I fear the person you see will be a terrible disappointment."

Edward raised an eyebrow and shook his head.

"For starters," said I, "the person within is chronically meddlesome."

"If that is so, it is only to right the wrongs of this land." He gazed upon his morsel and added, "Mmm, it is delicious. And so filling."

"Imagination?" said I.

"Truly."

"Yes?"

"Truly it requires imagination to make it so."

"I see. We should be going. The queen will soon discover you're missing," said I, standing up.

"Where will we go? For I fear there is nowhere in the land that the queen will not find me. It would therefore serve you better if I returned to my wheel. I would not for all the land wish to get you into trouble."

"Nonsense. We will make haste and find somewhere to hide you."

"Truly, is that your heart's desire?"

I replied by nodding and making off with haste.

It may or may not have come to your attention that, since meeting Edward, I have been more hungry than usual. And that the closer Edward was to my person, the more faint (from famishment) I felt. For this reason, as we made our way through the forest, I remained several paces in front. Striding purposely, every so often I would hear Edward call, "Truly, is hiding me your heart's desire?" In response, I would nod, and the back of my head would convey that it was. This went on for some hours, and I lost count of the number of times the question was posed. Then he asked another question entirely. "Truly, is that a house I see yonder?" I stopped walking and, as I looked through the many trees, Edward caught me up and stood beside me.

"Look," said he, pointing.

"Yes. I see it," said I, standing on tiptoes. Edward looked up and gauged the position of the sun, and also the position of the second moon (for there are two in this land). "Given our position relative to the sun and second moon, that house can only be the property of three people."

"Really? How ever do you know?"

"Before I was enslaved for the crimes of my father, I had made *the book* my life's study. I see you are surprised." I was about to explain that I was not in the least bit surprised, when he raised a palm and said, "I am just the son of a poor woodcutter. I have not the education of a Prince Charming. But I was fortunate to grow up in a shed that was close to where the little lamb hops, skips and jumps on his daily travels."

"You know the little lamb?" said I.

"I do. And he was kind enough to spare me a few minutes each day, to teach me how to read." Edward shook his head. "It was not easy."

"Learning to read?" said I.

"Learning to read whilst hopping, skipping and jumping about the yard. But I persevered. And so did my joints," said he, rubbing the small of his back.

As I watched him, I heard myself murmur, "Prince Charmings aren't so clever. Did you know they can only count to eight?"

"I had no idea."

“It's true.”

“Of course,” said he, rubbing the other side of his back. “It explains why they only ever cut figures of eight out of the air.” Edward forgot his promise and smiled at me. Not long after, I came round and Edward apologised for doing so. He said he must try harder not to smile, at least until my acute hunger had been satisfied. “Truly, do you like porridge?” he asked.

“Yes. The dwarves say it's particularly nourishing.”

“Quite so. As do the bears.”

“The bears?”

“Yes. The three bears who live in that house yonder.”

Some minutes later …

Some minutes later, we approached the house. It was a large brown house with a white front door, and large windows with white window frames. As I peered in through the window, Edward turned and rested his back against the side of the house. "Don't tell me," said he. "You see a table, and upon the table are three bowls."

"Yes."

"The bowls are different sizes: one is small, the second medium-sized, and the third large."

"Yes! Clearly, you have studied hard."

"As I said, I have made *the book* my life's passion. The bowls belong to the three bears. And now we must be going for she might arrive at any moment, and she should not for all the world discover us here."

"Who?" said I.

"Goldilocks."

"*Goldilocks?* Now you come to mention her, I believe I've heard of her." I shuddered. "What's wrong?" asked Edward.

"I just wondered what horrid fate *the book* has in store for her. I expect she's destined to fill those bowls many times over."

"Fear not, Truly, for the three bears are a kindly family. Goldilocks will be safe here. Now we really must be going."

"Safe here? Are you sure?"

"Quite sure."

"Safe sounds a very unusual fate for this land. But that being the case, I have an idea." I looked at Edward's golden hair. "Your name might have been Goldilocks," murmured I.

"It might. Although, I would have taken issue with my parents if it were."

"Be that as it may–" Edward held up a palm and silenced me.

"But don't you wish to hear my plan?" said I.

"It has already grown from an idea into a plan?"

"It has."

"Then you are correct. I do not wish to hear it."

"Not even if telling you my plan is my heart's desire?"

"Truly, you drive a hard bargain. If it's your heart's desire, then you must tell me."

"The three bears have not yet met Goldilocks?" said I, casting my gaze about for her arrival.

"They have not."

"So it seems to me that this is the perfect place for you to hide. At least until the queen grows tired of searching for you."

"I need not point out that this is not my story."

"It's true. You needn't. But you have studied her story, so

why not pretend to be her?" Edward cast his gaze down upon himself. He shook his head and said, "While it may be true that the colour of my hair may resemble hers, its length and style are wholly different. And as for the rest of me? I need hardly point out the obvious."

"But if the bears are yet to meet her, what does it matter?"

Edward looked at me and I could tell he was doing his best not to smile. "Truly, is it your heart's desire that I remain here with the bears?"

"Where you'll be safe from the evil queen. Yes."

"Then I shall do as you wish."

We entered the house and Edward sat before the smallest of the three bowls of porridge. He indicated the larger bowl with his eyes and said I should satisfy my hunger at once. Once all three bowls had been emptied, I followed Edward upstairs, where he lay first upon the smallest bed, then the medium-sized bed, and then the largest bed where I tucked him in. "Promise me you will remain here until it's safe to leave, *Goldilocks*," said I.

"Truly, is it–" I silenced him with a finger pressed to my lips.

On my way home, I kept my eyes peeled for Goldilocks, and made a point of trying to keep my mind *off* Edward. It was not easy, and even though I'd had a hearty bowl of porridge, whenever I pictured his smile in my mind's eye, I grew faint (with hunger). I therefore reasoned that my mind's eye was a distraction from my actual eyes, and my eyes needed to be alert if they were to spot Goldilocks. So, firmly but politely, I had a word with my mind's eye and asked it, "Would you kindly stop conjuring images of a smiling Edward?" My request must have worked because, out of the corner of my actual eyes, I beheld a flash of gold moving at pace. I turned and called, “Goldilocks?” A young woman with golden hair slowed to a stop and looked at me. I waved and beckoned her over and, having considered her options, she shrugged and made her way towards me.

“I must be close. Am I close?” said she, expectantly.

“Close to what?” asked I.

“To the house where I will find porridge?”

“You like porridge?”

“Of *course*. I'm also rather partial to a bed. For I find that forty winks are just the thing after a hearty bowl of porridge.”

“Are porridge and beds your favourite things?”

“In the whole world.”

“I see.”

She drew a deep breath and looked about anxiously. “I don't think you do. For I must find porridge and then go to bed as soon as possible.”

“You sound very serious, Goldilocks.”

She nodded. “How do you know my name?”

“I'm a student.”

“Of *the book*?”

"Is there any other?"

Her eyes grew wide, and she pleaded, "Then you *must* know where I will find my porridge and a bed? Please say they are close by."

"Indeed they are. I have just come from both."

"You *have?*"

"Yes. And I have a confession to make. I have eaten your porridge."

"You've done *what*? But why?"

"My options were scant, for I have passed out at least three times today from hunger."

"Who are you? And what in the name of oats is wrong with you?"

"My name is Orange Orange and, of late, my appetite has been humongous."

"That may be so. But do you even belong in my story?"

"As a rule? No."

She clapped her hands to her cheeks. "So my story's been changed? And Orange Orange has eaten all my porridge? Have you also slept in my bed?"

"No. But another has. His name is Edward, and he's in grave danger. So, if you don't mind, he'll be hiding in your story and pretending to be you. At least for a short while."

"But I do mind! For without porridge and a place to sleep, I shall go bonkers."

"Fear not, Goldilocks, for I shall take you home with me," said I, stepping in the direction of home.

"Why? Do you have porridge?"

"Oh, yes. All the porridge you can eat," said I over my shoulder.

"And a bed?"

"I'll make one up in the spare room as soon as we get back."

"And what about three bears?"

"No bears. But there are five dwarves."

"Are they kindly dwarves?" she called out.

"Yes. Very kindly." So it was that Goldilocks caught me up, and we locked arms and set off for home.

The next morning…

The next morning, I awoke to find Edward in my mind's eye, smiling. A little later, Not Particularly Hopeful shook me awake and said he'd never known me to sleep so late. "I'd convinced myself you must be poorly, or worse still, gone to a better place," said he.

"I'm neither ill nor have I gone to a better place. I'm just sorry for having neglected you all," said I, stretching. "I will get up and make breakfast."

Not Particularly Hopeful patted his stomach. "There's no need."

"You've had breakfast?"

"That's right. Best porridge a dwarf ever tasted."

"You must have met Goldilocks, then," said I, looking around him through my open bedroom door.

"You won't see her," said Not Particularly Hopeful. "She emerged from the spare room first thing this morning, saw the five of us sitting at the table holding our spoons, and…"

"Were introductions made?" I enquired.

"No. There was no one to make them."

"So what did she do?"

"She went to our supply oats and set about making several gallons of porridge. She sat with us and spooned down about a gallon herself, and then went straight back to bed."

"And she uttered not a word?"

"Not a word."

After the dwarves left for work, I told the songbirds to sing quietly as I did the housework. "Goldilocks needs her rest between porridge binges. It's the way she was written," said I, dusting. "And on no account are you to sing anything evenly *remotely* romantic. Love songs have a way of making me faint from hunger lately. And for some inexplicable reason, they return Edward to my mind's eye. And I need not remind you of the consequences should he smile." I laughed philosophically. "I have not been feeling myself lately." To which one of my songbirds tweeted that a walk in the fresh air would do me the world of good.

Later on, I stepped out onto the porch and looked to my right. The little lamb popped over his usual fence, and then skipped and bounced up to me. "I still haven't thanked you properly for saving me from Rumpelstiltskin, Orange," said he.

"Think nothing of it. Oh, what a lovely day! The weather is so very clement, don't you think so?" said I, appreciating its clemency. The little lamb bounced up to me and observed me at close quarters. "As I said to the grapevine yesterday, why don't you take a picture? It will last longer."

"Your cousin Snow would have expected me to help you."

"Help me? But why ever should I need help on a fine morning such as this? The finest of mornings!" I knelt and picked a bluebell from the ground. "*Help me*? I can't think what you mean," said I, holding it to my nose and breathing in its sweet scent.

"The grapevine tells me you have not been feeling yourself lately," said the little lamb.

"I suppose there has been the odd occasion when I have felt faint from hunger."

"It's not from hunger, Orange," said the little lamb, as though my diagnosis were ridiculous. I laughed in a good-natured way and said, "*Obviously* it's from hunger. What else could make a girl so light-headed?"

"Love," said the little lamb.

"*Love*?" said I, taking a step back.

"Love," repeated the little lamb.

"*Love*," said I, taking another step back and gripping the door frame for support.

"You're in love, Orange. With the woodcutter's boy, Edward."

"I most certainly am n–!" The sound of Edward's name brought an image of Edward's face to my mind's eye, and he smiled…

Some minutes later, I regained consciousness to discover that in his eagerness to wake me, the little lamb had been licking my face between bounces. As he descended to lick it once again, I rolled over and he licked up a mouthful of dust from the front porch. He bounced thrice, spat thrice, and said, "Do you believe it now? You're madly in love with the woodcutter's son."

I sat bolt upright and spluttered, “But,,, but,,, but,,, but…”

“Why else would you be talking about his butt?”

“I most certainly am not talking about *that*,” said I, standing up.

“The sooner you accept that you're in love with Edward the better,” said the little lamb as he hopped away.

“I thought you wanted to help me!” I called out.

“I did.”

“How is this helping me?”

“It's the truth.”

In response, I stamped my foot. It was in this mood that I began my walk. “Love Edward? Stuff and nonsense. I don't *do* love. Never have done love. Never will do love. Far too many issues for *love*. The notion alone is just too preposterous. One need only spend *two minutes* with my dwarves to know that!” I had not gone far when I spied two men in the distance. They were fighting over a single object and, sitting on a log and painting her toe-nails, was a girl whose face was obscured by her long blonde hair. As I drew nearer, I saw that *two* Prince Charmings were engaged in a tug of war over one slipper.

“Hello, Orange!” Cinders called from her log.

“Oh, it's you. What's going on?” I asked.

Cinders grabbed her ankle, raised her toes to her lips, and blew on the polish. “I'm making my foot as pretty as possible for the winning Charming to slip the slipper onto," said she between blows. I observed the Charmings who, for all intents and purposes, could have been identical twins. Cinders added, "My Prince Charming arrived early, just like yours did."

"Which one is which?"

"Beats me."

"Are we to be deluged by early Charmings?" said I.

Cinders admired her pretty foot and said, "Apparently, when news reached my own Charming that I'd fallen for another, my own Charming couldn't get here quickly enough."

I folded my arms and watched as one Charming tugged the slipper to his chest, and then the other did the same, and while they tugged they said things like, "The slipper *and* the girl are mine!"

"Were yours! But now they belong to me!"

"We'll see about that!"

"Indeed we shall!"

I looked at Cinders and said, "How long have they been tugging over you?"

"For what feels like an age," said she, sighing.

"Why don't you just pick one?"

"How to choose?"

"They're identical. So what difference would it make?"

Someone sitting on the branch of the tree above us cleared their throat and said, "Your cousin Snow has promised Cinderella's Charming to me. So I suggest you pick *Snow's* Charming, Cinderella." I looked up and beheld Little Red.

"Is that true?" Cinders asked me.

"My cousin may have made such an arrangement, yes."

"May schmay," said Little Red, climbing down and standing beside Cinders.

"I don't believe we've been formally introduced," said Cinders. Both looked to me for the introduction.

"Cinders, Little Red. Little Red, Cinders," said I. They shook hands and said the pleasure was all theirs. The formalities out of the way, I stuck two fingers in my mouth and whistled to get the attention of the Charmings. They paused mid-tug and held firmly to the slipper. "You must have noticed?" said I to them.

"Noticed?" repeated the Charmings in unison.

"That some changes have been made to the land of late."

The Charmings growled at each other under their breaths and said, "We've noticed."

"Chief amongst these changes is that the ladies of the land are now able to *choose* the Charming of their heart's desire."

The Charmings both looked gravely concerned and, when I asked what had perturbed them so, they said in unison, "For the love of all that's perfect, *please* don't choose either of us,

Orange."

Little Red chuckled. "Haven't you heard?" said she. "The grapevine has spoken of little else of late. Orange Orange has found her one true love." I looked at Little Red, and my expression must have been grave, for she quickly averted her gaze.

Cinders slipped her shoe back on and said, "I'm so happy for you! Unlike your cousin Snow, you have found your heart's desire."

I felt suddenly confused and spluttered, "But... but... but... but... and *but* with just one 't'." I glanced at the Charmings, who scattered like startled rabbits and flew into a nearby bush. "Don't pick either of us! Please! For we would not have our children resemble satsumas for all the world!"

"I have no intention of picking either of you," murmured I.

Cinderella stood up and moved to my side. "Little Red and I will choose our Charmings when we're good and ready," said told the Charmings. "In the meantime, we must take a walk with our friend Orange. For there are some things that girls must discuss in private."

"What *things*?" said I.

"Matters of the heart," said Little Red pointedly. With that the girls interlocked my arms with their own, and marched me away.

Once beyond the earshot of either Charming, Cinders said, "Do you know, your cousin Snow was exactly like you when it came to matters of the heart."

“I'm sure I don't know what you mean,” said I, glancing down at Cinders's arm, which held my own.

Little Red nodded. “I only met her a couple of times, but I got the impression she was *very* insecure.”

“How perceptive you are!” said Cinders. “Snow never could get to grips with her fairest-in-the-land status.”

“It must have been quite the burden for one with so many issues,” said Little Red.

I straightened my back and said, “So we both have our fair share of issues. If you have a point to make, then please make it.”

“The point is this,” said Cinders, tenderly squeezing my shoulder. “Feeling insecure about your appearance and being unable to love yourself must run in your family.”

“Rub it in, why don't you?” said I.

A well-intentioned Little Red did just that when she pointed out, “Neither you nor Snow think yourselves worthy of another's love.”

“The *point,* please?” said I, straightening my back to the point where a backwards cartwheel was a distinct possibility.

Cinders and Little Red glanced at one another and Cinders said, “The point is going to come as somewhat of a shock, Orange.”

Little Red grasped my shoulder and, having supported me thus, she said, “We have heard through a most reliable source…”

"The grapevine, no less," said Cinders.

"Yes, the grapevine," continued Little Red, "who assures us that he's spoken to the young man in question…"

"Edward," said Cinders helpfully.

"Yes, Edward, so his facts have come straight from the horse's mouth…"

"What *facts*?" said I.

"That Edward is in love with you too," said Little Red.

"…He can't possibly be," said I quietly, "for I resemble a mutated orange. And if he did, it would mean…"

"That he has fallen for the person within," said Cinders, placing her hand upon my heart.

I glanced down at her hand. "And he still thinks me worthy of... of..."

"His love, yes," said Little Red.

Tears overflowed from my eyes and rolled down my cheeks as I babbled, "The poor boy is clearly bonkers, but… no matter, for we will get him the *very* best help, but on no account is anyone to call the men in white coats."

"Hush, now," said Cinders. "Edward is perfectly sane. He's just the poor son of a woodcutter."

"Poor and perfect," murmured I.

The Return of Snow

I write this at midnight on the following day, and nothing has changed. And believe me it's not an easy thing to say, and more difficult still to write, but… I am in love with Edward. We had a date at the enchanted lake this afternoon. Cinders had arranged it, and she hid inside the hollowed-out tree, whispering words of encouragement through its peephole.

The fact is that before *you-know-what* happened to me, life seemed so much simpler. I did the housework each day, and then set off to help some poor character in need. Some might call it meddling (and many do), but this land is a cruel and terrifying place, and so many of its inhabitants need a happier ending. But since meeting Edward, I have been distracted. I blame my mind's eye, for it has been loath to let me think about much else. It is as though an enchantment has been placed upon me – an enchantment that I love *and* hate. Is it any wonder a person can't think straight when they fall in love?

This morning when I sat before my dressing table's mirror, I was no longer Orange Orange; I was Snow White again. My mirror welcomed me back (I presumed from the dead) as though I'd returned from the living room. It wasted no time in telling me that I was the fairest in the land. I didn't believe it, of course, but with my date with Edward only a few hours away, hearing it was a comfort of sorts.

My mirror might have taken my return in its stride, but the same could not be said of the dwarves. I decided it would be best to break the news to them quickly, like ripping off a plaster. Thus resolved, I drew a deep breath, flung open my bedroom door and shouted, "I'm back!" The dwarves, who had been waiting patiently at the kitchen table for their breakfast, spoons in hands, threw their spoons away and leapt for cover as though their spoons had become hand grenades. Goldilocks, who you may remember had come to stay with us, glanced up from the oats she was turning into porridge, observed my change in person, shrugged, and then returned to the serious business of porridge production.

Once I'd apologised to the dwarves for my Orange deception, and explained why it had been necessary, they gave me a hug and then returned to the table for breakfast. Insecure was quick to point out, "Once your evil stepmother discovers you're back, you're still going to be in terrible danger, Snow."

Not Particularly Hopeful drew a deep breath, as though a very large penny had just dropped. He began shaking his head and waggling his finger at me. "You've fallen in love with the woodcutter's son!"

Insecure smiled nervously. "No, she hasn't. It was Orange Orange who fell in love with the woodcutter's son."

"But Snow *is* Orange Orange!" pointed out Not Particularly Hopeful, not particularly helpfully.

Insecure looked at me like I'd betrayed him, and I could see the cogs turning behind his widening eyes. "You must be crazy," he murmured. "For while the woodcutter's son may be poor, according to the grapevine he's also perfect!"

"And?" I stammered.

"And?" said Insecure, turning as white as a sheet. "Don't you think that one so perfect deserves someone considerably less peculiar!?"

"Yes, of course I do, but..."

"But what?" said Insecure and Not Particularly Hopeful in unison.

I knew I had to think fast, otherwise they would ruin everything. And if everything was to be ruined, I would rather ruin it myself. The seed of an idea came to me. I grew it hastily and replied, "But I was Orange Orange when I fell in love with Edward."

"And?" said Insecure.

"And when I was Orange Orange, I wasn't feeling at all myself..."

"*And*?" pressed Insecure.

"And don't you see? It was *more* than just an orange disguise. Much more. The enchantment was so powerful that it turned me *into* Orange Orange. And it was she who fell in love with Edward. But, I'm Snow White again now, as you can see, so when I meet Edward today, I'm going to tell him there's been a terrible mistake."

"Would you like us to come with you?" asked Insecure.

"No! I mean, that won't be necessary. You've been taking far too much time off work because of me as it is. What with attending my funeral." As I smoothed out my apron, a general calmness fell over all. Which meant that Insecure and Not Particularly Hopeful must have believed me at least a little. Meddlesome, however, was in a dreadful mood. I knew why: I'd not had meddling on my mind. In fact, when it came to meddling, and without pointing any fingers, Cinders and Little Red had been the ones meddling in *my* affairs.

A little later, when the dwarves set off for work, I watched them until they were out of sight. I heard someone scream, and turned to see Cinders crumple to the ground, unconscious. Having just arrived at the cottage, she'd expected to see Orange Orange, not Snow White back from the dead. I hurried over and turned her onto her back. "Cinders? Cinders!?"

Cinder's eyes fluttered open. "*Snow*," said she softly. "You're alive?"

"Yes, it's me," said I, helping Cinders into a sitting position and sitting cross-legged beside her. She gazed at me askance, and slowly her senses returned. I placed a hand on her shoulder and squeezed gently. "It was I all along. I used powerful magic called fake tan, and with it I turned myself into Orange Orange."

"Fake tan?" she repeated, uncomprehendingly.

"Yes. They swear by it in a place called Essex."

"But why ever would they?"

I shrugged. "They must aspire to be orange there."

"But why? Orange is not the least bit an attractive colour for a person to be."

"That's why it was the perfect magic for me. I was no longer the fairest in the land, and my stepmother had no need of poisoning me."

"You could have told me, Snow. I'm your best friend."

"Little Miss Muffet thought it a good idea to keep my true identity a secret from all."

"Did she now? I can't say I'm surprised. That one's been acting very strangely of late. Hardly ever is she by her tree and eating her curds and whey. Now she spends all her days with the spider who was supposed to sit down beside her. Did you know that the no-eyed, no-brained toad that sells curds and whey has gone out of business?"

"Oh dear! No, I didn't. And it's all my fault for giving Little Miss Muffet a life beyond curds and whey."

Cinders brushed a stray hair from my face and said, "You do know what They say, don't you? That you can't make an omelette without breaking some eggs. It's so good to have you back, Snow!" *Technically speaking,* I thought, *I haven't been anywhere.* I opened my mouth to make that very point, but closed it again when Cinders lowered her voice and confided, "Truth be told, I wasn't particularly keen on Orange Orange. Oh, my!" She clasped her cheeks in surprise. "OH, MY!" she repeated, only louder and in capitals. "So it is *you* who has fallen in love with Edward!"

"Hush, keep your voice down," said I, glancing over my shoulder in the direction the dwarves had gone. "For Insecure and Not Particularly Hopeful must not find out for all the world."

“Snow in love? Oh, this is *big*. Perhaps you're destined to live happily ever after, after all!”

I shook my head. “Edward is sure to tire of me, particularly when he discovers that I've turned from Truly Orange into truly peculiar.”

“Whatever is the matter, Snow? You've turned the colour of an icicle.”

“Which reminds me, Edward is expecting to meet Truly Orange today, so he will also think me a liar.”

“Word on the grapevine is that Edward is poor and perfect. And perfect people are colour-blind.”

“You don't think he has a thing for orange girls, then?”

Cinders shook her head. “That would make him as peculiar as you are.”

Later that day…

Later that day, Cinders accompanied me to the enchanted lake for my date. I didn't make it easy for her, and kept coming up with excuses for turning back. The closer we got to the enchanted lake, the more I wanted to take flight and the tighter her grip on my arm became. And when the willow tree, within whose tumbling branches my date with Edward was to take place, came into view, poor Cinders had literally to drag me towards it.

Under its canopy, Cinders had laid out a magnificent spread: strawberries with cream, cream buns, cream cheese, cheese cakes, cheese toasties and many more cheese-based dishes besides. "What's with all the cheese?" said I.

"I know how much you love it. And you will recall how the no-eyed, no-brained toad had gone out of business?"

"Yes, of course. It was all my fault."

"Well, the toad had all this cheese to sell, and…"

"Say no more. What a lovely gesture," said I, squeezing Cinders's hand.

Cinders opened the secret door in the tree. "He was so *desperate* that he sold me all his cheese for an absolute bargain!" said she, stepping inside and closing the door.

"Oh, I see," said I.

Cinders waggled a finger through the little peephole. "Sit," she said sternly. I glanced behind to see the dog she must be talking to. “Sit!” said she again. “Edward is due at any moment.”

The notion of seeing Edward at any moment turned my legs to jelly, and I didn't so much sit as collapse into a heap. “I really don't need this,” groaned I from within my heap.

“For goodness’s sake!” said Cinders. “Rearrange yourself out of that heap. Didn't you hear what I said? Edward could arrive at any moment.” The reminder didn't help, but I managed to emerge from my heap somehow. “Do you hear that?” said Cinders.

“Hear what?” said I, my heart skipping a beat and my breath leaving me.

“Footsteps!” whispered Cinders.

I stuck my fingers in my ears until I saw Cinders's thumb emerge from the peephole and point downward, then withdrew them. “*Yes*,” whispered I. “Dry leaves are being trodden underfoot…”

“Under Edward's foot,” said Cinders, “and here he comes!”

A hand pushed aside the willow's hanging branches, and I beheld Edward wearing a strapless red dress and stockings. I had hoped Edward would not smile when he saw me, and those of you who read my last diary will know how his smile had a tendency to make me faint from famishment. On this point, I was relieved, for it was clear from his expression that there was very little chance of him smiling. I supposed it was his disappointment at finding me no longer orange, but pale enough to be visible from space most nights. But then he glanced down at his dress and shook his head as though he would have preferred one with straps. He looked at me, did a double-take, and said, “Truly, there is no cause for alarm. But it could be that you need a blood transfusion.”

I shook my head and confessed. “I am supposed to look like someone in need of a blood transfusion. You see, my name isn't Truly Orange, it's Snow White.”

“The fairest in the land,” murmured Edward.

“Well, yes, and *obviously* no. I have deceived you, Edward. And having deceived you, I would understand if you wanted nothing whatsoever to do with me…”

I was silenced mid-babble by Edward's raised palm. “Your colour, or lack of it, is unimportant, as I am colour-blind.”

“Metaphorically speaking?”

“Quite so,” said he. “Although the same could not be said for the eyesight of the three bears, whose own story mentions not a word of their acute myopia.”

“I see.”

“Like the three bears, I do not think that you do. They were expecting Goldilocks to be a girl, and would accept nothing I told them to the contrary.”

“Oh. So you aren't wearing a strapless dress and stockings by choice, then?”

“Is that a serious question, my love?”

“Deadly. For I know for a fact that the Big Bad Wolf likes to dress in women's clothes.”

“Perhaps you are mistaken, for the reputation of the Big Bad

Wolf is fearsome to say the least."

"Maybe so, but it's not as though anyone *forced* him to put on a nightdress and bonnet. He might just as easily have stood beside the door and devoured Little Red the moment she walked through it. I'm babbling, aren't I?"

Edward nodded. "And so fast that I barely caught a word of it." I opened my mouth, but closed it again when Edward added, "However, from the word or two I did catch, it seems that the Big Bad Wolf has more issues than your average wolf."

"Precisely so. And to think I wanted to go on a date with someone who wears a dress!" said I, glancing at Edward's.

"I am pleased to hear it isn't a preference, for I don't believe I can keep up this pretence for very much longer."

"It's a very nice dress," I pointed out.

Edward sighed. "Just one of the many that Mummy Bear has made for me… or rather, made for *Goldilocks*." Edward pulled at the side of the dress as though in discomfort.

"What is it?" asked I.

"Mummy Bear is so short-sighted that she mistook my muscular chest for something else… and *insists* on my wearing a training bra whenever I go out."

"I see," said I, endeavouring not to smile.

"I do not think that you do, for if you did you would know that for anyone to go through humiliation on a scale such as this on behalf of another could only mean that that person thought the world of that other person."

When I regained consciousness, I began to mutter, "But you cannot think the world of me, *must* not think it, for if you do it can only mean you are bonkers." I sat up and gazed beyond the branches of the weeping willow tree for the men in white coats who must surely be coming for him. "The men in white coats came for me once, but *that* was a misunderstanding," said I.

Edward brushed a stray hair from my cheek and said, "What has happened to make one so fair and so charitable so insecure?"

"I suppose I must have been written this way."

"Then I for one would like a word with the Author."

"Really? And if you met him what would you say to him?"

"I would give him a piece of my mind."

"Have him rewrite me, you mean?"

"Rewrite you? Never. Sooo," said Edward, sighing.

"Buttons on your training bra?" said I, feeling awkward and making a terrible joke.

"What was that?" asked Edward.

"Nothing. Just a terrible joke about embellishing your training bra with buttons."

"It already has buttons, believe me." Edward almost smiled, but stopped himself in time. "This cannot be easy for you," said he.

I nodded wholeheartedly. "The truth is that making jokes

under such stressful circumstances is extraordinarily difficult."

"Then maybe it's for the best if you do not try."

"So you don't think I'm the least bit funny, then? You will soon learn that not being the least bit funny is perhaps the most attractive thing about me." Edward's gaze seemed to take in every feature of my face, then settled on my lips. I rubbed at them vigorously. "Is there's something unsightly stuck to my mouth? Yesterday's porridge, perhaps? I'm such a messy eater. Compared to me, Insecure says that Awkward has excellent table manners. You may raise an eyebrow, but Awkward regularly stabs himself in the eye with his fork, and…" Edward leaned towards me, his lips parting close to mine. "I've had an idea," said he. I watched him, quite unable to move or speak. I blinked in a way that suggested he continue explaining his idea. "Perhaps," said he, "in a land such as this, where frogs can be turned into princes, and princesses can be woken from a hundred years of sleep with a single kiss…" He stopped talking and his gaze once again found my lips. I blinked, blinked again, and then sighed. "Well," he went on, "perhaps a kiss can magic away all your insecurities about living happily ever after." Edward leaned in closer, and I could feel his sweet breath upon my lips, and… *that's* when someone outside the tree yelled: "Edward, son of the woodcutter! Come out! You're under arrest by order of the Queen!"

A fraught moment later…

A fraught moment later, Edward was on his feet and I lay sprawled on my back. In my haste to join him, I had tripped over not just one but both of my size nines.

"You'd better stay there," said he, backing away.

"No! I'm coming with you. They are my stepmother's guards, so maybe I can help!" said I, clinging to his dress and pulling myself to my feet.

Edward backed away from me. "No," he said firmly. "It's much too dangerous. When the Queen discovers you're still alive, she'll start trying to poison you again. You know as well as I that she's written that way."

From beyond the tree's tumbling branches came the cry of the same guardsman. "This is your last chance! Come out with your hands raised above your head!"

"I will go and see the Queen!" said I. "I'll promise her *anything* if she'll let you go."

"Please. Do nothing foolish on my behalf…" said Edward, disappearing through the hanging branches.

He was greeted on the other side by laughter. I heard the door to the willow tree open behind me, and felt Cinders's hand upon my shoulder. "What has an insecure and not particularly hopeful girl to do to get a break in this land?" said she.

"You are not wrong."

“So what are you going to do?”

“Go straight to my stepmother and ask her to release Edward.”

“You heard him. It's much too dangerous.”

“That woman is going to find out I'm back sooner or later. She has so many spies that I suspect it will be sooner.” I stuck my fingers in my mouth and whistled.

“Barry?” said Cinders.

“Yes. There is no time to delay.”

Barry came trotting under the tree's canopy as though he'd been waiting to do so. Barry is faultless that way. When he clapped eyes upon me, he turned pale – not pale enough to be visible from space most nights, perhaps, but believe me when I tell you I have never seen a paler boar. “Is that really *you,* Snow?” said he, his piggy eyes welling up.

“Yes.”

“But *how*? And where is Orange Orange?”

“Orange Orange was me all the time. Little Miss Muffet gave me powerful magic that transformed me into her. I am very sorry for having deceived you, Barry, but I believed myself in great danger.”

“From your stepmother?”

“Yes. And I'd like you to take me to see her now.”

Barry looked at Cinders, who shrugged her beautiful shoulders. “She means to help Edward, the woodcutter's son.

And you know what Snow's like when she's minded to help someone in peril."

Barry nodded enthusiastically. "You'd better jump on. You wouldn't be Snow otherwise." I did just that, and Barry glanced at me over his shoulder. "It's good to have you back! I don't care what anyone says, this land needs you."

"Like a hole in the head, I should imagine. But thank you, Barry."

Forty-seven anxious minutes later…

Forty-seven anxious minutes later, I climbed off a hot and panting Barry. “You sure you want to do this, Snow?”

“I must. Edward needs me.”

“Alright, but I'm not going anywhere. I know swine are not permitted inside royal palaces unless roasted and served on a bed of rice, but if I hear you whistle, I'll batter down that door and find you.”

“Thank you, Barry.”

I knocked upon the door. My stepmother's butler opened it. You will remember how he is vertically challenged – so much so that he barely reaches my knobbly knees. Speaking of which, he must have recognised them right away, for he stumbled backwards, beheld my pale face, clasped his own and cried, “It can't be you!”

“I think you will find that it is me.”

“But if you're alive this is dreadful news! The very worst news imaginable!”

“You're pleased to see me, I can tell.”

“The Queen's been in such good spirits since she crushed you underfoot. Shoo!” said he, shooing me with his little hands. “Go! Just go. And if you know what's good for you, you'll go as far away as possible.”

“While I appreciate your advice, it isn't about me…” I

attempted to brush past him and, like the last time I visited, he thwarted my every attempt, and pretty soon it felt like we were out on *another* date, dancing. The idea of being on a *second* date was even more irksome than when it felt as though we were on our first date. I'm ashamed to admit that, when he did one of his impressive twirls, I stuck my foot in the small of his back and shoved him for all I was worth. I must be worth quite a lot when it comes to shoving vertically challenged butlers, for he shot away so fast on the polished floor that, when he finally made contact with something (it sounded like a cabinet filled with china cups, but who knew?) I could no longer see him. "Whoops," said I, brushing myself down.

As mentioned in my previous diaries, my stepmother's palace is very large. I might easily have got lost, if not for a loud party taking place in one of its many ballrooms. I followed the sound of merriment and eventually came upon two guards standing outside a set of gigantic doors. The guards were very tall, and held staffs that were taller still. The one on the right peered down at me. The fellow couldn't have been much of a scholar, for he didn't even recognise me. "By what name should I announce you, madam?" he asked.

"Snow White."

I had clearly underestimated his scholarly ways, for he opened the doors, banged his staff thrice upon the ground, and announced my arrival thus: "Snow White, the fairest in the land!"

Well, it would be no exaggeration to say that you could have heard a pin drop. And once the guest who had dropped a pin muttered an apology, the guests began to part and my stepmother emerged from among them like a spider from its lair. She fixed her evil gaze upon me and the colour drained from her face. "Orange Orange? Is this some kind of joke? Did you imagine this a Halloween party?"

I held my head high and shook it.

"Then have you recently been submerged in a vat of flour?" said she, looking past me into the hall as though expecting to see the vat of flour from which I had emerged.

I stood up as straight as possible and said, "No, I didn't. The truth is… I *am* Snow White."

"But I…" My stepmother glanced behind her and cast her gaze over her open-mouthed guests.

"You what? *Killed* me?"

"Don't be absurd. I was about to say I… I went to your funeral."

"It was not really my funeral. You buried an empty tube of fake tan." My stepmother smiled, and so false was her smile that it looked to have been painted on her face by an artist who could paint only glares. "Oh, it matters not! Thank goodness you're alive!" said she, summoning a servant with a crooked finger. When the servant was beside her, she leant in close and whispered, "Have the croquet lawn dug up immediately."

"Dug up, Your Majesty?"

"Yes, immediately. And then re-plant my apple orchard." Her servant bowed and left to carry out her orders.

"Sounds awfully urgent," said I.

"What does?" she asked.

"Your need for apples."

"What splendid hearing you have. You know what They say, don't you?"

"No. What does Frank say?"

"That an apple a day keeps the doctor away. They have never said that about a round of croquet," said she, getting a round of applause for Frank's insight. "Your father is going to be so relieved when he hears you're back. Where have you been?"

"Nowhere. I was disguised… as Orange Orange."

A dreadful penny must have dropped then, for she began laughing and pointing at me like I was the most ridiculous thing ever to disgrace her palace. Then she remembered her charm offensive and said sweetly, "So it is you, then."

"Yes. I believe we have already established that it is I."

"*You* and not Orange Orange have fallen in love with the woodcutter's son!" This she could not help but find funny, and her laughter must have been infectious for it quickly spread amongst her guests.

I stood as straight as possible under the circumstances and said, "I suppose I am quite fond of him, yes. Which brings me to the reason for my visit: I want you to let Edward go. For unless being poor and perfect is a crime, which I do not believe it is, then he has done nothing wrong and must be freed."

"Freed, you say?"

"I do say. And preferably into my custody. And right away."

"But my dear, Edward must be punished for the crimes of his father."

"And what crime did Edward's father commit?"

"The woodcutter was supposed to…"

"Yes?"

My stepmother glanced behind her at her assembled guests, all of whom were hanging on her every word.

"He was *supposed* to do what?" I pressed.

"It matters not what he was *supposed* to do, for his son has committed a serious crime in his own right now. And he must therefore remain in my dungeon until his trial."

"*Crime?* The crime of being poor and perfect?"

"No. If that were the case, I'd be half guilty of the same crime."

"Then what has he done?"

"He has impersonated another character – a very serious crime, and punishable by death."

"But that was all my idea!"

"Then maybe you'll be less meddlesome in future."

"How did you find out?"

"My soldiers knocked at your cottage this morning, and discovered that Goldilocks was living there. So they put two and two together, and then paid the three bears a visit. You are aware that Edward delights in wearing stockings and a training bra?"

"He does *not* delight in it. He only agreed to it because it was a part of…"

My stepmother leaned forwards on her throne. "Of what? Of his terrible deception?"

I removed my foot from my mouth and reattached it to the end of my leg. "I want to see him," said I.

"And so you shall. At his trial – a trial at which I am to be his only judge. A word of step-motherly advice: do not to get your hopes up. I have already found him guilty."

"And is that your final word on the matter?"

"It is."

I felt tears come to my eyes and, before I grew inconsolable, I turned and walked slowly from the ballroom.

I walked back through the palace with hands clasped behind my back and head bowed low. I soon came upon a green vase lying on its side in the middle of the corridor. The vase had on a pair of patent leather shoes, and it was talking to itself in muffled tones. This struck me as odd. I picked it up and put it back on its feet, whereupon it darted away and smashed against the wall. Out popped the butler like a booby prize. I say a booby prize, for any prize that bellows a string of words unrepeatable in a young woman's diary before it shoves you out the front door could only be described as booby.

The following morning…

I would like to say that I awoke the following morning with renewed hope in my heart that all would soon be well, but I didn't manage even a wink of sleep. This was due in no small part to my mind's eye, which *insisted* on showing me poor Edward in his dungeon every three seconds. I had never seen his cell (and neither had my mind's eye, come to that) but that did not prevent it conjuring the most horrid things. And as my mind's eye was quick to point out, Edward would never have been chained by his ankles to the ceiling over a pit of snapping alligators, if not for my meddling.

At breakfast the dwarves were all relieved not to have porridge again. "I'm glad Goldilocks has gone to live with the three bears," said Inconsolable.

"A real space-cadet. I fear for her," added Not Particularly Hopeful.

"You are wrong to fear for her," said I. "For Goldilocks is one of the few characters in this land who was always going to live happily ever after."

"It's alright for some," said Insecure.

Not Particularly Hopeful almost smiled. "It's just as well you're not Orange Orange anymore," he said.

"And why is that?" I asked.

"I should have thought that was obvious. Orange Orange fell in love, and nothing good ever came from falling in love."

“That's right,” added Insecure. “You need look no further than Edward the woodcutter's boy to see that.”

“Poor Edward!” cried Inconsolable, apparently on my behalf. “With all the trouble he's in, you're so lucky you're not Orange Orange anymore.” He blew his nose and then looked at me with tears in his big green eyes. “Poor Snow,” said he. “She looks miserable enough as it is.”

“Why *do* you look so miserable?” enquired Awkward. Insecure and Not Particularly Hopeful leaned forwards and looked at me, while Awkward leaned too far back on the bench and fell off onto the floor.

“Poor Awkward!” said I, standing up and rushing to his aid.

“Well?” pressed Insecure.

“Well what?” said I, helping Awkward to his feet.

“Why the long face?” asked Insecure.

“That is surely a question for *the book*'s illustrator,” said I firmly.

“Your face is actually more round than it is long, Snow,” said Not Particularly Hopeful.

“I wish you would make up your minds,” said I. “My face is either too long or too round, but I don't really see how it can be *both*. Although, come to think of it…”

“Where are you going?” asked Inconsolable, welling up.

“I'm taking my long round face out for a walk,” said I, heading for the door.

Inconsolable burst into tears. "But you haven't finished your breakfast!"

"She hasn't *started* her breakfast," pointed out Meddlesome. And then, true to his meddlesome nature he added, "In my experience, a lack of appetite can indicate that a person is in love."

"Not this time, it doesn't," said I, crossing my fingers and walking out the door.

I strode purposely through the woods. I didn't know where I was going but I knew wherever it was I needed to find answers there. *If only I knew the questions*, thought I. *Edward's fate is sealed? He's to be found guilty of impersonating Goldilocks – put to death for a crime that I practically* forced *him to commit.* I kicked a pebble and, as it sailed away, I thought, *Who says Edward's fate is sealed and can't be changed? Surely They must know better than Who*? It was then that I decided I must hear it from the horse's mouth. By that I didn't mean the horse's mouth in the west wood, but Frank the groundhog, known to all the universe as They.

I came upon Frank reclining in a hammock reading. "Hello Frank," said I, "what are you reading?"

"A very rare and old copy of *the book*," said he, licking a paw and turning the page.

"You don't seem the least bit surprised to see me returned from the dead," I said, standing at the end of his hammock.

"I'm not. And you know what They say, don't you?"

"No. What do you say, Frank?"

"That the early bird catches the worm."

"I must be the worm," nodded I. "I certainly resemble a worm first thing in the morning."

Frank rolled his eyes. "You are the bird, Snow."

"So who is the worm?"

"The worm is the useful information you seek."

"You know why I've come to see you, then? You have good news about Edward? That his fate is not sealed?"

"How can Edward's fate be sealed when we have an expert in the art of meddling in our midst?"

"And who might that expert meddler be?"

"Do you really need to ask?"

"It is *I*?"

"It is."

"So there is hope for Edward, then!"

"Yes. But at the same time you know what They say."

"No. What do you say?"

"That you should never count your chickens before they've hatched."

"I have chickens!"

"Just one chicken."

I held out my hands and turned them palms up in anticipation of my chicken.

"Your chicken is the Eighth Fairy," said he.

"The *who* fairy?"

"No, the Eighth Fairy. Have you heard of her?"

I shook my head. "Who is she, and how can she help Edward?"

"You've heard of Princess Aurora?"

"No."

"Many know her by her other name, Sleeping Beauty."

"I believe I have heard of *her*, yes."

"Sleeping Beauty is to be pricked by a cursed spinning wheel."

"Ouch," said I.

"It gets worse."

"It usually does in this land."

"The spinning wheel's curse will place her into a coma from which she can only be awakened by a kiss from her Prince Charming."

I scratched my head. "If you replace the spinning wheel with an apple, her story sounds very similar to my own. Are you *certain* you're not confusing her with me? For the deluded – and there are a great many in the land – think that I am a great beauty, and if my stepmother gets her way, then I'm to become a beauty of the sleeping variety."

Frank shook his head.

"So you mean there's a *genuine* beauty who is to sleep for a great many years?"

"There's another one, yes," said Frank.

"And does she have an evil stepmother who hates her?"

"No."

"Then who hates her enough to curse the spinning wheel?"

"The Eighth Fairy."

"The same Eighth Fairy who can help change Edward's fate?"

"That's right."

"But if she's as mean as you say, then why would she?"

"She won't, but she knows of a place where it can easily be done. And she will lead you there if you follow her."

"Follow her where?"

"To it."

"*It*?"

"Yes, to *it*." I placed my hands on my hips and fixed Frank with my most determined stare, and it must have done the trick, for he added, "*It,* the Author's Cabin it: the place where *the book* was written. It is where you'll find *the book's* original manuscript."

"Really?"

"Yes. And that's where you'll also find the Author's pencil and eraser. With them you can rub out Edward's current fate and replace it with one more to your liking."

"That's sounds *so* much to my liking! Not to mention right up my alley!"

Frank twirled his whiskers. "It has your name written all over it, Snow."

"And so too will *the book* if I get my hands on it."

It was Frank's turn to fix me with his most no-nonsense stare.

"Just my little joke," said I. "Of course I won't write my name all over it."

"If you do you'll write your name into every story in the land."

"I would never impose myself on the land in such a way. This land deserves better."

"Only rub out and alter the paragraph that relates to Edward's fate. Have I made myself clear?"

"As the finest crystal. So where might I find the Eighth Fairy?"

"She resides in the land that lies to the east, beyond the mountains."

"I wasn't aware there was a land to the east and beyond the mountains."

"Well, there is one. Why the long round face?"

"Because if that's true, I could have kept my promise to the woodcutter and left this land. So all this really *is* my fault."

"And now you must leave this land to put things right."

"Put things right…" murmured I. "Has the Eighth Fairy cursed the spinning wheel yet?"

"Oh, yes. She cursed it sixteen years ago when Princess Aurora was just a baby."

I felt a chill run down my spine. "So Princess Aurora has already been pricked by the cursed wheel?"

"Not yet. Her father the king found out about the curse and ordered that all the spinning wheels in his land be destroyed. If they don't spin they can't prick her." I opened my mouth in readiness to ask the obvious question, but closed it again when Frank held up a paw. "But *one* spinning wheel is still in use," said he.

"One?" said I. "And where is it located?"

"In the palace where Princess Aurora lives."

"But why? Could there *be* a worse place?"

Frank shrugged. "It's the way her story was written."

"I see. Who is this cruel Author? Might I find him at his cabin? I'd like a word with him."

"The Author left his cabin as soon as *the book* was finished. And nobody has seen him since."

"Too ashamed to ever show his face, I should imagine."

"Perhaps."

"So how does Princess Aurora come upon the spinning wheel?"

"First thing tomorrow morning, she's going to feel restless and explore the palace."

"Tomorrow morning!" I stuck two fingers in my mouth and whistled for Barry. "Then I should not delay for all the world."

"If you want my advice, it would be best if you didn't meddle with Princess Aurora's story."

"When her story is so much like my own?" I glanced about and could see no sign of Barry. I whistled again, and sure enough he emerged from the undergrowth.

"We must make haste to the land beyond the mountains, Barry."

"Who said there's a land beyond the mountains?"

"No. *They* said there is. Tell him, Frank."

"No doubt about it," said Frank.

"Well, I never," said Barry. "If that's what They say, then it must be true."

"If we've quite established that it's there, could we please make haste?"

Barry shook his head. "You know I'd help out if I could. But I'm not equipped to make that journey."

"Equipped?"

"With wings to fly over the mountains."

"Then how am I to get there?" said I, looking back and forth between Frank and Barry.

They came up with the solution: "You'll need to summon The Crow."

Barry nodded. "Frank's talking about The Crow as in as *the crow flies.*"

I jumped and flapped my arms, then remembered that that was how you summoned the men in white coats. I stopped and peered about nervously for them. Frank snatched a hair from his cheek and flicked it over his left shoulder. "Is that how you summon The Crow?" asked I.

Barry snorted. "If that's how They do it, then that's how it must be done." And lo and behold, The Crow appeared. It was considerably larger than your average crow – and it needed to be, what with all the weight I imagined I'd put on recently.

A good many fields and a mountain range later…

A good many fields and a mountain range later, The Crow landed in a forest clearing. I thanked it for getting me there in double-quick time and, in response, it squawked how the pleasure had been all mine – at least, I assumed that was what it said – then it flapped its great wings and took flight.

There was a well-trodden path that wended its way through the forest and, taking into account the way The Crow had brought me, I continued in that direction. I had not gone far when I came upon a little house. Outside of the house an old lady swept her porch while her dog danced a jig. "Hello!" she called.

"Hello!" replied I.

"I'm Old Mother Hubbard. And who might you be?"

"Snow White. My, what a talented dog you have! It's dancing a very impressive jig."

"It's the star of our nursery rhyme," said Old Mother Hubbard, rolling her eyes.

"That's nice."

"Not for me. All I do is run errands for it." Old Mother Hubbard looked at her dog and sighed. "I went to the barbers to buy him a wig, and when I came back he was dancing this jig."

It was then that I noticed her black dog had a mop of blonde hair. The old woman put down her broom and began to walk away. "Where are you going?" I asked.

“To fulfil the next verse, where else?”

“Which is?”

“*She went to the cobblers to buy him some shoes, and when she got back he was reading the news.*”

“Might I trouble you for some information before you go?”

“The dog troubles me all the time, so you might as well. I'm used to being troubled.”

“I'm sorry to hear that. If you answer my question, perhaps I might do something for you in return.”

“What might you do for me?”

“Oh, I don't know. Maybe change your nursery rhyme?”

Old Mother Hubbard rubbed at a crick in her bent back. “I don't think such a thing is possible.”

“I am certain that it is possible. I have had to make *teensy weensy* changes to stories before, and what's more, the place I must eventually find will make it easier than ever to change your rhyme.”

“Where must you eventually find?”

“The Author's Cabin.”

“I hope you're not going to ask me for directions to the Author's Cabin. No one knows where that is.”

I shook my head. “They say there is one person who does know, which is why I must find the Princess Aurora – aka the Sleeping Beauty – for she is acquainted with this person.

So my question to you is, do you know where she lives?"

"The Princess Aurora?"

"Yes."

"Her Royal Highness lives in the Grand Palace, of course."

"And is it far?"

"Not as The Crow flies."

"The Crow dropped me off a few minutes ago, and seemed in a great hurry to return to my own land."

"It's lucky for you I know a shortcut, then," said Old Mother Hubbard, walking back towards her house.

"Where are you going?" I asked. "I need to reach the Princess Aurora without delay, for she is in grave danger of being pricked."

"I'll be back in a mo. Just going to fetch a pencil and pad."

"Whatever for?"

"So I can rewrite my poem on the way, just in case you should find the Author's Cabin."

Sometime later

I waved goodbye to Old Mother Hubbard and put the new poem she'd written in my pocket. The path that led up to the Grand Palace was steep and winding, and when eventually I saw it, it stole my breath away. It was magnificent, and much grander than any in my own land. Its turrets were so high that they pierced the pink clouds floating over it. These same clouds were reflected in the water of its moat. A drawbridge began to lower and many men on horses rode out, paying me little attention as I crossed it – one of the benefits of being plain.

In the courtyard there were a great many doors leading into the palace. Some were grand, and I suspected that were I to knock upon one, a butler would refuse to let me pass. And I had to pass, so before long it would doubtless have felt as though we were out on a date, dancing. I therefore chose the smallest and shabbiest door I could find. Inside was a corridor lined with pegs, and he peg at the far end held a maid's costume. As I approached it, a portly woman appeared as if from nowhere and handed it to me. "You're late!" she said.

"Late? Oh, no! Has the Princess Aurora been pricked? Has she fallen into a coma?" The woman did not answer my question, opting instead to ask one of her own: "Are you quite normal?"

I shrugged. "Well, I'm obviously not *normal*, but I find that I'm able to function on a rudimentary level. Why do you ask?"

"Not only are you talking absolute *gibberish,* but you're dreadfully pale."

I nodded. "I'm visible from space most nights. So, Princess Aurora hasn't been pricked by a spinning wheel, then?"

"Of *course* she hasn't. The king banned them all."

It was clear that as well as being rude, this woman was considerably less well informed than I. "I won't be needing this costume," said I, handing it back to her. "And now, if you could just point me in the direction of Princess Aurora, I'll be on my way." I don't know if you've ever been boxed about the ears by a portly woman who is less well informed than you are, but I would not recommend it. It makes your lobes smart. "Get off me!" cried I, for that seemed the appropriate thing to cry under the circumstances. I crouched down, scrambled under her legs, and sprinted for all I was worth.

When I eventually slowed to a trot, I caught sight of my reflection and wondered why I was running like a pony. I stopped doing so and stood before a mirror. It was tall and grand, and I thought that boded well for my location in the Palace. I sensed that the mirror was about to speak, and stopped it with a raised palm. "Before you prove that you need your eyes tested, could you please just tell me where I might find Princess Aurora?"

The mirror yawned.

"Am I keeping you up?" I asked it.

"Now you come to mention it, yes."

"Hard work being a reflective surface, is it?"

"Of late. I blame the location."

I looked left and right down the ornate hallway. "What has the location to do with it?"

"It's the ideal place to stop for a chinwag. And whenever people stop and wag their chins, they keep me awake."

"I don't see why this should be such an ideal location."

"Really? Did you not just choose it to stop and wag your own chin?"

I could not deny it. "If you'd just tell me where I might find Princess Aurora, I'll be on my way."

"You're in luck. She wandered by here not five minutes ago."

"*Please* tell me that she didn't look the least bit restless."

"Now you come to mention it, I've never seen her look so restless. In fact, I've never seen her before. She's supposed to remain in her rooms."

"Then she must be about to come upon it!"

"Come upon what?"

"A room where an old lady is making clothes with a spinning wheel!"

"Relax. There is no such room. The king banned the use of spinning wheels sixteen years ago when the Princess was born. The Eighth Fairy placed a curse on her, you know."

"I had heard about the curse, yes."

"That Eighth Fairy is bad news. Wagging chins inform me that it all started when she went away to assist The Author at his cabin. She had been gone for such a long time that the king forgot to invite her to the Princess's christening. The Eighth Fairy was so angry that she placed a curse on the poor little Princess. That curse is the reason she's been confined to her rooms for sixteen years. It's the fear of her coming into contact with a spinning wheel, you know."

The mirror's reminder of that which I already knew was timely. "You must tell me which way she went!"

"That way," said the mirror.

"Past that grandfather clock?"

"No. The *other* that way."

"Past the cabinet filled with china cups?"

"If there's a third option in this corridor, I'd like to hear about it."

Several anxious minutes later…

Several anxious minutes later, I heard voices coming from behind a door that was slightly ajar. "Are you *sure* you want to touch my spinning wheel?" asked an old woman.

"Oh, yes please!" replied a younger woman.

"But why?" asked the older woman.

"It's just something I've always wanted to do," replied the younger woman.

"Be my guest, then…"

I burst into the room and saw Princess Aurora reaching for the spinning wheel. "Step away from that wheel!" I cried.

The Princess looked at me with the dulled eyes of someone who, having been confined to her rooms for sixteen years for fear of being pricked by a spinning wheel, reaches for the first one she sees having left it. "But why shouldn't I touch it?" she asked, looking down her beautiful nose at me.

"Two reasons," said I, endeavouring to look down my fat nose and still see her.

"And they would be?"

"Well, firstly it's a wheel."

"And the second reason?"

"It's *spinning*."

"So?"

"So the curse so!"

"Oh, that," said she, glancing down at her beautifully manicured nails. "Surely touching it *once* couldn't hurt."

I took hold of her hand and pulled her from the room into the corridor. She protested loudly but stumbled after me nonetheless.

I went back into the room, closing and locking the door. I picked up the spinning wheel and hurled it through an open window. It splashed into the moat, where it bobbed about on the surface. "Oh, now you've really gone and done it," said the old woman. "The Eighth Fairy is going to be furious."

"Maybe so," said I, sucking on my pricked finger, "but you know what They say: you can't make an omelette without breaking some eggs."

"*You* just volunteered to be the eggs," said she, pointing a gnarled finger at me.

"And not the first time," said I.

"You must be Snow White."

"I cannot deny it." We heard another splash, and when I poked my head out of the window, I saw Princess Aurora swimming towards the spinning wheel. "You have got to be kidding!"

"Has she jumped into the moat after it?" asked the old woman.

"Yes!"

The old woman nodded sagely. “She's been told so many times and by so many people to avoid spinning wheels that she's grown up to find them irresistible…” I've no idea what the old woman said next, for the very next instant I leapt from the window. Down I fell, my nose pinched between thumb and forefinger in anticipation of the smelly green water that fast approached it.

Several moments and a splash later…

Several moments and a splash later, we must have made quite a sight: two fairytale characters who were never even supposed to meet, let alone end up splashing about and screaming together in a smelly green moat. The reason for our screaming (and to a lesser extent our splashing about) was this: neither of us could swim. Apparently, we hadn't been written that way, so it came as a relief when we realised the moat was only four feet deep and we could stand up. Aurora made a splashing lunge for the spinning wheel, and I made a lunge for Aurora. Despite my efforts, the princess landed flat upon the wheel. Fortunately for her, the wheel was no longer a spinning wheel but a bobbing wheel. I folded my arms and asked the Princess what she was bobbing and sobbing about.

"How am I to become the Sleeping Beauty now?"

"That wheel was *cursed*. Wouldn't you rather be a waking beauty than a sleeping one?"

Princess Aurora climbed off the wheel and stood up. "Like you, you mean?"

I shook my head. "All that bobbing and sobbing must have affected your vision. But all things considered, you're a very fortunate person."

"Yes, you are!" said an angry voice.

I looked up and beheld a young woman with short dark hair. She was wearing a pink dress and holding a purple wand. "The Eighth Fairy, I presume?" said I.

"Snow *White*, I presume?" said she. We placed our hands on our hips, a body language that said we'd presumed correctly.

"Well, this is a first," said she. "Not only are you in the wrong story, but also the wrong land!"

"I will travel anywhere to prevent an injustice." The Eighth Fairy pointed her wand at me and went red in the face. "You can't frighten me with a silly wand," said I, preparing to duck.

She lowered her wand. "There is somewhere I have to be, so I'll decide what to do with you later. Unlike you and your *meddling*, some of us have useful work to do." With that she turned and stomped off.

I moved swiftly to the edge of the moat and tried to climb out. The edge was steep and muddy, and no sooner had I hurled myself upon it than I had slid back down into the water. I turned to Princess Aurora. "Would you mind giving me a hand?"

"Not at all," said she, wading over to me. "Where are you going?"

"After the Eighth Fairy," said I, craning my neck and watching her stomp into an immense forest.

The Princess cupped her hands, and a glance from her pretty green eyes told me it was quite alright to place a foot in them. As I climbed out, she said, "She's headed into the forest of a million and one trees."

"A million and *one?* Sounds awfully precise."

"It's the *one* that counts the most."

"And why is that?"

"It leads to the Author's Cabin. And you must not for all the world even behold it."

"And why not?"

"Because it's forbidden. Don't you know Anything?"

I shook my head. "I've never had the pleasure of meeting him, but if there's one thing I do know, it's that *nothing* should prevent us from changing things for the better." I reached down and pulled her from the moat.

"You must be very brave," said she.

"Brave? No. Just meddlesome."

As I walked away, she called out, "Thank you! All things considered, I think being a waking beauty might be better after all."

I nodded. "You know what They say."

"No. What do They say?"

"That no one has ever had a fabulous time in a coma."

"Is that what They say?"

"I expect it is what Frank would say if he were here, yes."

"And what of my Prince Charming? He's expecting to come upon me in a coma."

"If he loves you he'll understand."

"And if he doesn't?"

“Then you hold out for a Charming who does.”

“Alright! I will.”

About an hour and some ten thousand trees later…

About an hour and some ten thousand trees later, I observed the Eighth Fairy stomp up to a cluster of five trees. As I watched her, it occurred to me that perhaps she wasn't in a bad mood after all. "Maybe she just has a ridiculous walk," murmured I. I crouched behind a tree and watched the Eighth Fairy cast her gaze about to check that she hadn't been followed. She must have considered the possibility a slim one, for she quickly stomped through the centre-most of the five trees and vanished.

I stood before the tree – which, to all intents and purposes, resembled a normal tree – and reached out to touch it. I was not surprised when my hand vanished inside, and relieved when the rest of me followed it…

I emerged into a pretty little garden with a picket fence. At one end of the garden was a white house, and at the other end a log cabin. The Eighth Fairy stomped up the steps towards the white house, opened the door with a key on a chain, and went inside. I breathed a sigh of relief and turned towards the log cabin. "That must be the Author's Cabin," said I, walking towards it. The door to the Author's Cabin had a round brass knob, which to my delight turned. The door opened…

Inside was a study with a desk, and upon the desk was a single book. Closer inspection revealed it to be a manuscript held together by a brass clip on its left-hand side. On the front was written, "*The Manuscript of The Book*, sole property of *The Author*." By the manuscript's side was a pencil with an eraser tip. The notion of holding *the book* alone was enough to give me goose bumps. After all, this was where the world of fairy tales had been created. Over time, and through word of mouth, its stories had been told in many lands, including your own. I opened the manuscript and flicked through its many pages until I came upon one where the names Happy, Grumpy, Sleepy, Bashful, Sneezy, Dopey and Doc had been written in the margin. They had been crossed out, and on the actual page were the names of my dwarves.

I remembered why I was there. "I must save Edward," said I. I was about to turn the page and find the part where the Queen was to find Edward guilty, when I paused and looked over my shoulder to make sure I was alone. I was. Steeling myself, I picked up the pencil and changed Insecure's name to Secure, then erased the *Not* in Not Particularly Hopeful's name. Even as I looked upon their new names, Secure and Particularly Hopeful, I felt different: as though I might as well feel secure and hopeful as feeling any differently was counter-productive. I added brackets above the changed names and in the brackets I wrote: "*and feeling secure and particularly hopeful should also apply to anyone who reads these words, for they are an important part of this story too*." "It's a good thing I didn't change Meddlesome's name," said I, smiling and turning the page. *And it's a very good thing I came*, I thought, as I read how the Queen was to find Edward guilty and sentence him to death by a thousand wolf bites. *Talk about overkill*. I erased all of that and replaced it with: '*and it came as a complete surprise to everyone in the land when the Queen found Edward innocent. And what's more, all the mirrors in the land were gifted with improved vision and as a result could see that they'd made an error: Snow White was not the fairest in the land at all, the Queen was, and from that day on they told her so.'* "I'm hopeful that will do the trick, "murmured I.

I flicked through *the book* and made one or two more changes. Sometime later, I yawned and stretched and said, “Meddlesome will be very pleased.”

When I left the cabin, I came upon the Eighth Fairy using her wand to water flowers in the garden. When she saw me, she looked very confused. I had read in The Book how, when I left the cabin, she would discover me and, in true fairytale style, would transform me into a rat as punishment for following her. And not just any rat: the rat *I* was to become was the fairest rat in the land. The poor rat was to live with four mice, and their names would reflect its – that's to say *my* – personality. The names of the mice were to be Flea-Ridden, Festering, Claustrophobic and Agoraphobic. Which basically meant that I would spend my days in a festering, flea-ridden panic whether I stayed in or went out. I had erased all that, choosing new words and actions for the Eighth Fairy. I therefore had an excellent idea of what she was going to say and do when she saw me. “Oh, it's you!” said she, as though surprised to see a long-lost friend.

“Yes, it is I.”

“Have you just visited the Author's Cabin?”

“I have.”

“Hope you found it to be clean and tidy?”

I nodded.

“Did you make any changes to *the book* while you were there?”

“Yes. And I have tried my best to do right by others.”

“And having done right by others, I expect you’re keen to get back to your own land to see how it's all panned out?”

“That's right. So, if you wouldn't mind waving that wand of yours and doing the honours…”

A moment later…

A moment later, I was back in my own land, and the first two people I came upon were Little Miss Muffet and the spider. They were in the midst of a passionate embrace, the spider's arms wrapped around her and their lips pressed tightly together. I imagine you must be grimacing, but there really is no need. Thanks to a *small* alteration on my part, the spider was no longer a spider but a handsome prince. And Little Miss Muffet's prince was no one-dimensional Charming either: he was a person of great imagination and wit. Indeed, he had the personality of the spider. When they saw me, they broke their embrace and before he had a chance to ask I said, "Yes, it was I who turned you into a handsome prince."

The prince bowed low. "However can I thank you?" he said.

"You can thank me by always remaining true to Little Miss Muffet."

"Consider it done," said he who had no name, and then asked if I might give him one.

Without a moment's hesitation, I replied, "Prince True of Hearts."

"Thank you!" said Little Miss Muffet, hugging her Prince True of Hearts.

"You have turned my worst fear into my true love!" said she, releasing her prince and opening her book of fairytale poems. She read aloud the amendments I had made to her poem (for they were in every copy of *the book* now): "*Little Miss*

Muffet sat on her tuffet eating her curds and whey, along came a spider who was turned into a handsome prince and they lived happily ever after."

"I'm sorry it doesn't rhyme, but I was pressed for time," said I, rhyming after I needed.

"Who needs a rhyme when you can live happily ever after with your one true love?"

"That was my thinking," said I. "While you have *the book* to hand, would you mind looking up Old Mother Hubbard's poem? I pasted a new one she'd written over the top of the Author's, but had no time to read it."

Little Miss Muffet flicked though *the book*. "Here it is," said she, scanning the poem.

"Well?" said I.

"It seems Old Mother Hubbard has a maid who waits on her hand and foot… yes, her maid brings her presents in every verse."

"And what of her dog?"

"Dog? There's no mention of a dog." I felt a little guilty for allowing Old Mother Hubbard to erase the dog from existence, but fortunately Little Miss Muffet was on hand with the most famous of They's quotes: "You can't make an omelette without breaking some eggs."

As I went on my way, I thought about that and decided that, despite the dog's erasure from existence, I was rather chuffed with the way my omelette was turning out.

The next character I came across was the no-eyed, no-brained toad. You may recall how he used to sell curds and whey down by the enchanted pond? And how, since Little Miss Muffet no longer spent her waking hours eating curds and whey, he had gone out of business. Having no eyes and no brain had proven an obstacle to starting a new career, but thanks to my alterations that was no longer the case. The no-eyed, no-brained toad now had 20/20 vision and an IQ of 240, which meant he had perfect eyesight and the biggest brain in the land. This went some way to explaining why he was hurriedly writing equations while simultaneously examining the surface of both moons without the aid of a telescope. I thought it best not to disturb the perfect-eyed, big-brained toad and continued on my way.

I hadn't gone far when I heard the most beautiful whistling I had ever heard. Barry the Boar came trotting from the undergrowth with his lips pursed. "My, what a fine whistle you have, Barry!"

"Thank you, Snow. No idea how it happened. One minute I was blowing raspberries, and the next…" Barry pursed his piggy lips and whistled the most enchanting melody. He stopped and said, "There's something different about you too, Snow."

"There is?"

"Yes. You look… happier."

"I cannot deny that I am feeling particularly hopeful."

"No one deserves to feel particularly hopeful more than you," said he. Then he pursed his lips and whistled on his way to work.

I little further on, I met the dwarves on *their* way to work. Meddlesome hurried over and shook my hand. He sounded awestruck as he said, "We heard through the grapevine that you found *the book*, and did some rewrites!"

Awkward, who was not far behind him, tripped over his own feet and stumbled to the ground. "Couldn't you have changed *my* name too?" he lamented, glancing over his shoulder at Secure and Particularly Hopeful.

"I didn't see the need," said I. "You are so very endearing the way you are, and everybody loves you."

Particularly Hopeful and Secure took hold of an arm each and lifted Awkward back onto his feet. "And you will always be well liked," said Particularly Hopeful.

Secure reached out and squeezed my shoulder. He smiled and said, "And the same goes for you, Snow."

"Thank you. And you no longer have any objections to my falling in love with Edward?"

Secure and Particularly Hopeful glanced at one another and shook their heads. "Why should we object?" said they.

I waved goodbye to the dwarves and set off along the path that led home, and had not gone far when I came upon the little lamb. My rewrites doubtless had something to do with the fact that he was no longer hopping about like a crazy thing with fleas. The little lamb was reclining in a hammock and enjoying the shade of a sunny day with a glass of milk. "Hello, Snow," said he, sipping from his glass.

"Hello, little friend," said I.

"I can tell by your smile that you've noticed there's something different about me."

"I have noticed."

"And do I have you to thank for my being able to relax and enjoy the moment?"

"I may have made a *small* amendment to *the book* concerning you, yes."

"I cannot thank you enough. This feels like what life ought to be about. Not rushing about and never sparing a moment to appreciate anything. Thank you."

"It was my pleasure."

"Where are you off to?"

"To find Edward."

The little lamb nodded. "The Queen pardoned him."

"I thought she might."

The little lamb smiled knowingly. "He's a lovely young man. I've known him since he was a boy."

"So he told me. You taught him how to read."

"Yes. And here he comes now."

"He does…?" said I, turning as Edward stepped from the woods into the clearing. He smiled as he walked towards me, but his smile no longer made me faint from famishment. Now it just made me smile too – which I considered not only a vast but also a workable improvement.

“Hello, Snow,” said he.

“Hello, Edward,” said I.

“Little lamb,” said Edward.

“Edward,” said the little lamb. “It seems we both owe a debt of gratitude to Snow and her meddling ways.”

“Agreed,” said Edward. “And what a sight for sore eyes you are,” he told me, which I believe to be a compliment. He approached me, took hold of my hands, raised them to his lips, and kissed them. I felt a little famished and wobbled slightly, but managed to stay on my feet. He raised a perfect eyebrow. “I wondered,” said he, pausing to ponder his wonder.

“You wondered?” enquired I.

“Yes. If you might spare me a few minutes of your time and walk with me.”

I had no timepiece, but had I one, I would not have had any great need of it at that moment. “Yes,” I replied. Edward offered me his arm and I took it – that's to say I held onto it as we walked.

“I bumped into your dwarves earlier,” said he.

“You did?”

“Yes. And I couldn't help but notice that a great change had come over two of their number.”

“And which two might that be?” said I, as though I had not even the first clue.

"Let me explain," said he. "You can imagine my surprise when Not Particularly Hopeful patted my back and said he was *particularly hopeful* about our future together."

"Yours and his?"

"Mine and yours."

"I see. I can only but wonder at your confusion."

"And that wasn't all."

"It wasn't?"

"No. Secure shook my hand – very firmly, I might add – and told me that you were up to the task of living happily ever after."

"With my dwarves?" said I.

Edward shook his head. "With me."

I drew a deep breath and smiled. Edward stopped walking and turned to face me. He studied my face and looked deeply into my eyes. "It's true, then? You do feel ready to live happily ever after?"

"Yes, I believe I do."

"Tell me," said he. "How did this miraculous change occur? And why are you smiling?"

"I am smiling because I discovered how to change those things within myself that stop me being happy and, having discovered how to change them, I …" I stopped talking because Edward had moved his head closer to mine, and wherever his head went his lips tended to go also. "Are you going to kiss me?" I asked.

"Truly, is that your heart's desire?" I could not answer, but something about my expression must have answered for me, for the next moment our lips touched. It would be inappropriate to go into too much detail about our first kiss. But when I tell you what They say about it, I think you'll understand: that no kiss before or after was ever as gentle or as passionate.

After our kiss, Edward walked me home. He was about to kiss me goodbye when Awkward stumbled out of the front door and landed in a heap. As we helped Awkward to his feet, he apologised for being so clumsy. Edward would hear nothing of it. "To be flawed is to be human, and beyond those flaws that would keep us apart, I would not change any of Snow's for anything in the land."

"Is that true?" said I.

Edward brushed a stray hair from my eyes. "You would not be the person I love without them."

That night when I went to bed, I thought about how fortunate I'd been to find and change *the book*, and also about all the friends who have accompanied me on this journey. It occurred to me that there might be one or two changes you'd make if you could find your own book. Well, you know what They say: that everyone has a book inside them. Frank assures me that people have misinterpreted what he said, and that he didn't mean that anyone can write one great novel. He said that's ridiculous. What he *actually* meant was that everyone has a book inside their imagination. And once conjured, changes can be made to those things that stand between them and their happiness. Frank has assured me that those things are almost always in the mind, and that anything in the mind *can* be changed. Best wishes. And goodnight to all. Snow.

Snow & Alice in Wonderland

Dear friends and confidants, several months have passed since I completed my last diary, The Return of Snow, and these words are the first I have written since. Edward, to whom I am betrothed, persuaded me it was no longer necessary to keep a diary.

"But why not?" I enquired as we strolled hand in hand by the enchanted lake.

"I should have thought that obvious. You see, in three short weeks, we are to be married."

"And?"

"And, my love, do you really think that anyone is going to be interested in reading a diary about someone living happily ever after?"

"Well ..." said I, preparing to make my case.

Edward stopped walking, looked out over the enchanted lake, sighed and said, "Your daily routine is to become one of unceasing happiness, Snow."

"It is? Can you really be so certain?"

Edward nodded and explained his reason for doing so. "So much so that each and every day might best be summed up with a smiling face." He gazed down at me, and smiled that smile of his that, as you may recall, used to make me faint from famishment. "How likely is it that anyone is going to be interested in seeing page after page of smiling faces?"

"I suppose your point is a reasonable one," said I.

Three weeks have passed since we had that conversation. And so much has changed! I write these words on what was to have been our wedding night. I'm at the cottage that I share with my dwarves. But Edward is not here with us. He has been swapped! With a stranger called Alice. I will endeavour to order my thoughts and explain how this came to pass. Several hours ago, I was standing at the altar, blushing beneath my veil as Edward repeated the vows spoken by the high priest. It was a grand occasion, and the cathedral was packed to the rafters with dignitaries from all over the land. Even my father, who is known for being absent (for he has been written that way) returned for my wedding. He sat beside my stepmother looking just as proud as she looked disdainful. I focused all my attention on the sound of Edward's voice as he repeated his vows. Then, when it came my turn to do the same, and despite my nerves, I spoke my own vows loud and true. Finally, the high priest asked Edward to place the ring on my finger, and through the ringing in my ears, I heard Edward say, "I do." But then, when it came time for me to say that I did, or rather, I do, Edward had vanished into thin air! Standing beside me on the same spot, I beheld a girl of similar age and height to myself, dressed in a blue and white dress. She observed me as though my expression had led her to believe that I had lost my wits. "Did you see a white rabbit come this way?" she enquired of me matter of factly, as though an absence of wits was commonplace where she'd come from. Her enquiry prompted gasps from the congregation and, in response, the girl, whose name I've since learned is Alice, whispered out of the corner of her mouth, “Look. Have you seen a white rabbit come this way, or haven't you?”

“*Edward*?” said I, as though in a trance.

“*Edward*?” repeated she, casting her gaze about, I presumed, for sight of a fleeing rabbit. “Is that the rabbit's name?”

“Edward is the name of my true love,” murmured I. “And we're to be married this very day.”

“You're to marry the rabbit this very day? I've seen some peculiar things since I fell down that hole but *really* … is it quite legal to marry a rabbit?” I felt my senses returning, and along with my senses, a keen sense of injustice. I gripped her shoulders and shrieked, “Edward is a person! A beautiful person! A poor person. And perfect! What have you done with him?”

“Unhand me this instant!” exclaimed she. I felt a hand upon my shoulder and looked askance into the worried yet determined expression of my friend, Little Red. She motioned with her head towards my stepmother and said, “*She's* responsible for this. I'd bet my bonnet on it.” Little red is more than a little attached to her bonnet, and would not enter it into a bet unless confident of winning.

“Excuse me,” said I to Alice, “I need a word with someone.”

“With who?”

“With *her*,” said I, darting a glance in the direction of my stepmother.

"Why? Does she know where the white rabbit went?"

"I think it unlikely. But I bet she knows where Edward is." I marched down the steps that led up to the altar, the great train of my wedding dress swishing over the ground behind me, and made a beeline for my stepmother. The horrid woman sat beside my father who, as usual, looked rather less compos than mentis, that is to say, he smiles a lot but hasn't had much to say for himself in years. In comparison, my stepmother looked like the cat who'd got the cream.

"Is there a problem?" enquired she, doing her best not to smile.

"A problem? Why should there be a *problem*," said I sarcastically as Alice pitched up beside me.

"And who have we here?" enquired my stepmother looking Alice up and down.

"This is Alice. The young woman I *almost* married just now. What have you to say to *that*?"

"Whatever makes you happy, dear. We're very forward thinking here in the land."

Ignoring this, I enquired pointedly: "Where is Edward?"

"Edward?" said she, glancing about as though the name rang a bell.

"Edward! The boy I was to marry today. Why else are we all here?" said I, balling my hands into fists.

My stepmother chose to ignore my question and instead spoke to Alice. "Why do you keep gazing about? Have you lost something?"

Alice nodded. "Have you seen him?"

My stepmother leaned forwards in her seat. "Seen who, dear?"

"The White Rabbit."

"My my, what careless young women you are! You've both lost things. You ought to get on like a house on fire."

"I have not *lost* Edward," said I.

"Really? Then perhaps you can tell me where he is?"

I felt a sense of dread descend upon me. "*That* I do not know. But something tells me that you do. So? Where *is* he? TELL ME WHAT YOU HAVE DONE WITH EDWARD!?" To this, gasps rang out around the cathedral.

My stepmother lowered her voice to barely a whisper. "I suggest you lower your voice, dear *stepdaughter*. That is, if you want your dwarves to see another sunrise."

"I knew it … *where* … where is he?"

"Switched," whispered she, menacingly.

"Switched?"

My stepmother glanced at Alice. "With *her*. And that is all I am going to say on this matter." Then, in a voice loud enough to echo about the cathedral, she added, "There is to be no wedding today. The careless bride has mislaid the groom!"

The events that followed are somewhat of a blur. But I seem to recall an irresistible urge to bop my stepmother on the nose, but being thwarted in my attempt by someone (turns out it was Little Red) who grabbed me from behind and dragged me from a spinning cathedral. I must have fainted for I woke up not ten minutes ago and found myself back at the cottage. I discovered Alice asleep in the spare room, and have resolved not to wake her until the morning, when we shall get to the bottom of all this.

The following morning …

At sun up, I climbed out of bed and walked forlornly from my bedroom into the living room. As you may recall, at the end of my last diary, I discovered the book in which all our stories are written, and I took the opportunity to do some *tiny* re-writes. First and foremost, I made sure my stepmother would pardon Edward so that he might live happily ever after. I also took the opportunity to change the names of two of my dwarves so that I might join him. And so, under my penmanship, Insecure became Secure, and Not Particularly Hopeful became Particularly Hopeful.

This morning, I came upon my dwarves, whose names are Awkward, Meddlesome, Inconsolable and the recently renamed *Secure* and *Particularly* Hopeful, sitting at the table and eating their porridge. You may recall how their names reflect aspects of my own personality. This explained why Inconsolable had not touched his porridge, and why his eyes were puffy from crying. Indeed, looking into Inconsolable's eyes was like looking into my own troubled soul. Thankfully, it was the new and much welcome influence of Secure and Particularly Hopeful that provided the strength I needed to remain compos mentis. Particularly Hopeful finished the last of his porridge, placed his spoon beside his bowl, wiped his chin with his napkin and said, "Not to worry, Snow. Wherever Edward is, whatever the queen has done with him, you'll find him. All will be well again. You mark my words."

"I couldn't agree more," said Secure.

“The queen has left you with NO choice,” chipped in Meddlesome.

“No choice?” said I, slumping down into my chair at the head of the table.

Meddlesome puffed out his chest. “No choice but to meddle with her evil plans, and restore some much-needed order.”

“I agree!” exclaimed Awkward banging his fist upon the table, catching the end of his spoon, and sending it spinning into the wall behind. As I watched a clump of porridge ooze down the wall, Alice emerged from the spare room. She pulled up a chair and sat down at the table next to me as though she'd been a part of our family for years. No prizes for guessing what the first words out of mouth were. “I don't suppose any of you have seen a …” She was unable to finish her question due to the chorus of “NO's!”

“I take it you've all met Alice then?” said I, “and that no introductions are necessary?”

Secure picked some porridge from between his teeth with a tooth pick and said, “Little Red made the introductions after she carried you into your room and put you to bed.”

Meddlesome nodded. “Alice came here from another land.”

“Wonderland,” said Alice.

“What's it like in Wonderland?” asked Secure.

“I hadn’t been there long but long enough to know that it's perfectly bonkers,” replied she.

“You don't strike me as being *particularly* bonkers,” said Secure, scrutinising her.

"That's because I'm not from Wonderland. I was only visiting there."

"Then what land *are* you from?" enquired Particularly Hopeful.

"England."

"*England*? That rings a bell," said I, as the dwarves began nodding.

"I should hope it rings a bell," said Alice. "I should think that everyone must have heard of England."

Particularly Hopeful licked his clean spoon and placed in down in his bowl. "Yes, you may be right," said he, "but none of us can quite place it. Which way *is* England exactly? I mean as the crow flies?"

"Interesting question," said Alice. "If you tell me where I am, then perhaps I might answer it?"

"You're in *The* Land," said I with a sigh.

"*The* land?" repeated she none the wiser.

"The Land of Fairytales," said Meddlesome.

"I *am*? Really?!"

"Why the excitement?" murmured I.

"Because where I come from …"

"England?" interrupted Meddlesome.

"Yes, England. You see, where I come from in England, the

land of fairytales only exists in the pages of books." All present, including myself, leaned forwards in our seats and peered closely at Alice, our mouths fallen open. "Are you saying …" said I, "are you *saying* that you're from *the real world*?"

"Yes. Of course. Via Wonderland." A heavy silence descended, a silence that was punctuated by the sound of Awkward falling backwards off his chair and landing upon the ground with a clunk. Alice sat up and peered over the table. "… Is he alright?"

"Perfectly alright. He falls of off things on a regular basis," said Particularly Hopeful.

Alice slid back in her seat. "If you say so."

"But you *can't* be from the real world," said I.

"I can assure that that is precisely where I am from," said Alice, casting her gaze down forlornly. "All this talk of the real world only reminds me that, well that …"

"That what?" asked Awkward, climbing back onto his chair.

"That I am more lost than anyone has ever been," said she, lifting her gaze from the table and looking at each of us in turn. "That is why I need to find the white rabbit. You see, I followed him down his rabbit hole to Wonderland, and he alone knows the way back. I fear he is still in Wonderland, and that I may never find my way there, let alone home to the real world …" Tears came to Alice's lovely blue eyes. I stood up slowly. "We will find a way to Wonderland. We *must*, for I feel it in my water …"

"Feel what?" said Awkward, making himself comfortable.

"That just as Alice was brought here against her will, so Edward was transported to Wonderland against *his*, and that our going there is the only way I will find him. The queen said as much. And I believe her."

"And find the white rabbit?" said Alice, brightening somewhat.

"Yes, of course the white rabbit," said I.

Reassured thus, Alice asked, "So, if this is *truly* the land of fairytales, who might you all be?"

"Need you ask?" said Meddlesome, puffing out his chest with pride. "You're sitting with *the* dwarves."

"What dwarves?"

"Only the most famous dwarves in all creation," said Secure.

"Isn't it obvious who we all are?" added Meddlesome.

Alice looked at me, furrowed her pretty blond brow, and said, "*Snow*?"

"Please to meet you," said I, discovering I could still smile.

"You're Snow *White!* The fairest in the land? Really?"

"That is what they tell me."

"Now you come to mention it, I *thought* I recognised you from somewhere. Of course, your illustrations! But … what of the dwarves," said she, scrutinizing them.

"What of us?" said Secure.

"Well, for starters, there's supposed to be *seven* of you. And your names, your names …"

"Their names were changed by the book's author. Presumably *after* it found its way to the real world," said I. "As you can see, in reality, there are *five* dwarves."

Alice jumped up and ran to the kitchen window. "So? Who else lives here? I mean from the land of fairytales who I might have heard of?"

I sighed. "Just about *everyone* else, I should imagine."

After breakfast …

After breakfast, Alice and I set off for the one person in the land who might shed some much-needed light on how we might reach Wonderland. I refer, of course, to They (as in you know what They say), better known in these parts as Frank. We had not gone far when we heard the little lamb call from behind us. “Hello Snow!”

I turned around. “Hello little lamb.”

“So what news if any of Edward's whereabouts?” asked he.

I shook my head, then nodded. “Yesterday, in the cathedral, my stepmother whispered that he'd been switched with Alice. Where are my manners? Little lamb, may I introduce Alice, Alice this is my good friend the little lamb.”

“Pleased to meet you,” said they to each other.

“Alice was brought here against her will from a place called Wonderland,” said I.

“Although, I'm from *England* originally,” said Alice.

“England?” said the little lamb, “in the *real world*.”

I smiled. “How well informed you are on the whereabouts of lands.” You may recall how the little lamb used to hop, skip and jump all the time but how, since I found the book and made a *tiny* alteration, he can now stroll normally and appreciate the moment like other lambs. And, so it was, that the little lamb stood perfectly still as I explained Alice and I’s shared predicament. Once I'd finished, he said, “I take it you're on your way to consult with They then?"

"That's right …" said I, as Barry the boar came flying out of the undergrowth with Little Red on his back.

"Thank *goodness* I caught you!" exclaimed she.

"Why? Whatever is the matter?"

"It's bad news, I'm afraid," said Little Red climbing off Barry's back.

"The queen, the queen!" panted Barry, trying to catch his breath.

"What of her?" I asked. Little Red smacked her right fist into her left palm. "Your *stepmother* guessed that you might attempt to restore order by consulting with They, and has sent her guard to arrest him."

"She's done what!" exclaimed I.

"And has he been arrested?" asked Alice.

Little Red and Barry shook their heads. "Course not," said Barry, "you know what They say, don't you?"

"No. What does Frank say?"

"That forewarned is forearmed," said Little Red, narrowing her eyes.

"And who forewarned him?"

"The Grapevine. Who else?" said Barry.

"Frank's taken refuge then?"

Little Red nodded at me.

“Where?” asked Alice.

“In the one place in the land where a happy ending is always ensured,” said Little Red.

“You mean with the three bears?” said I.

Barry nodded. “Jump on Snow. You too, Alice. I'll have you both there in three shakes of a lamb's tail.” Alice climbed onto Barry's back behind me, and Barry took off at speed, leaving Little Red and the little lamb in the clearing.

Alice clung tightly to me and above the sound of clomping hooves said, “Can it be true?”

“Can what be true?” said I over my shoulder.

“That we are going to visit the three bears?”

“We are.”

“Crikey. And might Goldilocks be there?”

“Where else?”

“I've always wanted to meet her.”

“Well, brace yourself for a bit of a disappointment.”

“What do you mean?”

“The sad truth is that Goldilocks is only interested in two things: porridge and bed.”

“Of course! Everybody knows that. But she must have other interests.”

"None that I'm aware of. And she lived with me for a time."

As we approached the cottage where the three bears live with Goldilocks, Barry slowed to a trot. "I'll keep watch out here," said he, sniffing at the air. "You two go and have your talk with Frank."

"Thank you, Barry," said I, climbing down off his back with Alice.

I knocked on the door. Daddy Bear opened it and, standing on his hind legs, peered over our heads. You may recall how Edward had taken refuge with the three bears for a time, and how, during that time, he had turned up for our first date wearing a dress. This had been entirely due to the three bears having acute myopia. That's to say, they're as blind as bats, and mistook Edward for the female Goldilocks they had been expecting. Which explains why Daddy Bear asked, "Is there someone there?"

"Yes. We're down here," said I.

"Hello Daddy Bear," said Alice, gazing up in delight. Daddy Bear squinted down at her and sniffed at the air. At that moment, They, also known as Frank the groundhog, scrambled up onto Daddy Bear's shoulder and said, "You *are* here. Alice of Wonderland!"

"Indeed, it is her," said I. "Where are my manners? Alice, may I introduce They and Daddy Bear."

"But he *can't* be They," blurted out Alice.

"Frank and I have already had this conversation," said I. "You think it odd that *They* is plural and Frank here is singular."

Alice nodded. “Why don't you call yourself I?”

“Because if I did then every time someone quoted me they'd sound like an English gentleman,” Frank pointed out.

“You’d better demonstrate Frank,” said I.

“Alright. ‘I say, a bird in the hand is worth two in the bush.’ ‘I say, there's no time like the present. Or, ‘I say, you should never count your chickens before they've hatched.’”

“I do see what you mean,” said Alice, scratching her head. “And I thought Wonderland was a bonkers place.”

“I can assure that when it comes to bonkers that Wonderland has nothing on this place,” said I, barging past the myopic bear with They on his shoulder.

Once inside, we came upon Goldilocks sitting at the table, scraping her bowl for any last vestige of porridge. “Goldilocks! It really is you!” said Alice quite taken aback.

Goldilocks placed her spoon down in her bowl and yawned. “Have we met?”

Alice shook her head. “No. But mother and father used to read your story to me when I was little. It was my favourite. No offence,” said she, glancing at me.

“None taken,” I assured her.

Goldilocks stood up, stretched, and said, “Then you'll know that it's time for bed.”

“But won't you stay …?” said Alice as Goldilocks turned towards the stairs.

"Absolutely not. No can do," said she, stifling a yawn.

As we watched Goldilocks ascend the stairs, I placed a hand of Alice's shoulder. "It's nothing personal, it's just the way she's written: porridge followed by bed followed by porridge followed by bed."

Alice sighed. "It's probably a good thing her story ended when it did then."

"A *very* good thing, I should imagine."

Once Daddy Bear had explained that Mummy and baby bear had gone out early to fetch oats and honey, and that he too had chores to attend to, Alice and I sat at the kitchen table with Frank.

"Before we begin there's one more person I've invited," said Frank glancing at the open window.

"Who?" said I.

"No. Who wouldn't have been any use in solving this conundrum." Just then, the mystery guest came slithering through the open window.

"What is *that*?" said Alice, shrinking back in her seat.

"Fear not," said I, for it is just the Grapevine. I glanced at Frank who had raised his rabbit-like nose in a superior fashion. As Alice watched the Grapevine creeping over the ground towards us, she whispered, "Doesn't Frank like the Grapevine?"

I shook my head. "They fell out when the Grapevine said that you should take everything They (Frank) says with a pinch of salt."

"How rude of the Grapevine," said Alice who added quietly, "Although, I believe I've heard my mother say as much."

"I must confess," said I, "that I had not expected to see the two in the same room."

"I heard that *They* wished to bury the hatchet," said the Grapevine as its tentacle came to rest on the back of a chair.

"What? Through *yourself*?" said I, stifling a chuckle and convinced that such a marvellous joke must relax the tension. It didn't. But it was pleasing to hear Alice chuckle nonetheless.

Frank cleared his throat and exhaled slowly as though composing himself. "The problem at hand is enormous. And you know what They say, don't you?"

"No. What do you say?" said Alice and I in unison.

Frank twirled his groundhoggy whiskers. "That a problem shared is a problem halved."

"Excellent!" said I. "For if any problem needed halving it is this one."

The Grapevine nodded the tip of its tentacle in agreement, then slithered towards Alice whose face it seemed intent on taking in every feature of. I remembered what being under such intense scrutiny from the Grapevine was like from my time as Orange Orange.

"Is there something the matter with my face?" asked Alice going a little boss-eyed as the Grapevine's tentacle touched the tip of her button nose.

"Just making sure you are who you say you are."

“Who else would I be?” enquired Alice.

“Who indeed,” said the Grapevine glancing in my direction.

Feeling a little awkward, I blushed and said, “Convincing all the land that I was no longer Snow White but a new character called Orange Orange was a tactical necessity.”

“I realise that now,” said the Grapevine turning its attention back to Alice.

“Alice is from the real world,” said I keen to change the subject. My pronouncement was met with silence from Frank and the Grapevine.

Alice looked back and forth between them. “I am from the real world you know. Via Wonderland.” The Grapevine nodded at Frank as though to confirm Frank's suspicions.

“What is it?” said I.

Frank twirled his whiskers. “Alice is *sort of* from the real world.”

“And she sort of isn't,” added the Grapevine.

“*What*?” said Alice. “I'll have you know that there's no sort of about it.”

“Well, yes and no,” said the Grapevine.

“Oh, for goodness sake!” exclaimed I, “If you know something then tell us what it is.”

Frank placed his paws down upon the table. “I strongly suspected, and now I've had it confirmed by the Grapevine, there can be no doubt about it.”

"About what?" huffed Alice.

"That Alice is a *fictional* character just like the rest of us," said the Grapevine.

"A fictional character whose story begins and ends in the real world," added Frank.

A fraught moment later …

A fraught moment later, Alice had gazed about fitfully for someone of whom a second opinion to this ludicrous pronouncement could be asked, and a glance had passed between Frank and myself that had left me in little doubt that their pronouncement had been correct.

“You are Alice of the *fictional* story Alice in Wonderland,” said Frank.

“What’s more,” added the Grapevine, “your story was written in the 19th century by a man called Lewis Carroll.” At the mention of Lewis Carroll, Alice jumped to her feet as though pricked by a pin, stumbled a couple of steps, and then collapsed in a heap as though felled by an arrow.

“Whatever is the matter with her!?” exclaimed I as I knelt beside her.

The Grapevine’s tentacle hovered over her. “Alice has heard the one thing that no character is ever supposed to hear,” said he.

“And that would be?”

“The name of her author.”

“Lewis Carroll? Then why bring her author’s name up?”

“The answer to that question is your territory, Frank,” said the Grapevine.

Frank twirled the ends of his whiskers before making

perhaps his best known and most profound statement: "Because you can't make an omelette without breaking some eggs." As I gazed down at the slumbering eggs in question, Frank added, "She will know for certain that she's a fictional character now. You are both facing a very tricky conundrum. And time is of the essence."

Alice came round with a start, sat bolt upright and exclaimed: "I do not exist! I am fictional!"

I took hold of her hand. "Don't be silly. Of *course,* you exist."

"As a fictional character like the rest of us," added Frank.

"Can there *be* such a thing as a fictional character who exists!" cried Alice.

"Why shouldn't there be?" asked the Grapevine.

"Because it's *such* a contradiction!"

"Now listen here," said Frank, "just because you're a contradiction, it doesn't mean you have to shout."

"Is that what They say?" the Grapevine asked Frank.

"That is what I say, yes," replied Frank.

"I shall pass it on to all in sundry then," said the Grapevine.

"You do that," said Frank.

"You're both bonkers!" cried Alice.

"Look," sighed I, "fictional contradiction or not, Alice needs to return to Wonderland to find the white rabbit. And I must accompany her, for my one true love has been banished there. So, how do we get there?"

Frank lay on his back, placed his front paws behind his head and, gazing up at the ceiling said, "It's a tricky business travelling between lands."

The Grapevine's tentacle rose up from the floor and hovered over him. "It's a matter of direction," murmured he.

"Well, it's *obviously* a matter of direction," huffed Alice.

"Not any direction. The *correct* direction," said Frank.

"The correct direction to leave this land and arrive in Wonderland," added the Grapevine. To this, Frank lifted a paw from behind his head and pointed it at the ceiling.

"The entrance to Wonderland is upstairs? I must say that would be awfully convenient," said I, hopefully.

"I'm afraid it is not ..." sighed Frank.

"Why don't you tell them what you heard through me once upon a time," said the Grapevine.

Frank nodded. "You have to travel a good deal higher than the bedroom of the three bears to find the entrance to Wonderland."

"How much higher exactly?" enquired I.

Frank narrowed his eyes, and said mysteriously, "There is only *one place* in all the land which comes close to being high enough."

Alice and I glanced at one another. “And that place would be?” we asked.

“You're familiar with the story of Jack and his Beanstalk?” asked Frank.

“I believe I've heard of that particular story,” said I uncertainly, “but like most stories in this land, the specifics are a little hazy.” Following a hunch, I looked at Alice whose expression confirmed my suspicion that she was well acquainted with the story. Frank and the Grapevine must have followed my own train of thought for they too focused their attention on Alice. “I know Jack’s story,” she said.

“We're all ears,” said I.

“But you live here, in the land of fairytales. Don't any of you know it?”

“Yes, but only in the vaguest of terms,” nodded the Grapevine.

Frank scratched behind his left ear. “The stories of the land are like half remembered dreams to those of us who live here.”

“Half remembered? Rather less than a quarter remembered,” added the Grapevine.

Alice placed her hands behind her back, paced up and down the kitchen, and related the story. If you're reading this, it doubtless means you're in the real world, and must therefore already be well acquainted with it. And being acquainted with it, you will know that it's not Jack and *his* Beanstalk but Jack and *the* Beanstalk. You will be aware how Jack's mother sent him to market to buy a cow, but how, having met an unscrupulous person on the way, Jack swapped the money his mother gave him for some magic beans. You will also have heard how, when he cast them to the ground, they grew into a beanstalk, a beanstalk down which a terrible giant descended.

“So,” mused I, “in order to reach Wonderland, we must find and climb Jack's beanstalk?”

“That’s absolutely right,” said the Grapevine. “And you know what They say.”

Alice and I looked at Frank and braced ourselves.

“That you can't reach Wonderland without climbing Jack's beanstalk and avoid being torn asunder by the homicidal giant who lives up there in a castle.”

“I see,” said I. “It's not one of your better-known sayings, is it?”

“Give it time,” replied Frank.

“Time may be a luxury you can’t afford,” said a voice above us. We looked and beheld Little Red swinging on the chandelier. She leapt off it, landed on the table, leapt off the table, did a somersault, and landed upon the ground where she whipped out her copy of the book. She opened it at a bookmarked page, stabbed a finger upon it, and said, “It’s bad news, I'm afraid. Jack has already planted his magic beans.”

“And?” said I.

“And, in just a few days’ time, he's going to chop down the beanstalk.”

"Time must be of the essence then," surmised I.

"Exactly!" said Little Red heading for the door.

"But how are we to find the beanstalk?" asked Alice.

Little Red reached the door and turned to face us. "Fear not for I know the way to Jack's village."

"It lies beyond the furthest reaches of the Woods of Utter Despair," said the Grapevine.

"I know," said Little Red.

"The Woods of Utter Despair?" said I. "Isn't it close to where Hansel and Gretel live?"

"Their cottage lies at the southernmost tip of the Woods of Utter Despair," nodded Little Red.

The grapevine's tentacle rose up majestically and said, "You must travel *through* the wood and exit it in the north. Jack's village is located close to its northernmost boundary."

Ten minutes later …

Ten minutes later, Alice, Little Red and myself were sat atop Barry who, if I'm honest, was struggling to trot as fast as a canter. Still, his effort was such that I needed to clasp hold of his tusks, just as Alice clasped hold of Little Red, and Little Red held onto me. It was while we three sat as just described, that the following question occurred to me: “The Woods of Utter Despair?” said I over the sound of Barry's clomping hooves.

“What of them?” replied Little Red.

“I take it that whoever named them did so because of their scant knowledge about them?” At that moment, I detected a swaying in Barry's gait, and a glance over my shoulder provided the reason for this: Little Red was shaking her head with gusto.

That can't be good,” thought I.

“That can't be good,” said Alice as though she’d read my thoughts.

“Well then,” said I, “it must surely be that whoever named them was a pessimist.” Barry's gait, which, moments before, had returned to normal, once again went topsy turvy.

“Not a bit of it,” replied Little Red as Barry missed colliding with a tree by centimetres. “In fact,” Little Red went on, “the fellow in question was considered to be the greatest optimist in the land.”

“Really?” said I.

“Bar none,” replied Little Red.

"Well, who was this person? And what made *him* such an expert on these woods?"

"The fellow's name was Eustace Eustace Eustace," said Little Red. "Although his friends called him Todd. Todd dedicated his life to the study of the woods. It was on his death bed that Todd re-named them The Woods of Utter Despair."

"How sad. So what did Todd die of?"

"Utter despair. He spent way too much time in those woods."

"I see. Are you going to ask the obvious question or am I," I asked Alice over my shoulder.

"Be my guest," replied Alice, politely.

I drew a deep breath, braced myself, and enquired, "So what were the woods called before Todd renamed them the Woods of Utter Despair?"

"Are you quite certain you wish to know?" replied Little Red.

"Quite certain, yes. I would not have enquired otherwise."

"As you wish. They were called The Prepare to Lose Your Grip On Sanity If You Dare Enter These Woods Woods."

"Bit of a mouthful …" mused Alice.

"Yes. But highly effective," said Little Red, "for it prevented people from entering them and travelling to the lands in the north for hundreds of years."

"And why was that so important?" I asked.

"It ensured that no one from the south would meddle with the stories in the north."

I shuddered. "How dreadful." A house that I recognised hove into view. A house that you would recognise too if you saw it, made, entirely as it is, from gingerbread.

Barry skidded to halt and we all three jumped off his back. Above Barry's panting, I heard a sound similar to the one that I heard when I first visited. "It sounds like Gretel's chopping wood with the axe that proved so useful in changing her story to one with a happy ending," said I. "Well, happy for everyone except the witch."

"And a fine bit of meddling that was too," said Little Red. "Second only to how you meddled in my own affairs and ensured that I wasn't eaten by the big bad wolf."

"And how you meddled in my affairs, and ensured that I can whistle despite my piggy lips," panted Barry.

Alice looked at me. "My my, you *have* been busy."

"You don't know the half it," said I, turning and striding purposefully towards the sound of chopping.

Behind me, I heard Alice ask little Red, "So, you're not going to be gobbled up by the big bad wolf then?"

"That's right. I'd like to see him try. And what's more, Snow promised me Cinderella's Prince Charming. We've already been out on a couple of dates."

"And how does Cinderella feel about that?"

"She couldn't care less because Snow gifted her her own Charming."

"You gave your Prince Charming to *Cinderella*?" came Alice's bewildered voice from behind me.

"I cannot deny it."

"Very generous, I'm sure," said she.

"Not really. I have never been keen on Charmings. Much too one dimensional for my tastes."

"So how's it going with Cinderella's Charming?" Alice asked Little Red.

"I dumped him."

I stopped in my tracks and turned around to face them. "You did *what?*"

"I think you heard."

"But why? You seemed so keen on having a Charming to live happily ever after with?"

"I've had a change of heart. It's adventure I crave. Not sweet nothings."

"For what it's worth, I think you've made the right decision. Adventure suits you very well," said Alice.

I smiled. "In that we are all in agreement."

When we came upon Gretel, she was not chopping wood but hurling axes, one after another, into a tree with a witch's head carved into it. "Oh bravo!" cried Little Red. Gretel spun about to face us, axe in hand. When she saw that it was I, she lowered her axe and smiled. "You're a sight for sore eyes," said she. Which, as I've mentioned in my previous diary, I believe to be a compliment.

“Ditto,” said I, rubbing at my own peepers. “This is Alice, Little Red you already know. Alice, this is Gretel.”

“Hello!” said Alice, walking forwards with hand outstretched. “I’m very pleased to make your acquaintance. And happy to hear that the witch didn’t eat you, after all.”

“Thank you,” said Gretel placing the axe in her belt and shaking her hand. “Nice to make your acquaintance, too. The grapevine passed through here recently. I'm sorry to hear about what happened on your wedding day, Snow. Whatever does the fairest in the land need to do to get a break in this land?”

“You're not wrong,” nodded I. “Edward was switched with Alice, and now they're both far from those they love.”

Gretel’s hand went to the axe in her belt. “Word through the Grapevine is that your evil stepmother was responsible.”

I nodded.

“Maybe I should deal with her?”

“Whatever do you mean?” asked I.

“I mean you were right about an axe being the solution to my own woes. And since then, I've made axe combat my life's study. *So, woe be tide* any evil witches,” said she, casting a furtive glance about her.

I straightened my back. “Thank you for your kind offer. But I don’t think that it’s such a good idea. I mean, evil witches are one thing but vindictive queens are quite another.”

Gretel shrugged. “So, what brings you here, to the boundary of the Woods of Utter Despair?”

I swallowed a lump that had risen into my throat. “We must pass through them,” said I, looking through the trees in their direction.

“*What*? But why?” said Gretel.

“To travel to the land to the north, for that is where we will find the beanstalk.”

“Beanstalk?”

“*Jack's*,” said Alice.

“Yes, Jack’s,” said I. “We have it on good authority that the entrance to Wonderland is located at its top.”

Gretel scratched the side of her head thoughtfully. “Doesn’t an angry giant live up there?”

I nodded bravely. “And we must avoid him at all costs.”

Gretel shuddered. “That's supposing you even make it through the Woods of Utter Despair. You do know what they used to be called I suppose?”

“We do,” said I, stoically.

“It's just …” said Gretel.

“It's just what?” asked Little Red narrowing her eyes.

“The sounds I hear coming from those woods at night …”

“They are not happy sounds I take it?” said I.

Gretel shook her head. "They are the sounds of … well of …"

Little Red planted her fisted hands on her hips. "Utter despair?"

"I'll say."

"Well," said I, "we shall just have to make sure that we do whatever's necessary to keep our spirits up as we pass through them. *And* adopt a zero-tolerance policy towards anyone or anything that attempts to inflict despair, utter or otherwise, upon us."

"With that in mind, I'm coming with you," said Gretel.

"Oh, no you're not," said I. "You're needed here in this land. Let's face it, the place is teeming with evil witches that need your attention. And besides, it's unlikely we shall be returning through the woods, which means you'd have to travel back alone."

"No, she won't. She'll travel back with me," said Little Red.

I shook my head. "I won't allow you to take such a risk either."

Little Red and Gretel glanced at one another. "I think you'll find the choice is not yours but ours alone to make. If not for you we would both have been digested long ago," said Gretel.

"Which is why we're going to see you safely through the Woods of Utter Despair whether you like it or not."

And so it was that, sometime later, we four girls set off into the Woods of Utter Despair. We walked purposefully so as not to betray any apprehension (or despair). The woods themselves were comprised of those things that are generally associated with woods: trees, stumps of trees, bushes, ponds and brooks. Alice was the first to speak. “Is anyone despairing yet?”

“No,” said I.

“No,” said Gretel.

“Absolutely not,” said Little Red, “but we must all remain on our guard …” added she, her hand coming to rest on the axe in her belt that Gretel had given her.

“Agreed,” said Gretel, “despairing thoughts are tricky customers.”

“Don't I know it,” nodded I.

“Nasty things. Prone to sneaking up on you when you least expect it …” said Little Red.

“Oh, very much so,” concurred Alice.

“And usually from within,” said I.

“More's the pity we can't swivel our eyeballs and keep watch the other way …” said Little Red, lifting the axe from her belt and attempting to do just that.

I raised an eyebrow in her direction. “Yes, more's the pity. Oh, Look! Over there,” said I, pointing past her to a humongous tree with a black door. Little Red grasped her axe with both hands, and Gretel pulled her own from her belt. “Oh, for goodness sake,” said I, striding towards the door. “We come in friendship. Now put those away.”

I knocked upon the door. A shutter slid up and the darkness beyond was occupied by the face of an old man, an old man with the largest, most despairing eyes I had ever seen. We're talking a veritable kaleidoscope of despair here.

“What are you doing here!?” exclaimed he, despairingly. I opened my mouth to reply but closed it again when he said, “Look into my eyes, look into my eyes, look into my eyes. What do you see?”

“You poor, *poor* man,” said I, “for I see only despair!”

The old man nodded profusely. “You’re not wrong, you’re not wrong. And don’t forget the utter. And unless you want eyes like mine, I suggest you turn around and go back the way you came. Now go! Shoo!” And with that he slammed the shutter back down.

“I have never *seen* such despair,” shuddered I. I turned to see that Alice alone among my companions was shaking her head. “What is it?” I asked her.

“That man isn’t despairing at all. He’s a liar.”

“Oh, come now, Alice,” said I, “have more respect for the despairing.”

“Agreed,” said Little Red, “did you not see the poor fellow’s eyes?”

“Since you ask, no, I didn’t see them.”

“Why? Are you short sighted?”

Alice tutted. “Couldn’t you tell? They were *fake*.”

"What were fake?" asked Gretel.

"His eyes of course."

I folded my arms. "It does not become you to mock the despairing in this way, Alice."

"Stand aside," said she, brushing past me, and rapping on the door. The little shutter rose up. The old man's face appeared. "What's this? You're still here? Go away! Back the way you came. That's very important. If you venture any further into these woods, you too will have a face as despairing as mine!" Alice reached through the little shutter, and whipped the old man's eyes clean off his face! Much cringing and gasping ensured from Gretel, Little Red and myself who could not bring ourselves to look in the wretched fellow's direction. "Oh, for goodness sake!" said Alice, "look! It's just a pair of *glasses!*"

"Give those here!" shrieked the old man whose new eyes, while vexed, were a considerable improvement over his despairing ones.

"You snatched away his *glasses*?" said I, "however did you know?"

Alice put the glasses on, and looked just as despairing as the old man had. "Joke glasses are *very* common where I come," smiled she.

"We've never seen anything like them," said I, to my nodding companions.

"Well, they're ten a penny in the real world." This revelation that Alice was from the real world had quite a sobering effect on the old man. "Did you say you're from the *real world*?"

enquired he.

Alice nodded. “Well, the *fictional* real world anyway.”

“Dicey semantics. It’s pretty much the same thing. It's no wonder my disguise didn't fool you.” The shutter went down and, a moment later, the door opened. The *little* old man stepped down off the box he'd been standing on and beckoned us inside.

Inside the hollowed-out tree, we followed him down a flight of rickety wooden stairs into a warren of rooms. “Please sit down and take the weight off your weary legs,” said he, motioning to a settee covered with pillows stuffed with leaves that poked from little tears. The old man was not wrong about our weary legs, and we were happy to oblige. “My name is Oscar Zoroaster Phadrig Emmanuel Ambroise Diggs,” said he, placing his thumbs inside his braces and studying our faces for recognition. His gaze passed over Gretel, Little Red and myself before settling on Alice. “Surely you must have heard of me? You’re from the real world, and I'm extremely famous there.”

“The fictional real world,” replied Alice. “I suppose your name *sort of* rings a bell.”

“A rather quiet one?” observed I.

“Very,” nodded Alice.

Oscar rose up, rather self-importantly onto tiptoes, pressed his thumbs in his braces, and said, “I expect you will have heard of me by my *other* name.”

“I might,” said Alice, “What is it?”

“The Wizard of Oz.”

Alice clasped her hands to her cheeks. “No!”

“Yes,” said Oscar, proudly.

“Am I to take it that you've heard of Oscar by his other name?” smiled I.

“Of course! But you can't be the Wizard of Oz. You simply can't,” said Alice.

“And why not?” asked Oscar.

“Because this isn't Oz. It's the land of fairytales.”

“I take it you are familiar with how my story ends?”

“Yes,” said Alice. “Dorothy, the hero of the story, discovers that you’re not an all-powerful wizard, just a little old man hiding behind a curtain.”

“That's right,” said Oscar, “and what do you imagine happened to me after Dorothy clicked her heels and returned home to the fictionalised real world you both share?”

“No idea,” said Alice.

“I was out of a job. That’s what.”

“Oh, I think I understand,” said Alice, “so your work experience must have made you perfect for this job.”

“The Keeper of the Woods of Utter Despair? Where there is no despair? None. Utter or otherwise? Of course. So much so that they head hunted me. Oh dear,” said he, sitting down upon a stool rather dejectedly.

“Whatever is the matter?” asked Alice.

“Once again, I've been rumbled.”

“Rumbled?” asked Little Red.

Oscar nodded sadly. “Just as it was discovered that I'm not an all-powerful wizard, it has now been discovered that the Woods of Utter Despair contain no despair. They’re actually a charming place to picnic. Not that anybody ever does.”

I placed my hand on Oscar's shoulder. “Let me assure you that your secret will remain safe with us. Won't it girls?”

“We shall take it to the grave,” said Little Red.

“And beyond if necessary,” added a nodding Gretel.

“You'd do that for me?” said Oscar.

“You sound surprised?” said I.

“I am surprised. You approached from the south. Word through the Grapevine is that the south is a cruel and heartless place.”

“It's true that there are a great many rogues where we come from, rogues that can make living happily ever after a tricky business. But we are not at all like them. In fact, *we* are on an errand of mercy.”

“Someone needs your assistance in the north?”

“In a manner of speaking,” said I.

“Maybe you could sum up the reason for your quest in two words or less?” said Oscar to me.

I raised my chin. “True love.”

“True love, you say?”

“I do say.”

“Yours?”

“Yes. My true love’s name is Edward. He has been banished to a place called Wonderland. And Wonderland can only be reached from the land in the north.”

“Wonderland?” said Oscar his eyes opening wide.

“You've heard of it then?” asked Alice, hopefully.

“Oh, yes.”

“And?” said I.

“And everyone who lives there is bonkers. Or so I heard.”

“You heard correctly,” said Alice.

“Alice in Wonderland?” said Oscar as the penny didn't so much drop but clank.

“That’s me,” grinned Alice.

“Then, I take it that *you’re* seeking the white rabbit?”

“How well informed you are,” said Alice.

“Speaking of which,” continued Oscar looking at Gretel, “weren’t you supposed to be eaten by a witch?”

Gretel drew the axe from her belt and began to sharpen its

blade with a pumice stone. “There was a change of plan. One that involved my axe.”

“If only Dorothy had adopted a similar strategy,” mused Oscar.

“Why,” asked Little Red, “did she come a cropper at the hands of an evil witch?”

“No. She clicked her heels and scarpered home. But many others did come a cropper. And still do,” replied he with a shudder.

Gretel narrowed her eyes. “Sounds a bad sort that witch.”

“The Wicked Witch of the West? The very worst.”

“And which land does she reside in?”

“Oz, obviously,” said Alice.

“Can’t say I miss the place much,” said Oscar. “And what’s more, I met the best friend I’ve ever had when I came here.”

“*Todd*?” said Little Red.

“You knew him?”

“I only knew of his work studying these woods,” replied she.

“Lovely chap. He kept my secret to the bitter end.”

“We heard he died from utter despair?” said I.

“Not at all. He died of old age. Only he was wearing a pair of these at the time,” said Oscar, putting his despairing glasses back on. “Now, who fancies a hearty bowl of soup?”

Following a delicious supper of vegetable soup …

Following a delicious supper of vegetable soup, we said our goodbyes to Oscar and continued on our journey north.

"What a pleasant fellow," said I as we all turned and waved goodbye.

"Pleasant maybe, but not particularly trustworthy I should imagine" said Gretel.

I glanced at Gretel. "While his line of work maybe unusual, I believe he has a good heart. And that's why we must keep his secret and tell no one of the true nature of the Woods of Utter Despair."

It was dusk and, as the light began to fade, we felt reassured by the knowledge that the Woods of Utter Despair were no such thing. I suppose this goes some way to explaining why what happened next caught us completely off guard. We'd been having a tete-a-tete with Alice about the merits of being fictional. "You will live on in the hearts and minds of people for as long as there are well, people with hearts and minds," I reassured her.

"I suppose there is that."

"What's more, people may find comfort and inspiration in your brave deeds," added Little Red.

"Brave deeds?" said Alice.

"Oh, come now," said I, "you fell down am enormous hole and found yourself in a scary and, by all accounts, bonkers place. But did that dampen your resolve to find a way back home?”

“I suppose not,” said Alice.

“What a wonderful example to us all …” I was interrupted by the wind that whipped up suddenly, knocking us off our strides. I looked at Alice, whose long blond hair trailed like ticker tape behind her and, above the howling winds I shouted, “This sort of wind is not at all common in the land …”

“Indeed, it is not,” said Little Red drawing her axe from her belt.

“If not utter despair, what do you suppose is causing it?” asked Gretel steadying herself against a tree. As if by way of reply, we heard a cackling that swirled all about us on the wind.

“I … I recognise that cackle!” shouted I.

“Your stepmother?” said Little Red, raising her axe.

I nodded and gazed about for any sign of her. There was none. But her cackling grew louder and then burst into hateful speech: “Did you really think I'd let you get away with this ‘plan’ to rescue Edward?”

“You can't stop me!” cried I.

“Really? We shall see about *that*. Goodbye thorn in my side! Goodbye for all eternity!” Such was the venom in her voice that I closed my eyes and braced myself for the worst. This explains why, when I opened them seconds later, the sight that greeted me was so unexpected. Lying asleep atop a four-poster bed, I beheld a beautiful young woman. She was wearing a magnificent red and green dress, and her extraordinary golden locks were tied up in the biggest bun you've never seen. I realised that Little Red, Alice and Gretel were standing by my side.

"Not at all what I expected," murmured I.

"You and me both," said Little Red casting her gaze about the large, round turret room. She stepped towards the open window behind us and looked down. Gretel joined her. "My … it *is* a long way to the bottom," said Gretel, backing away from the window. "I never have been one for heights."

"They've never bothered me …" murmured Little Red stepping aside so that Alice and I might behold the drop.

"This must be the tallest tower in all the land," proclaimed I, looking out over the green meadow far, *far* below.

"We must find a door," said Alice.

"There doesn't appear to be one," said Gretel.

"From my experience, there never does but …" replied Alice making her way around the outside of the circular room. I approached the splendid four poster bed where the sleeping girl lay. At close quarters, it was clear that she was a damsel of some sort.

"Wake her," said Gretel, "she must know where the door is."

"My thinking precisely," said I, giving her shoulder a shake. The damsel stirred a little and muttered something about a dread of dandruff. I shook her more firmly, her lovely eyes fluttered open, and she sat up with a start.

Her first question was not unexpected. "Who *are* you? Tell

me immediately!" cried she, gazing wide eyed about the room at her visitors.

"You're absolutely right," said I, "for introductions should be made first and foremost. My name is Snow …"

"As in *White*?"

"Yes. And this is Gretel …" said I motioning to her.

"Hansel's sister?" said she, her exquisite blue eyes opening wide.

"For my sins," replied Gretel.

"And this is Little Red," said I, motioning to Little Red.

"Riding Hood?" murmured the damsel.

"Present and correct," replied she.

"And last, but by no means least, this is Alice," said I, pointing to Alice who, having satisfied herself that the room had no doors, smiled at the damsel on her bed. "*Alice*? I don't believe I've heard of you."

"I'm not from these parts. But I've certainly heard of you, *Rapunzel* …" replied Alice, her smile widening.

"You recognise her then?" said Gretel.

"Of course. Where I come from she's as well known as the rest of you. Don't you know of her?" We all shook our heads.

Rapunzel looked at Alice. "It's a comfort to know that *someone* is aware of my terrible plight."

"Take heart," said I, "for terrible plights are extremely common in the land. But, if I'm entirely honest, yours doesn't look so bad."

"Then think again. For I am prisoner in this tower," sighed she, "a prisoner for all eternity. And one that has committed no crime."

"That's pretty harsh," said I. "Whatever does a damsel called Rapunzel have to do to get a break in this land?"

"Tell me about it," she sighed.

Little Red placed a hand on her chin. "That explains the absence of a door."

"Quite so. There *is* no door," said Rapunzel, sitting and dangling her lovely legs over the edge of the bed. "What is more there are no stairs. And even if there were stairs they would be to no avail. You see, there's no door at the bottom of the tower either. So, I'm afraid that I, *we,* are trapped here for all eternity."

I looked at my ashen faced companions. "It's no wonder my stepmother cackled so when she banished us here." Only Alice amongst them had some colour in her cheeks, made more so, I should imagine, by the effort she was clearly putting into remembering the finer points of Rapunzel's story.

"What is it?" I asked her.

Alice folded her arms, scrunched up her brows, and appeared even deeper in thought.

"There's no need to trouble yourself so, Alice," sighed

Rapunzel, “this tower is *it* for us.” Alice spun about and looked out of the open window behind her. She stepped forwards and tapped a knuckle against the window frame as though trying to jog her memory. It must have worked for she spun about and, looking at Rapunzel, asked, “Just how long *is* your hair anyway?”

“*Long*,” replied Rapunzel, centring the enormous bun that made her head look exceptionally dainty.

“Why so long?” I asked her.

“It's just the way my story was written,” shrugged she.

“Exactly!” cried Alice in such a way as to make us all jump.

“Now look here,” Gretel admonished her, “if we're to spend an eternity together in this tower, you really must moderate your reactions.”

Alice composed herself and, in a considerate yet knowing tone said, “I have just remembered the finer points of Rapunzel’s story.”

“And?” asked I.

“And her long hair is an exceptionally positive finer point.”

“*Positive*? My hair is nothing but a high maintenance thorn in my side. I hate it.”

Alice smiled at Rapunzel. “I have such good news. The *best*. Confinement in this tower is not how your story ends.”

“I beg to differ,” replied she, scratching at her hair.

“You may beg to differ all you like. In the meantime, come

over her.”

“Leave my bed you mean?”

Alice nodded.

“But why?”

“So I can take down your hair.”

“Take down my hair,” replied Rapunzel aghast.

“That's right.”

“Not likely.”

“Why ever not?” asked Little Red.

“Because my hair is simply MASSIVE. It’s like setting loose a creature. Do you have any idea how long it took me to capture it and place it back upon my head the last time?”

“No idea,” said I.

“*Two* whole days.”

“It's not going to take two days to round it up this time,” said Alice. “In fact, it's not going to take any time at all.”

“And why's that?” asked Rapunzel.

“Because we're going to cut it all off.”

“What? *All* of it?” gushed Rapunzel.

Alice looked out of the window. “That's right. We're going to use it to make a rope.”

Ten minutes later …

Ten minutes later, during which time much excitement ensued, not least from Rapunzel herself who had to be persuaded that Gretel and not she would be the best person to wield the axe that severed her thorn, we'd gathered up the sea of hair and twisted it into a rope. "That should do it …" said Gretel whose hair twisting ability had impressed us all. "The witch … she used to make me braid her hair …" explained Gretel, tongue pressed into her cheek, as she knotted the final strands of hair.

"Which reminds me," said Rapunzel, running her fingers through her bob, "wasn't the witch supposed to eat you?"

"Yes. But there was a change of plan," replied Gretel, gazing about for a place to tie the end of our hair rope.

"Your story was changed?" said Rapunzel.

"Yes. Snow let it be known that I might make some *teensy-weensy* changes."

"Well then, I suppose," said Rapunzel thoughtfully, "that we're making some *teensy-weensy* changes to my story now. By helping me escape I mean."

"Teensy weensy is actually an accurate assessment," said Alice, "you were going to be rescued by a handsome prince anyway."

"Really," replied Rapunzel, blushing.

Little Red rolled her eyes. "*Gormless* Charming en route or not, we can't just leave her here to wait for him."

"Yes, you can. It's not as though I'm a prisoner anymore. I can come and go as I please now. How long till my Charming arrives do you think?"

"How long's a piece of string?" said I. "They tend to do their derring-do in their own time. But when he does show, my advice would be not to let him know that you don't need rescuing."

"Snow's right," nodded Gretel. "Prince Charmings pretty much exist to rescue their damsels. Take that away and what does it leave them?"

"Not a lot," said Little Red.

We all climbed down the rope of hair, including Rapunzel, who immediately knelt and picked the bluebells that grew around the base of her tower. "I shall pick flowers every day, and place them in my hair to make myself pretty for my Charming."

"Your Charming is going to be besotted, bluebells or not," said I.

Rapunzel placed a bluebell to her nose and, having sniffed its sweet scent, enquired of me, "Is something the matter?"

As I swallowed the lump in my throat, Little Red said, "Bluebells are Snow and Edward's flower …" Rapunzel handed me a bluebell. "Keep your spirits up for you *shall* see him again."

"I will do my best," said I, taking it. "Speaking of which, we really must be on our way." Having shaken hands with each of us in turn, Rapunzel began to climb, hand over fist, up her hair. As she climbed, Alice called out, “Oh, I almost forgot! Be sure to sing every morning …”

“Okay. But why?”

“Because it's the sound of your beautiful voice that first attracts your Charming.”

“Will do!”

Sometime later …

It goes without saying that, sometime later, when we had reached the northernmost point of the Woods of Utter Despair, that not one among us had experienced any despair. To the contrary, our above average spirits were raised further upon the sight of the town that we had come to find. We had arrived at a high vantage point at its southern end, and were comforted by the sight of a tremendous beanstalk that rose up to pierce the clouds to the west.

"We've actually arrived at the right place," said I.

Alice gazed up at the beanstalk and swallowed hard. "And now we must find Jack before he gets to work with his axe." The reminder was a timely one, and we walked briskly down a long slope into town. Once there, we discovered the streets awash with people discussing the sudden appearance of the beanstalk.

"Excuse me," said I to one of the townsfolk, a plump woman wearing a pinny, her hands covered with flour.

"Hello, young ladies," said she to us. "If you're curious to know about the beanstalk, I'm afraid I can't help. I'm as much in the dark as anyone about where it's come from."

"We quite understand," said Alice, "we're looking for a boy who lives in this town. His name is Jack."

"Jack?" mused the woman. "Jack what?"

"Jack and his beanstalk," ventured Gretel.

The woman narrowed her eyes. "Jack and *his* beanstalk?"

"Yes. He's a young man of about our age. Rarely does what he's told?"

The woman turned rather red in the face. "Oh, *that* Jack," tutted she.

"Yes, *that* Jack," said I, "would you mind pointing us in the direction of his abode. It's rather urgent."

"Next street along. The cottage with the green door. So, the beanstalk is Jack's doing, is it?"

I shook my head. "Whatever gave you that impression? And now we must be going. Goodbye."

Upon our approach, the cottage's green door burst open, and a young man with dishevelled hair and ruddy cheeks ran out holding an axe. We all converged at his garden gate, the four of us blocking his path. A fact not lost on him. "Move aside! You must let me pass!" cried he.

"Sounds urgent," said Little Red.

"You have no idea!" said he, seeking a route through us but failing when we closed ranks. "Please! You must stand aside!"

"No can do," said Little Red.

"But you don't understand!"

"We understand only too well," said Gretel.

The young man glanced at her and, the moment his eyes met hers, his anger seemed to evaporate. “You do?” said he, quietly. Gretel answered his enquiry with a sigh.

“Yes, she *does*,” said Little Red narrowing her eyes at them both.

“She does what?” asked the young man as though in a haze.

“She understands that you're on your way to cut down the beanstalk,” said I.

“Yes. Yes, of course. The giant!” replied he, regaining his senses. “I must chop down the beanstalk otherwise the giant will destroy the town.”

Little Red folded her arms. “We know all about that, *Jack*. And that the beanstalk was your doing.”

“Then you will know that I must make amends!” said he, glancing up at it.

“And make amends you shall,” said Gretel quietly, “but before you cut the beanstalk down, my friends, Alice and Snow here, must climb it.” The sound of Gretel's voice seemed to soothe and confuse the young man in equal measure. “But why would they want to?”

“Because they need to reach a place called Wonderland. And it can only be reached from the top of the beanstalk.”

“Oh, I see …” murmured Jack, gazing into Gretel's eyes.

“Oh, for goodness sake!” cried Little Red. “There'll be time enough for you two to get better acquainted later. We must be going!”

Ten fraught minutes later …

Ten fraught minutes later, during which time, much scrambling, huffing and puffing had taken place, we arrived at the base of the beanstalk.

“You really planted this thing?” said I, craning my neck and endeavouring but failing to see to its top that lay beyond the clouds. Jack cast his gaze towards the ground, and sighed miserably.

Gretel placed her hand on his shoulder, “Don’t be sad, it was an accident.”

“An accident that would never have happened if I hadn't bought those magic beans from that witch.”

“Take heart. It was just the way your story was written,” Gretel reassured him.

“Are *you* a part of my story?” said Jack, brightening somewhat.

“Technically? No, she wasn’t. But she is now,” said I, reaching for a vine and pulling myself a little way up the beanstalk. “Come on, Alice. Edward and the white rabbit await,” continued I, extending a hand down to her.

“Right you are,” said she, taking it.

“Gretel, Little Red, thank you for everything! I shall see you soon when I return having rescued Edward …”

“Thank you both! For everything!” said Alice.

"Good luck you two," cried Gretel.

"Take no prisoners! Do you hear me?" stomped Little Red.

"Indeed, we shall not …" said I. "Oh! One more thing …"

"Yes?" said Little Red.

"If you could refrain from chopping down the beanstalk until we've reached the top it would be most appreciated …"

"But we can't let the giant descend it to the bottom," Jack pointed out.

"It won't come to that, for we shall make haste," said I, making haste.

"Don't look down!" cried Gretel. Those words of advice were the last we heard from our friends as, before long, we were out of earshot, and climbing for all we were worth. Halfway between the ground and the clouds, I wished I'd followed Gretel's parting advice. The distance was dizzying.

Once we'd passed through the clouds, the sight of the soft bed of soft 'cotton wool' that stretched as far as the eye could see was comforting. My comfort was short lived, however, for soon after, I heard a grumbling that grew steadily louder, and it came from the stomach of a hungry giant. Squinting up, I beheld the soles of his monstrous boots. "We must climb to the other side of the beanstalk …" said I, scrambling to its other side.

"Yes!" replied Alice doing the same just below me. We stopped climbing, held out breaths, and listened to the giant's huff and puff as it descended towards the town. "Come on!" whispered I, glancing up to the top of the beanstalk, "for they will cut the down the beanstalk as soon as they clap eyes on him …" Alice, who, in her eagerness to be clear of the beanstalk before it plummeted to earth, had reached the vines alongside my own. "Do you think they've already begun chopping?"

"No idea. But the clouds have hidden us from view."

Alice glanced down. "The giant has passed through them, Snow."

"Which means they'll be able to see *him*," said I, as we continued our climb towards the top some fifty metres away. That's when the beanstalk began to sway in a way that, hitherto, it had not swayed before. "It's just the wind …" said I, trying to hide the concern in my voice.

"But there *is* no wind. Not unless you're referring to the giant's as it climbed down past us," murmured Alice, wrinkling her nose. The beanstalk lurched forward suddenly, and then backwards, and then forward …

I looked up. "We're almost at the top! Come on …" But before I could grab hold of the vine above me, the beanstalk toppled sideways as though someone had just yelled TIMBER!

Following the most terrifying few seconds later imaginable …

Following the most terrifying few seconds later imaginable, Alicc and I had lost our grip and plummeted earthbound, only to have our falls broken by something warm, black and feathery. “Fear not!” cried I, grabbing hold of her, “for it is just the crow!”

“What crow!?”

“The crow as in as the crow flies!” The crow flapped its mighty wings and climbed towards the land above us. “Hang on tight!” squawked he, “I'll have you back on terra firma in a jiffy.” True to his word, the crow swooped up and then down upon the ground atop the beanstalk. Alice slid off him and, stumbling backwards she observed, “You’re the biggest crow I've ever seen!”

“Which is just as well. Frank sent me.”

“*Frank*?” said Alice.

“Yes. *Frank,*” said the crow

“Do you mean They?” said Alice.

“The one and only,” said I, climbing down off the crow’s back.

“You know, I've heard my father say that ‘*They* have a lot to answer for’ many times,” mused Alice. “The next time he does, I shall tell him that it simply isn't true.”

"You do that," squawked the crow flapping its wings and rising a little into the air.

"So where are you off to now?" I asked it.

The crow shrugged. "Wherever it is, you can be sure that I'll be taking the most direct route. And you?"

"Alice and I must find the entrance to Wonderland. Apparently, it's around here somewhere," said I, glancing up at a castle atop a hill. Now reader, I'm sure you will appreciate that any castle is going to be pretty large, the clue being in the word castle. But I'd like you to take a moment and imagine a *giant's* castle. That's to say, a castle that is so vast that a regular castle is the size of a dog's kennel in comparison. Truly, this castle blotted out the land and sky beyond it.

"As you're seeking the entrance to Wonderland," squawked the crow, "would you like the good news or the bad news with a silver lining?"

Alice and I glanced at one another. "We'd like the good news," agreed we.

"The good news is the white rabbit will lead you straight to the entrance."

"And I suppose the bad news is that the white rabbit is already in Wonderland?" said a nervous sounding Alice.

"Not at all," squawked the crow. "And what's more, the white rabbit in this land is the size of a building. Which means you can't miss it."

"So, what's the bad news with a silver lining then?" asked I.

"That the white rabbit belongs to the giant's wife."

I took several steps over to the edge of the land in the clouds, looked down at the tremendous drop, and said, "Surely you mean the giant's *widow*?"

The crow nodded. "Exactly. But you know what They say?"

"That you can't make an omelette without first felling a giant?" said I, taking liberties with the most famous of They's quotes.

"No," replied the crow, "That every cloud has a silver lining."

"And the silver lining in this instance would be?" asked Alice.

"That the giant's wife loathed him."

"Really?" said Alice.

The crow nodded. "She despised him. I heard it through the grapevine."

"News from the grapevine does tend to be accurate," mused I.

"So you two can be the bearers of the good news," squawked the crow as it rose higher.

"The *good* news?" said Alice.

"That her husband has fallen and lies dead in the land below." As the crow flapped away it said, "She'll be so happy, she might give you permission to follow the white rabbit."

“Indeed, she might! And thank you!” cried I.

A few minutes later, Alice and I were squeezing through the iron gate that led into the castle. Well, I say squeezing, but in truth the railings were so far apart that you needed to squint to see those to the left and right of you. “This must be what the world looks like to an ant,” said Alice philosophically, as we hurried towards the castle's towering black doors. They were closed but, when you're ant-sized, you can mosey beneath the gap at the bottom of doors, and not even worry about bumping your head.

Beyond the doors, the castle's entrance hall spanned like an ocean of dark stone to a staircase. Climbing the staircase would have been impossible without professional climbing gear, not to mention weeks of tuition, which explains our relief at hearing a thunderous pounding coming from our right. “The giant's wife?” said Alice.

“There's only one way to find out,” said I, stepping purposefully in the direction of the pounding.

Half an hour, much thunderous pounding, and a headache later …

Half an hour, much thunderous pounding, and a headache later, we scurried under a door into a kitchen. And there, making dough, was a giant woman, snub-nosed and buxom. “She could be the giant's wife,” said Alice.

“She could … although, with a grand abode such as this, she might also be his cook. Only one way to find out,” said I, cupping my hands either side of my mouth. “Excuse me!” yelled I. The giant paused mid pound, shook her head as though she suspected she must be hearing voices (inside it) and then began her pounding again.

“Hello! We're down here!” cried I.

“Go away,” muttered the woman. “Go away and leave me alone!”

“But we need your help!” shouted Alice.

“Help, *help*,” said the woman shaking her head that was easily the size of a cottage. “No, you don't. You're not real. It’s the stress. Now stop your jabbering. You hear? Stop your jabbering and leave me be.”

“She's growing rather distressed,” Alice pointed out.

“I know more than anyone what it's like having issues,” nodded I.

“So, what should we do?”

“Get her attention another way … come on,” continued I, making for a broom that was propped up against the counter just behind her. Alice and I stood at the foot of the broom, the handle of which towered so far above us that we had to squint to see its end. We squinted from the top of the handle to the giant's head, and back again. “It would certainly reach …” mused Alice.

“Yes. But how to topple it …” said I, reaching out and feeling a bristle that was as tall as we were.

“We need something like a rope …” said Alice, casting her gaze about for something like a rope.

“A rope? Or something like one?” said I.

“Yes. If we had a rope we could wrap it round the back of the bottom of the broom's handle, and heave the broom over.”

“That's very clever.”

Alice shrugged. “I have an undoubted advantage when it comes to solving puzzles of a peculiar sized nature.”

“You were written that way?” said I quietly as I too cast my gaze about for a rope or something like one.

“Quite so,” said Alice. “The room that I found myself in at the bottom of the rabbit hole was at first too large and then too small. I somehow knew how to deal with both situations. It was when I finally found the solution to getting through the small door, the door through which I might add, I spied the rabbit making off into a wood, that I found myself standing beside you in that cathedral.”

"Indeed, it sounds as though spatial conundrums were your author's favourite type," said I, spying a length of twine lying on the ground beneath a counter on which sat the biggest stuffed chicken you've never seen. Moments later, I was holding the end of the twine over my shoulder, and dragging it towards the broom.

Alice proved very nimble in jumping up onto the bottom of the broom and wrapping the twine around it. Being rather awkward myself, I imagine I would have kept sliding off. Eventually, there we stood, each holding an end of the twine. "On three," said I, preparing to tug on the twine for all I was worth. When it comes to tugging twine, it seems that Alice and I are worth rather a lot, for the broom toppled forwards and bopped the giant on her head with a meaty CLUNK.

"Arr!" cried she, which seemed entirely appropriate. As we'd hoped, she cast her gaze about for the cause of her pain, and saw it in the form of two tiny figures waving their hands above their heads. The giant was a good deal nimbler than she appeared, for she bent down and scooped Alice and I up in a trice. "What's all this then?" said she, bringing us to eye level. I opened my mouth to answer her question but closed it again when she answered it herself. "Mice people! A great delicacy in these here parts!" said she, rubbing at her head and smiling at her mixed fortunes.

"We are most certainly *not* mice people," said Alice.

"Course you are my tasty. What else would you be? My husband loves the taste of tiny folk."

"So, you *are* the giant's wife and not his cook then?" asked Alice.

"What an impertinent question. But if you must know, I am

his wife *and* his cook. Not to mention his cleaner and general dogsbody. Now where did I put that cook book?" mused she, casting her gaze about for the book that apparently contained a recipe for which Alice and I were an important ingredient.

"You are not going to need that cook book," said I.

"I beg to differ," said she, "the finer points of mice people soufflé are lost on me."

"Be that as it may, you aren't going to eat us because we've just done you a big favour," said Alice.

"That's right," chimed in I, "and now it is beholden on you to return it."

"Oh, yes? And how is giving me a bump on my head doing me a favour?"

"That wasn't the favour,' said Alice. "We understand that you're not awfully keen on your husband?"

The giant's wife cast her gaze about and, having satisfied herself that he wasn't around, said, "For mice people you're very well informed. I loathe the oaf. Always have. Always will."

"Then it is my great pleasure to inform you of your husband's demise," said I, placing my hands on my hips.

"His what?"
"His demise," repeated I.
"What are you telling me? That he's *dead*?"
"As a dodo," nodded Alice.

"A *dead* dodo," clarified I, as the giant's widow seemed rather slow on the uptake.

“But he can't be dead. That oaf is practically indestructible. I doubt I shall ever be rid of him.”

“Well,” announced I, “your practically indestructible oaf of a husband just fell a *very great height* to the land below.”

“Our friends chopped it down to prevent him from reaching the bottom,” said Alice.

The giant’s widow scratched her head thoughtfully. “That would certainly have been very forward thinking of them. If he’d have made it to the bottom, the greedy so and so would have eaten them all.”

“Our friends are nothing if not forward thinking,” said I.

“Which explains why your husband was D.O.A.,” smiled Alice.

“D.O.A?” repeated the giant's wife.

“D.O.A? repeated I.

“Dead on arrival,” said Alice.

“In the land below?” said the giant's wife.

“Yes,” confirmed we.

“Well then, it seems I have no need for that cook book after all. Or any cook book! I'm free!”

“You are free,” said I. “And, in return for being the bearers of such wonderful news, there's something we'd like you to do for us in return.”

“Anything!” bounced the giant's happy widow.

“We need to follow your white rabbit,” said Alice.

“Follow Clementine? Where?”

“To the entrance to Wonderland.”

“And Clemmie knows where it is?”

“We have it on good authority that she does, yes,” said I.

“Whose authority?”

“The crow's,” said Alice.

“As in as the crow flies,” added I.

“Well, if anyone knows the best way to get somewhere it's him, I suppose.”

And so it was that the giant’s widow fetched her rabbit, Clementine, and Clementine led us all up to a room in the attic that contained a missing floorboard. The giant's widow knelt and put us down beside the floorboard. Alice knelt also, and sniffed at the darkness beyond it. “The unmistakable whiff of Wonderland,” said she, wrinkling her nose. I knelt and sniffed alongside her. “It smells like a *very* peculiar room filled with very peculiar things …”

“That's the one, yes.”

I turned and looked up at the smiling face of giant's widow. “It's time we took our leave. You enjoy the single life.”

“Oh, I will. You two take care of each other now.”

“We shall,” said Alice, and with that she winked at me, jumped in, and disappeared.

“Goodbye!” I called up to the giant's widow.

“Goodbye! And thank you again for the wonderful news!”

“It was our pleasure,” said I, squeezing my nose as though about to leap into water …

Wonderland

A minute later, having fallen at first through darkness, and then past alcoves lit by candles, I dropped lightly into a room and landed on my feet. The room was not round but neither did it have any corners. “What a curiously shape this room this is,” murmured I. The furniture in the room was brightly coloured, oddly misshapen, and labels were attached to everything. “Looking for something,” said I to Alice who was scurrying about on her hands and knees.

“It's still here!” exclaimed she.

“What is?” asked I, bending down and picking up a label with two words written on it: 'Drink me.'

“The door … the one through which the white rabbit went.”

“The door you passed through just before you found yourself about to marry me in the cathedral?”

“Yes! Come on!” I took one last look at the room, scratched my head, and then followed Alice through the knee-high door. On the other side was a path that wended its way through a wood. The trees and plants in this wood were *considerably* more colourful than those in my own land. “Why are you squinting? The sun is obscured by the trees,” said Alice, as she brushed some dirt from her knees.

“Everything's so colourful here …” mused I, doing the same.

"Compared to the moody woods where you come from maybe," said Alice. "Come on! When last I saw it, the white rabbit was headed this way," continued she, walking briskly along the path.

We had not gone more than half a dozen steps when a voice startled us. It was a male voice that sounded as though it was enjoying a mouthful of squelchy peaches. "What's all this then?" said the voice as just described. Alice and I stopped in our tracks.

"What's all what?" replied Alice, looking hither and thither for the owner of the voice.

"*This*," said the voice.

"Who and *where* are you?" said I, stepping closer to Alice.

"Where and, more to the point, *who* are you?" the voice asked me.

"Snow asked you first," Alice pointed out.

"Snow!" said the voice. "Snow! Snow? Snow!?"

"That is my name. I would appreciate it if you *didn't* wear it out, for in a land such as this the wearing out of names is commonplace."

"Ah, harrr!" said the voice, "that's where you're wrong."

Alice leant in close and whispered, "This is a different land, remember?"

The voice must have had exceptional hearing for it said, "Different, indeed! As in *Wonderland*. Alice?"

Alice nodded. “Are we acquainted?”

“Never seen you before in my life.”

“Then how did you know my name?”

“How did I know her name she asks!”

“It seems a fair enough question,” said I.

“One of you is where you're supposed to be. Better than none of you, I suppose. You hoo! Behind you.” Alice and I turned and beheld a caterpillar the size of a child. He was sitting on a gigantic mushroom and puffing on a contraption that created plumes of smoke.

“You weren’t there a moment ago,” observed I.

“That all depends,” said the caterpillar taking a long, thoughtful drag on his smoke making contraption.

“Depends on what?” asked Alice.

“On where you were a moment ago.”

Alice placed her hands on her hips. “We were walking through that very spot.”

“My point precisely!”

“What is your point?” asked I.

“That X marks the spot,” said the caterpillar, looking down at the X that now marked his spot.

I nodded. “They do say that X marks the spot.”

“You know Frank?” asked the caterpillar, slyly.

“I do. He's a dear friend of mine.”

“You admit it then?” said the caterpillar, puffing so hard that the smoke obscured it.

“Admit what?”

“That you’re nothing but a rotten cantalouper!” said he, appearing from within the smoke.

Alice raised an eyebrow. “Isn’t a cantalouper a fruit?”

“I believe that’s a *cantaloupe*,” said I, lowering my voice. “It’s very much like a melon. Awkward loves them so much that, in his eager eagerness to eat them, he frequently almost chokes on them.”

“I called you a rotten *interloper*,” puffed the caterpillar.

“No, you didn’t. You called me a rotten cantaloper.”

“Nonsense. There's no such thing as a cantaloper,” said the caterpillar.

“Look,” said an impatient sounding Alice, “Did you by any chance see the rabbit pass this way?”

“Finely and timely!” exclaimed the caterpillar.

“What's finely and timely?” asked I of it.

“A question I was expecting from someone I was expecting it from!”

“Oh. I see. So, you've noticed that, strictly speaking, and *technically*, I'm not supposed to be here.” The caterpillar puffed furiously on its smoke making contraption. “It's not as though you're the first today."

I felt my heart race. "There was another?"

"Yes, there was a Nother. He climbed that tree yonder and promptly fell out of it. That explains the red stain below it. But what's that got to do with the polite young man who came along after the rabbit?"

"Edward! Was his name Edward?"

The caterpillar removed the smoking contraption from its mouth with one of the hands it did not have. "Now let me think …" pondered he.

"Think?" said I. "Did he tell you his name or not?"

The caterpillar opened one of the eyes it did not have and peered at me like I was the biggest idiot it had ever seen. "Have you been paying attention?"

"Indeed, I am hanging on your every word."

"Upside down?" asked the caterpillar.

"Well … no, obviously not upside down."

"Just checking."

"Just checking?" said I.

"That you're quite sane."

"That's rich," said Alice. "So, was his name Edward, or wasn't it?"

"I somehow think it *was*," said the caterpillar placing the end of his smoking contraption back in his mouth and puffing furiously.

I felt tears stinging my eyes and Alice's hand upon my shoulder. "Did you speak with him? Is he alright? Did he mention me?" I asked.

"Who are you?"

"Snow White."

"The fairest in thc other land?"

"You've heard of her then?" said Alice.

The caterpillar shook itself. "Whatever gave you that impression? The young man didn't say much. Seemed rather keen to be on his way."

I glanced up and down the path. "Do a lot of interlopers pass this way?"

"This way? No. Absolutely not. Quite unheard of. Only you. And that fellow whose name escapes me. And what a dreadful mess you've both made of everything."

"What mess? I have only just arrived. And Edward can only have been here a short while."

"Tell that to all the characters that Alice was *supposed* to meet when she was *supposed* to arrive here."

"Why? Would they be interested?" asked Alice.

"In the short time they have left, yes."

"Short time? Are they in some kind of trouble?" said I.

"Not some kind. All the kind."

"Oh, dear," said Alice. "I had no idea my late arrival would cause anyone any problems."

"You didn't arrive late," said I, "you were on time and then you were abducted." I fixed the caterpillar with my most determined stare. "So, who are these characters and what is to become of them?"

"These characters are too numerous to mention. But the Queen is to make a *particular* example of three of them: the mouse, the dodo ... *and* the white rabbit," puffed the caterpillar philosophically.

"The white rabbit!" said Alice.

"Yes, *and* the mouse *and* the dodo."

"I'm very sorry for the mouse and dodo, of course I am, but I followed the white rabbit here, and he alone knows the way back home." Alice was growing distressed so I thought it best to change the subject. "Who is this dreadful queen?" asked I.

"Of Hearts," replied he caterpillar.

"You surprise me. She doesn't sound particularly big hearted."

The caterpillar nodded. "You know what They say about her, I suppose?"

I shook my head. "I don't believe Frank has ever mentioned any queen by that name."

"Well, They say that the Queen of Hearts is the very

definition of an oxymoron."

"I have no idea what that means but it doesn't sound at all good," said Alice.

"And what's more, it sounds a good deal better than it is," puffed the caterpillar.

I placed my hands on my hips. "So, what *crime* have the mouse, the dodo and the white rabbit been charged with?"

"The very serious crime of being superfluous."

"To what?" said Alice.

"To the requirements of this story. What else?"

"That's hardly their fault," said I, looking back and forth between Alice and the caterpillar who suddenly shouted, "Off with their heads!"

"Ours?" said I, glancing nervously at Alice.

"Yours? No, no, no, no. Being deprived of their heads is the fate of any character deemed superfluous to requirements by the queen."

"Oh, that's pretty grim," huffed I. "What do superfluous to requirements characters have to do to get a break in this land?"

"Maybe the queen's bluffing," said Alice, hopefully.

"Bluffing? Bluffing?" said the caterpillar, "The Queen of Hearts likes nothing better than a beheading. Any old excuse will do."

“Be that as it may, I, *we*, shan't allow it,” said I to Alice.

“Meddling in affairs of state is a serious business,” pointed out the caterpillar.

I raised my chin. “Maybe so. But it's never stopped me before. So please point us in the direction of the Queen's palace. I, *we*, are desirous of a word with her.”

“Is this true?” the caterpillar asked Alice. Alice nodded, uncertainly at first, but then defiantly.

“When are the executions to take place?” she asked.

“Tomorrow at noon. Just before the croquet tournament. The Queen of Hearts likes nothing better than an execution to get her in the sporting mood.”

Not long and an exclamation that does not belong in a young woman's diary later …

Not long and an exclamation that does not belong in a young woman's diary later, Alice and I were making haste down the path that the caterpillar had assured us was the most direct route to the Queen's palace. We had not gone far when we heard laughter, high pitched and, if I'm perfectly honest, its owner sounded a little unhinged. We stopped and peered through the trees in its direction. "Do you see what I see?" asked Alice.

"Only if you see a table in a clearing … a table laid for a tea party."

"And what of the hare, the dormouse lying face down in a bowl of trifle, and that fellow with masses of red hair and bulbous green eyes?"

"Is the fellow wearing the biggest top hat you've never seen?"

"I should say so," said Alice.

"And is it purple?"

"Exceedingly. Look, I realise that we're on an urgent mission, but I feel *compelled* to talk to them …" said Alice, scratching her head.

"Well, this is your story so, if you feel …" I stopped talking because Alice had stepped into the clearing. The man in the top hat was walking up and down the length of the table, avoiding, rather skilfully I might add, all the food laid out upon it. As previously mentioned, the Dormouse was face down in a bowl of trifle and, at closer inspection, he appeared to be sleeping. In contrast, the Hare was tapping his fingers upon the table in a most agitated manner. At the sight of Alice, he exclaimed, “Hatter! Hatter! She's here! At last! Alice!”

The Hatter spun about and beheld Alice. “And what time do you call this?” said he, pointing wildly at an enormous clock nailed to a tree behind him. The clock's hands were moving hastily both forwards and backwards.

“Why? Am I expected at this tea party?” said Alice.

“Not only expected but required!” said the Hare.

I leaned in close and whispered. “It must be how your story was written.”

“It is *precisely* how!” said the Hatter, “but not, I might add, how *your* story was written,” continued he, stamping his foot upon the table and pointing at me. It was then that the Dormouse woke with a start, gazed at me through a face covered in trifle, and said, “Alice?”

I shook my head. “No, I'm Snow. This is Alice,” said I, placing an arm about her shoulders.

“Oh yes, so she is,” replied the Dormouse, slamming its face back in the trifle.

“Don't mind him,” said the Hare, “he has issues concerning sleep and trifles.”

I nodded. “Maybe he's a relation of Goldilocks? She has similar issues with *porridge* and sleep.”

"Goldilocks, you say? Goldilocks!" said the Hatter, folding his arms so tightly round himself it was a wonder he could still breathe. He unclasped himself, hurried to the end of the table, knelt, gazed at me and asked, "Goldilocks and Snow … of the *White* variety?"

"Clearly, she is," said the Hare. "Clearly!"

"I cannot deny that I am visible from space most nights."

"Alice!" said the Hatter tuning his big hypnotic eyes upon her.

"Yes?" replied she, startled.

"You were supposed to come here alone."

"I did. But then I found myself suddenly marrying Snow in her land …"

The Dormouse lifted its head from the trifle. "So you're married then?" said he, "how very modern," he concluded, before passing out in his trifle.

"Actually, Alice and I are not married. I was about to marry my one true love, *Edward*, when my stepmother swapped him for Alice."

"You know Edward?" said the Hatter.

I nodded vigorously. "Did he pass this way?"

"I should hope not," shuddered the Hare.

"Why do you shudder so?" said I. "Edward is a lovely young man. Poor and perfect."

“Maybe he is and maybe he isn't,” said the Hatter. “And whether he is or whether he isn't will matter not a jot to the Black Bandit.”

“The Black Bandit?” said Alice.

The Dormouse lifted its head from its trifle and cried “Is the Black Bandit here!? Oh, for the love of trifle, tell me that he isn't!”

“No. He isn't,” said the Hatter. Reassured thus, the Dormouse slammed its face back down into its trifle.

“What has this Black Bandit got to do with Edward?” asked I.

The Hatter shook a finger at me accusingly. “You are *both* responsible! Don’t deny it.”

I swallowed hard. “If you're referring to the danger that the superfluous characters find themselves in, then you should know that Alice and I are on our way to visit the Queen of Hearts. We are going to sort all that out. You see, there's been a terrible misunderstanding.”

“I don't think the Black Bandit's going to see it that way,” said the Hatter.

I gazed at him imploringly. “Who is this Black Bandit? And what has he to do with Edward and I?”

“The Black Bandit is the cruellest rogue to roam this land or any other,” said the Hare. “He's a giant! Seven feet tall. Utterly without mercy. Or pity. Loves to run people through with his sword. For sport!”

The Hatter turned his hypnotic gaze upon me. “The Queen

has placed a bounty on both of your heads. And the Black Bandit means to collect it." I deduced that either I had grown a second head which, let's face it, would not exactly be anything out of the ordinary in Wonderland, or else the Hatter was referring to mine and Edward's head.

"Dead or alive," said the Hare.

"What's that supposed to mean?" asked Alice.

"That the Black Bandit will get his reward whether he delivers you and Edward to the queen dead *or* alive."

"To my knowledge, the Black Bandit is yet to deliver anyone to the queen *alive*," said the Hatter racking his brains for an exception to the dead option.

"Are you telling me the Black Bandit will *kill* Edward if he finds him?"

The Hatter sat down in his chair, put his feet up on the table, picked at the dirt beneath his nails and murmured, "Oh, yes. He'll delight in it I should imagine."

Five fraught minutes later …

Five fraught minutes later, I was hurrying down the path that led to the queen's palace, while Alice made every effort to keep up. “We *must* reach the palace and talk to the queen,” puffed I. “Tell her that there’s been a *terrible* misunderstanding. That she must remove the bounty on Edward's head. We’ll explain that all this is my stepmother's fault. That none of this would have happened without her meddling. Surely the Queen of Hearts must listen to reason?”

“Yes, surely,” said Alice, uncertainly. “And, in the meantime, we'd better keep our eyes peeled for thc Black Bandit. You’re wanted dead or alive too.”

“Psssssst!” came the sound of pssssssing. Alice and I stopped in our tracks. “Psssssst! Over there! I’m over there!” said a male voice that sounded like it belonged to an absent-minded professor.

“Over *there*?” said I, turning and gazing over ‘there’ into the woods. My eyes widened as I beheld a plump cat that hung upside down in mid-air. The cat was grinning from ear to ear and believe me when I say I have never seen a bigger grin.

“That’s weird,” murmured I.

“Exceedingly,” agreed Alice.

“Yes! You're looking right at me. I'm over there!” said the cat.

“You mean you're over *here*,” said Alice, stepping towards it.

"I was over here but now I'm clearly over there."

"But we were just over there," protested Alice.

"Not from where I'm hanging."

"Look," said I, "as interesting as this philosophical discussion about the whereabouts of *here* and *there* is, we really must be on our way."

"Would you be interested to learn who else is over here?"

"Who?" said Alice.

"The Black Bandit. Hide!" Alice and I glanced at one another and then dived into a bush below the cat. We held our breath as a man rode into view. He was atop a stallion and dressed entirely in black, including a black mask that obscured his doubtlessly spiteful face. He rode slowly, as though he hadn't a care in the world, and had a smugness about him that was more than a little unsettling. I was relieved to see that he was all alone, that's to say, there was no one with him, *dead* or alive, which boded well for Edward.

Once he was out of earshot and well on his way, the cat said, "Allow me to introduce myself, I am the Cheshire Cat. It's not only an honour but also a relief to meet you, Alice." Alice and I climbed to our feet and brushed ourselves down.

"You're very kind," said Alice.

"No at all. If we hadn't met, then I would have been superfluous. And my head would be for the chop, too." The Cheshire Cat, that had hitherto been hanging upside down in mid-air, floated the right side up.

"Thank you for warning us about the approach of the Black Bandit," said I. "And you're not wrong about the superfluous characters. They are in considerable danger. Which is why Alice and I really must be going."

"And where are you going?"

"To see the Queen of Hearts. And explain that none of this was their fault," said Alice.

"And to ask her to remove the bounty on Edward's head," said I.

"And your head," said Alice.

The Cheshire Cat went boss-eyed. "Alice is quite right. You are *both* wanted dead or alive. But you can forget the alive. The Black Bandit prefers to deliver his captives cold."

"So we've already been told," shuddered I.

The Cheshire Cat whipped a scroll of paper from somewhere within its fur. A scroll fastened by a length of red ribbon.

"What's all this then?" said Alice.

"It's a decree issued by the queen," replied the Cheshire Cat pulling off the ribbon and unfurling the scroll with a flourish. "You might say that it's hot off the press. And if you did you'd be right," continued he, as the scroll burst into flames and disintegrated in its paws.

"Was that something we should know?" asked Alice.

"That all depends," said the Cheshire Cat.

"On what?"

“On how well you're able to take bad news.”

Alice and I glanced at one another, then fixed the Cheshire Cat with our most no-nonsense stares. “We are well used to it by now,” said we.

The Cheshire Cat's grin turned upside down. “Oh, dear me, why so glum?”

“To the contrary,” replied I, “experience has turned us into …”

“Realists?” ventured Alice.

“Yes, realists,” said I, folding my arms and bracing myself to hear something, well, *real*. “Well?” I asked it. “We haven’t got all day.”

The Cheshire Cat produced a pocket watch, opened it, and then gulped at the dial. “Indeed, you haven't! In fact, you have just forty-eight minutes.”

“Till when?” asked Alice.

“Until 11pm.”

“And what happens at 11pm?”

“That's when the Queen is going to yell 'off with their heads.'”

I swallowed hard.

“Whose heads?” asked Alice.

“The heads of the superfluous characters. Who else? Unless …”

“Unless what?”

“Unless you two give yourselves up before then.”

Several minutes and a great deal of huffing and puffing later …

Several minutes and a great deal of huffing and puffing later, Alice and I sprinted round a bend in the path and skidded to a halt: before us, atop a hill, we beheld a sprawling castle with brightly coloured turrets that soared into the sky. "This looks like the place," said I, rubbing at a stitch in my side.

"It's where the big bad from my story lives, I feel it in my water. I'm so glad you're here, Snow. I'm quite certain your experience is going to prove invaluable when dealing with *this* evil queen."

I shrugged. "I hear evil queens are pretty similar. I wouldn't be at all surprised if there's a factory that makes them for stories such as this. I know there's a factory that makes Prince Charmings. Did you know that?"

Alice shook her head. "I had no idea."

I took a step towards the castle but stopped when Alice grabbed my arm. "I have a horrible feeling *this* queen is going to be rather different from those in your own land."

"My track record with those in authority in my own land isn't so great. So maybe that's a good thing? Come on, we must make haste."

Not long after, Alice and I ran up to a closed gate. Through its iron railings, we saw a beautiful lawn where two portly young men; identical twins, were playing croquet. Alice took hold of the gate's bars and peered through them.

"Do you recognise those twins?" enquired I.

"No, not *exactly*. But like all the other characters we've encountered so far, they look oddly familiar. Does that sound strange?"

"Not at all. They must be important to your story. I *sort of* recognised my Prince Charming when he arrived early."

"And you'd never seen him before?"

"No, never."

Alice nodded. "Yoo hoo!" cried she through the gate.

The plump twins, both wearing skull caps, scrunched up their eyes and peered in our direction. "Who goes there?" said the one wearing a blue cap.

"I'm Alice." The twins dropped their croquet mallets, high fived one another, clicked their heels (no mean feat) and then trundled over the lawn in our direction.

"I get the impression they've heard of you …" murmured I. Our view of the trundling twins was suddenly obscured by a couple of flat surfaces. Alice and I stumbled backwards and beheld two playing cards. The playing cards were taller than us, considerably so, and had arms, legs, and a head. Their heads were the same shape as their suit. In this case, diamonds and clubs. The three of diamonds drew a sword from a scabbard and cried, "Halt! Who goes there?"

Whereupon the four of clubs added, "Fiend or foe?"

To this the three of diamonds rolled his eyes and whispered, "It's *friend or foe*. You only had to learn one line. I'll have to tell the Queen."

"Oh, please don't! She'll have my head. Let me try again!"

"Oh, go on then," said the three of diamonds, begrudgingly.

The four of clubs drew breath, and his pained expression suggested he was concentrating awfully hard. "Fiend of foe!?" cried he again.

"I give up. You're toast," said the three of diamonds.

"Stand aside! Stand aside! Make way!" said the trundling, out of breath twins. The playing cards turned sideways and all but disappeared. "Masters Tweedledum and Tweedledee," said the cards bowing their paper-thin heads.

"Don't you know who this is?" said the twin whom I deduced must be Tweedledum for the letters TDUM were stitched into his cap.

"That is what we were just trying to ascertain," replied the three of diamonds.

"She's neither fiend nor foe. She's *Alice*," said Tweedledee.

"Oh, yes, so she is," said the four of clubs, peering at me.

"Not her! *Her*! That's Alice!" cried the twins, pointing at Alice. "Now open these gates!" The gates were swiftly opened, whereupon the twins were all over Alice like a friendly rash, and the playing cards were all over me like an angry one.

"You must be the female interloper!" cried the three of diamonds, twisting my arm behind my back.

"Ouch! Unhand me this instant!"

"Let go of her!" demanded Alice.

"Not likely."

"Have you time for a round of croquet?" Tweedledum asked Alice.

"*What*? Of course not."

Tweedledum tutted. "We thought you might say that."

"Yes. And it's all *your* fault she doesn't have time," added Tweedledee, glaring at me.

"No, it isn't," replied I. "If it's anybody's *fault* then it's the queen's." The collective intake of breaths that followed gave me the impression I'd said the wrong thing.

"The Queen will have your head now for sure," said Tweedledum.

"And talking of heads," said Tweedledee glancing at his wrist watch, "The superfluous characters are due to lose theirs any minute."

"Then we have no time to lose! You must take us to Queen of Hearts," cried Alice. Knowing that the superfluous characters would lose their heads unless I presented myself to the Queen asap, strengthened my resolve to grin and bear being painfully manhandled in her direction.

We rounded a hedge and came upon a beautiful garden where the Queen of Hearts sat upon a raised throne. Around the edge of the garden, there stood an army of playing cards with fearsome-looking pikes. The three superfluous characters that were to be beheaded: the mouse, the dodo and the white rabbit, were trembling with heads bowed before a masked brute who leaned nonchalantly on an axe. The Queen of Hearts, not yet having seen our approach, stood suddenly and yelled, “It's time! Off with their heads!”

“No!” cried I.

“What’s this?” said the Queen, peering at our approaching party. I should explain that this evil queen looks nothing like the ones in my own land. This queen is neither hunched nor haggard, willowy nor beautiful. The unsettling truth is this: she is mostly head. I’m talking a good two thirds of her. The remaining third (well, just about) is a mass of red hair. Her arms and legs, while dainty and perfectly formed, are absolutely minute. There she stood, hands upon a tiny waist that, by all the laws of nature, should not have been able to support the weight of that bonce. Sitting beside the queen, on a throne a little lower down, was a playing card: The Ace of Hearts. “It’s really her, aunty! It’s Snow White!” said the Ace, clapping silently in delight. The Ace was unique from the other cards in that he was plump (for a playing card), and had a handlebar moustache. “Release her this instant!” the Ace ordered the three of diamonds. He then rushed over and skipped about my person like a happy bird. “She looks *just* like she does in the book in the library! Oh, *can* I? Please say I can, aunty! I really want to!”

“Really want to do *what*?” said I.

“I think there must have been a terrible mistake,” said Alice. “Snow isn't even supposed to be here. I have been led to believe that this is my story?” A collective sigh reverberated around the garden, and the queen’s face lit up as though on fire. “I see. This is YOUR story is it! *Yours*? Tell me, *whose* story is this?” bellowed the queen to her courtiers.

“It’s your story, your Majesty!” replied they.

“Did you hear that? This is my story. Mine, you hear. You, *Alice*, are nothing but an upstart. A *bit* player. A walk on part. An extra! Do you understand?” The queen began tapping her foot impatiently and added, “You have less than one second to say that you do, otherwise that impertinent head will be severed from those diabolical shoulders.”

“I understand,” nodded Alice, wisely.

“I'm glad.”

“Aunty!” cried the Ace of Hearts.

“Yes, my petal?”

“Well, *can I*?” said he, looking at me in a way that made me feel more than a little uncomfortable.

“I suppose so,” replied the queen, whipping out a pair of opera glasses from somewhere on her person. “Although, are you *certain* you want to? She's dreadfully pale.”

“She is *Snow White*, aunty.”

“You can say that again.”

“Look,” said I, “there's obviously some confusion. I've only come here to ask you to spare the lives of the superfluous characters. And to implore you to send word to the Black Bandit to stop hunting Edward.” A silence descended, and out of this silence came the cruellest laughter you've never heard from all present. As is usually the case with these sorts of stories (it's the way they are written) everyone continued to belly laugh until the queen, whose own belly laugh was more of a chin laugh due to her chin being where her belly ought to be, stopped. “So, you wish me to spare the superfluous characters? *And* remove the bounty from the other interloper's head? Is that all?”

“Yes, that about covers it,” said I.

“I will grant you *one* request but not the other,” snapped the queen. “And the one comes with certain terms and conditions,” continued she, winking at the Ace of Hearts.

“Oh, yes,” said I, glancing at the Ace.

The queen raised her chin. “I will spare the superfluous characters on the following terms and conditions,” said she, snapping her fingers. A playing card, the Jack of Clubs, darted forwards, bowed low, and handed the queen a scroll. The queen unfurled it and read the following: “This, my decree, as written on this day the 21st of June, 1888, does solemnly promise that I will spare all superfluous characters, including the mouse, the dodo *and* the white rabbit,” said she, glancing at Alice, “if the interloper known as Snow White marries my nephew the Ace of Hearts.”

“But I *can't!*”

“And why not?” demanded the queen.

“Because I am betrothed to another; to Edward, my true love.”

“I see. Well, the news is not good on the Edward front,” replied the queen rolling up the scroll.

“Maybe,” said I, “but it will be greatly improved when you remove the ransom from his head.”

“Are you *certain* you want to marry her? She's not very

bright," said the queen to her nephew.

"Very sure," nodded he.

The queen tuned her steely gaze upon me. "Weren't you listening? I said could grant *one* of your requests but not the other. I can spare the superfluous characters but I cannot prevent the Black Bandit from killing the other interloper."

"*Wh … what*? But you're the queen of this land. You can do as you please."

"Within limits. Last night, The Black Bandit demanded a ransom be paid for … what's his name again?"

"Edward," said Alice, placing a comforting arm around me.

"Yes, Edward. And the Queen of Hearts does not pay ransoms. It sets a bad example. A note that stated as much was delivered to the Black Bandit several hours ago."

"Maybe …" said I, breathlessly, "maybe he will take pity on Edward. Make him the exception. Edward *is* the exception."

"Nonsense," barked the queen, "the Black Bandit has a reputation to uphold. As far as he's concerned there *are* no exceptions. So, regarding your *Edward* …" The queen drew a finger across her throat, and only Alice's arm about my waist prevented me from falling to my knees. "So, you see there *are* no barriers to your marrying my nephew now."

"I won't do it!" said I, clinging to Alice.

"You will because if you do not I will have the heads of the superfluous characters on spikes! As for Edward, word is he has already met his maker."

The following morning …

Shortly after the queen had told me of Edward's fate, I fainted, not from 'famishment' but from grief. I awoke the following morning in a turret room not unlike Rapunzel's and, like Rapunzel, I too was a prisoner. But unlike her, my heart felt as though it had been torn, beating from my breast and stamped into dust. The thought of never looking into Edward's knowing eyes again was almost too much to bear. I say almost because I was still able to draw breath, and therefore must have been bearing it. It seemed as though my stepmother had finally got what she wanted: she had banished me to another land and destroyed any chance I might have of living happily ever after. I heard a knock on the door, and then the sound of Alice's friendly voice, "Snow? Are you awake?"

"C … come in," said I, my throat bone dry.

The door opened and it was a comfort to see Alice's sympathetic face. "I'm so sorry," said she, coming over and sitting beside me on the edge of my bed. She reached for a jug of water on the bedside table and poured some into a glass. She handed it to me and, although dreadfully thirsty, I found I had not the stomach for more than a few sips.

"You have nothing to be sorry about," said I, quietly.

"If not for me, you and Edward would never have been in this cruel place."

"You're wrong. If not for my *stepmother* we …" I felt tears come to my eyes and a frog to my throat.

“Take heart,” said Alice, placing a hand upon my own. “You can’t know for sure that the Black Bandit has hurt Edward.”

“I know,” nodded I, “but the queen seemed so certain. And, unless I receive word to the contrary, what choice will I have but to marry her nephew? The queen said she will execute the superfluous characters if I do not. I could not for all the world let them perish in the hope that Edward lives. How selfish would that make me? And I need not remind you that the white rabbit is amongst them. You would be trapped in Wonderland forever.” We were both started by a loud rap on the door. “Who is it?” said Alice.

“The Ten of Spades, I am personal assistant to his highness the Ace of Hearts. His highness requests the pleasure of Snow White’s company in his Parlour of Things.” I could tell by the expression on Alice’s face that she was about to tell the Ten of Spades where to go, and in no uncertain terms.

“No,” said I, sitting up, “I had better do as he says. If only for the sake of the superfluous characters.”

“I hope that one day I shall be as kind as you, Snow.”

“You are already so,” said I, standing unsteadily. I clung to Alice’s arm, and we followed the Ten of Spades down a sweeping staircase, through a great many palatial rooms, and into the Parlour of Things. The parlour was red and sumptuous and looked out over a garden where a fountain sprayed multi-coloured water into the air. All around us were objects hidden beneath red satin sheets. The Ace of Hearts was standing before an easel, upon which sat a portrait of yours truly. “Do you like my portrait of you?” asked he.

“Your painting does me great justice,” said I, for it did.

The Ace nodded in agreement. “I have a confession to make.”

“You do?” said I, glancing nervously at Alice.

The Ace puffed out his chest with pride. “*This* is not the only portrait I have painted of you.” He skipped about and removed several more sheets to reveal yet more paintings of me, each identical to the first. “I can see you're impressed,” said he, mistaking my perturbed expression for something that suited him better. “How I have dreamt of this day!” continued he, clapping and bouncing on the spot.

“You have?” said I, gripping Alice's arm.

“I have! Welcome Snow White, the *fairest* in all the lands, to my Parlour of Things!” said he, skipping about his parlour and removing the remaining coverings. The objects beneath included: three life sized statues of me, four busts of my head and shoulders, an armchair with my face carved into its wooden back, a croquet mallet with a Snow White shaped head, a carving of a flamingo with my own head where its flamingo head ought to have been, and many more me orientated things besides. Finally, he hurried over to the last object, and whipped away the covering to reveal a plinth with my name carved into its base. “Chop chop, as aunty likes to say to her executioner!” said he, gesturing to the knee-high plinth.

“What? You wish me to …”

“Yes! Stand upon your plinth. I know we’re yet to be married but please, indulge me, try it out for size, and let me behold my collection of things complete!”

“But … I am not your *thing*.”

“I beg to differ. You are easily the most important thing in my collection.”

“Snow will *never* be a part of your collection of things!” said Alice stepping before me.

“Oh, I think she will,” said the Ace, tapping his foot impatiently.

“Over my dead body!” said Alice.

“Not yours. But certainly over the dead bodies of the superfluous characters. Indeed, if Snow does not indulge me with this preview of where she’s to live happily ever after, then at least *one* superfluous character will be separated from his head before the day is out.” I walked unsteadily to my plinth, stepped upon it, and turned around. As I gazed out from the place where I was to live happily ever after, I thought of Edward, and felt tears come to my eyes.

An hour later …

An hour later, I was led exhausted to a gathering in the Queen's Garden. My wedding to the Ace of Hearts was to take place the following day, and this was to be our rehearsal. A great many packs of playing cards were present, dressed in uniforms with gold braid, and *dozens* of courtiers dressed as chess pieces. Not to mention a whole host of stony-faced characters too numerous to mention here. If truth be told, such was my grief that much of the rehearsal is a blur. The one thing that I can remember with clarity, however, is the conversation I had with Queen. She was sitting beside an altar, where a bald vicar stood in a purple frock.

"And here the happy couple are now," said the queen. It was only then that I realised that the Ace of Hearts was not only walking alongside me but had an arm interlinked with my own. "Cheer up, Miss White, it might never happen," chuckled the queen.

"If what you have told me about the Black Bandit is true, then, the worst *has* happened," murmured I.

The queen rolled her eyes. "I have some news that will improve your spirits." I gazed at her expectantly, hoping beyond all hope that she had some good news concerning Edward. "As the bride to be, you're allowed to choose your own bridesmaids. I can see my news has cheered you a little." This improvement was due to my having spotted the superfluous characters: the white rabbit, the mouse and the dodo, clasped in irons with their heads bowed. I imagined they had been placed there to remind me how their fates lay in my hands. It was not the sight of these characters in their wretched states that had improved my countenance, rather the idea that had taken seed in my mind.

"I can choose *any* characters to be my bridesmaids?" murmured I.

"That's what I said, didn't I?" snapped the queen.

Marshalling all my strength, I fixed my most determined gaze upon her. "Well then, I choose the white rabbit, the mouse *and* the dodo."

"*What* did she say?" the queen asked her page.

"I believe that she wishes the white rabbit, the mouse *and* the dodo to be her bridesmaids," your Majesty.

"Oh, she does, does she?"

"You did say I could choose. So, I choose white rabbit, the mouse and the dodo."

"Is she mad?" the queen asked the Ace of Hearts.

The Ace shrugged, bit off a loose fingernail, and replied, "Does it matter?"

The queen looked down her nose at me. "I suppose you realise they will be required to wear bridesmaid's dresses?"

"And?" said I.

"And they're *males*. Would they do it?" said she, glancing over her shoulder in their direction.

"Yes, I'm sure they would," said Alice, cottoning onto my

plan, “after all, as Snow's bridesmaids they will no longer be superfluous. They'll be *perfluous* again. And free to live out their lives.”

“*Perfluous*? Does such a word even exist?” the queen asked her page.

“No, Your Highness. I believe Alice just made it up.”

“Actually, I just *invented* it. So, it must exist,” insisted Alice.

The queen leant in close to her page. “Is Alice’s logic sound in this matter? Her logic sounds sound.”

“One cannot argue that she just invented the word. And, once invented, I suppose it must exist, your Majesty.”

“Then don't just stand there. Add the word to the Royal Dictionary! This instant! What is the meaning of this request?” said the queen to me.

I straightened my back. “I wish only to ensure that, following my wedding to your nephew, that the now *perfluous* characters will be freed.”

“But that was already to be part of the arrangement,” replied the queen, unconvincingly.

“And now I'd like your word that it *is* part of it, and that they *shall* be freed.”

“You would, would you? Perhaps you’d like it in writing?” replied the queen, sarcastically.

“Actually, she would,” said Alice.

The queen looked at her nodding nephew. “Oh, very well,”

replied she, “have the royal pardon drawn up. But it is only to come into effect once the vows have been taken. And now we must begin the rehearsal, chop chop!”

The following morning …

The following morning, I woke from a nightmare about spending the rest of my days as an object in a collection of things dedicated to myself, only to find myself destined to become just that. But I was determined to stay compos mentis long enough to speak my vows, and ensure the freedom of the now perfluous characters. I supposed that my grief over Edward would take hold soon after, and that I would end up, for want of a better term, a broken exhibit in the Ace of Heart's collection.

There came a knock at my door. I sat up in bed and somehow found my voice. "Come in," said I. The door opened and the glue of my sanity entered in the form of the white rabbit, the mouse and the dodo. Alice was hot on their heels and her sorrowful expression led me to believe that she must have been concerned for my well-being.

"Snow? Did you sleep well?"

"Yes, very well," said I, putting on the bravest face I had to hand.

The mouse stepped forwards. "I can't thank you enough for making me perfluous again," said he. At this juncture, I should point out that the mouse of Alice's story is not a tiny rodent that scurries around in search of cheese: *this* mouse wears a waistcoat, walks about on its hind legs, and is as big as a great dane. In this regard, it is very much like the white rabbit. Speaking of which, the white rabbit began to hop up and down and enthuse that he too couldn't thank me enough. "I therefore intended to thank you as regularly as clockwork," said he, checking the dial on his pocket watch. "Thank you!"

"There really is no need," said I, "for it is my nature to be meddlesome where the happy endings of others are concerned."

"Meddlesome?" said the mouse darting forwards to shake my hand, "not a bit of it. You've done nothing less than save our bacon."

"I like bacon," said the dodo as though he wasn't quite sure what bacon was. He stumbled forwards to shake my hand also. I grabbed it in the nick of time for the poor fellow, who reminded me of Awkward, would have fallen flat on his great beak otherwise. I shook the dodo's hand warmly. "Saving your bacon was the very least I could have done under the circumstances."

Alice smiled solemnly. "The white rabbit will soon be free to lead me back home. I too owe you everything."

"Then why the face like you've been sucking on a lemon," said I, remembering how Cinders used to ask me the same question. At the thought of Cinders, I felt a pang of homesickness.

"Why?" said Alice, "because your sacrifice it's … well, it's simply too great."

I smiled as best I could. "A great many characters have suffered worse fates than mine." I turned to the white rabbit, "You will lead Alice back to the real world, won't you?"

"Of course! Right away! Well, at her earliest convenience."

“The *fictional* real world,” Alice reminded me.

“It matters not for that is where home is. I can at least take comfort in knowing that you’re there following my …”

“Wedding,” sighed Alice, miserably.

The hours that followed are little more than a blur. But later, as the fog began to clear, I found myself standing in a grand anteroom within the palace. I remember seeing my reflection in one of the room's many mirrors and, realising that I was wearing a wedding dress, I had reacted as if smelling salts had woken me from my haze. The dress was red and black with a long and bulbous train in the shape of a clover. My makeup had been liberally applied in red and black also. I felt certain that had the mirrors voices like those in my own land, that they would have pronounced me the scariest, not the fairest in the land.

The room's other inhabitants came into focus in the room behind me. I turned to see that Alice too had been made a bridesmaid and that she looked perfectly lovely in her dress. However, the sight of the white rabbit, the mouse and the dodo in their dresses, pink and strapless, struck me as so absurd that I found myself doubled over in laugher. "She's delirious!" I heard Alice cry. "Quickly, we must hold her to prevent her falling!" I remember the clutch of my bridesmaids' hands, keeping me on my feet until my delirium had passed. And a rap on the door which opened to reveal four playing card guards.

"It's time," said one amongst them.

"Time?" said I, wiping the moisture from my face.

"For your wedding. Your groom awaits your arrival at the altar," said another. My bridesmaids were instructed to pick up my train, and I began to walk slowly towards my date with dreadful destiny. Take heart, reader, for dreadful destiny, it seems, is not always as we imagine. Our party, which consisted of myself, four bridesmaids and four guards, were halfway across a small, walled in courtyard that led out into the queen's garden, when we were ambushed! The offender was a giant of a man; none other than the fiend himself: *The Black Bandit*. His reputation had clearly been well earned for he set about our guards with a fury the like of which I had never seen, separating each from his sword and rendering them unconscious with a blow from the handle of his own. Once our guards had been dealt with in this way, he came over to where I stood amid my cowering bridesmaids and proclaimed the following in a voice laced with gravel, "*You're all coming with me.*" In reply, I found myself reaching up and slapping him *hard* across his masked face for all I was worth. And, when it comes to slapping seven feet tall kidnappers who, rumour has it, have killed your one true love, I must be worth quite a lot for he stumbled sideways.

"What have you done with Edward!?" cried I. To this the Black Bandit replied not with words, but with a lasso that he drew from a pouch on his back. A moment later, having snared us, he grasped the end of the lasso over his shoulder, and dragged us towards a door. Once through this door, which was not an easy fit for five hostages lassoed together, the fiend shoved us into the back of a covered wagon. As we fought to free ourselves, we heard the sound of a whip lashing at the air, and tumbled onto our backs as the carriage moved swiftly away.

Once free of the lasso, I made a lunge for the back of the wagon, drew back the cover, and saw that we were thundering along a path into the woods. Alice and the white rabbit were suddenly either side of me. "Should we jump?" said a wide-eyed Alice.

"Jump? Not you!" implored the white rabbit clutching its

pocket watch. "I might survive at such speeds, but the rest of you would not." The carriage hit a bump and we all flew up and came crashing back down again.

"Come away from there if you don't want to fall out!" cried the dodo.

"The dodo's right," said Alice glancing over her shoulder at the large bird cowering in the rear of the wagon.

"I'm, right?" said he, "Are you sure? Only, I've never been told I was right before. About anything."

"Well, you're right now," said Alice, smiling at the dodo and ushering us back towards him.

"Do you think we're all doomed?" the mouse enquired of the dodo.

"What are you asking me for?" asked the dodo.

"You were right once. Maybe you're on a roll?"

"Of course we're not *doomed*," said Alice.

"What do you imagine the Black Bandit wants with us?" the mouse asked the dodo who buried its head in its chest and exclaimed, "I'm not used to being asked so many questions!"

"Why does the Black Bandit want anyone? To hold them to ransom," said Alice.

"Which means you must all be valuable," said I, "for he wouldn't have kidnapped you otherwise." A moment later, the carriage came to such an abrupt halt that we found ourselves in a heap on top of the dodo. As we scrambled to disentangle ourselves, the sheet at the back of the wagon was torn asunder and the shadow of the Black Bandit fell upon us.

About a minute and much shoving later …

About a minute and much shoving later, I stood huddled amid my bridesmaids beneath a tree. “Now look here,” said Alice, “it’s not too late to do the right thing and let us go.”

The white rabbit nodded. “Snow might be valuable to the Ace of Hearts, but as for the rest of us? No one is going to pay a ransom for any of *us*. So, you may as well let us go.”

“I won't be going anywhere without Snow,” said Alice, edging between me and the seven-foot brute.

“That's where you wrong,” growled he. “A ransom has been paid for everyone present *except* Snow White.”

“What splendid news!” said the white rabbit, opening its pocket watch, “I’m late for a very important date.”

“Yes, you are,” growled the Black Bandit through his mask.

“I am? And what date might that be?” asked the white rabbit who sounded genuinely intrigued by the possibility of having somewhere to go.

“You are expected, and without further delay, by Alice’s father who has paid your ransom.”

“What? *Just* mine?”

“Pay attention! All of you *except* Snow White.”

“What even me?” said the dodo.

"Yes, even you," growled the Black Bandit in such a way as to make the dodo shrink backwards.

"But why not Snow? My father would have paid …"

"Silence!" barked the Black Bandit, "Snow White is worth more to the Ace of Diamonds than she is to you father."

"But this is wonderful news, Alice." said I, bravely, "for you are all to go somewhere safe."

"I won't leave you with this *fiend*! How could I?" cried Alice.

"But you must. You know as well as I that now they've escaped, leaving Wonderland may be the only hope that our new friends have of keeping their heads," said I, smiling at the blushing dodo.

"Well then," said Alice, "I'll go with them as far as the entrance that leads back to my home, but no further."

"You'll do as you're told *little girl*. The ransom has been paid for four and *four* will be delivered. Four or *none* at all," said he, drawing his sword.

"Alice *please*," implored I, "you must see our friends safely out of Wonderland."

"How did you even contact my father in the real world?" Alice asked the Black Bandit.

"I could not have contacted him in the real world. But he lives in the *fictional* real world. You think the queen would have spared any of you? She'd have had all your heads in time. Beheading is her addiction." I felt my own fingers brush against my neck. "It will serve you best not to displease the Ace of Hearts," said the Black Bandit whose attention was clearly focused on me beneath that terrible mask.

The white rabbit clicked open the clasp on its pocket watch. "Is that really the time? I'll be late! We'll all be late!" said he, glancing at those he was now tasked with leading to Alice's home.

"Is the conduit far?" asked the mouse.

"Far? That all depends on how late we are," replied the white rabbit winding its pocket watch.

"You are VERY LATE," growled the Black Bandit.

"Yes!" agreed the white rabbit, clicking its heels. "Late enough for the entrance to be right around here …" continued he, making his way around the tree to the other side. We all followed and, lo and behold, the white rabbit was gazing down into a large rabbit hole.

"This hole will deliver you to Alice's garden?" growled the Black Bandit.

"Yes. In no time. Which is just as well as we have no time to lose!" replied the white rabbit leaping in and disappearing.

"It's your turn," the Black Bandit told the mouse.

"You think it's safe," murmured he.

Alice spoke up, her voice filled with sorrow. "I'm sure we can trust the white rabbit when it comes to rabbit holes that lead between worlds such as this."

"Well, if *you* think it's safe," said the mouse who then closed his eyes tight, and stepped into the hole. The mouse was followed swiftly by the dodo who had been given a nudge by the Black Bandit. Alice threw her arms around me and clung so tightly as to force the breath from my lungs. "Thank you, Snow! Stay strong!" pleaded she, "and say that we shall meet again!"

"I hope that we shall, with all my heart," said I, hugging her tightly.

"I know I shall never make another friend like you," she murmured into my shoulder. Alice released her grip on me and took a backwards step towards the hole. "Have faith, Snow White," said she, welling up, "faith that even if you're not reunited with Edward in this world then …" Alice's comforting gaze continued to meet my own until she too had climbed into the rabbit hole and disappeared. I turned and looked up into the mask of the brute with whom I was now alone. "Tell me," said I, "must I cling to the hope that I will see Edward again, not in this world, but in the next?" The Black Bandit nodded and I fainted away.

Sometime later …

Sometime later, I came around to find myself in a small boat being rowed across a vast lake. I sat up and gazed over the still waters. Even though his eyes were hidden by his mask, I could feel the fiend's gaze upon me. "Where are you taking me?" I asked, sounding as though it did not matter.

"To my hideaway on the north side of the lake. The queen's soldiers will soon be searching the south side."

I gazed out over the water. "Did he, did Edward mention me before you …" The Black Bandit replied with a nod.

"Then tell me, what did he say?"

"Are you certain you wish to know?" A glance in his direction indicated that I did. "He told me that never before had the son of a poor woodcutter loved another so passionately and so deeply. He said that he'd looked into the depths of your very soul and …"

I felt a tear fall from my cheek. "And what?"

"And that the compassion, beauty and strength he'd seen was the like of which he'd imagined he would never see."

"I see ..." said I, blinking away my tears.

"Above all else he said that the very worst thing he could imagine in all the world would be your suffering. To this end, he pleaded with me to treat you mercifully. He seemed a decent enough fellow. And that is why I will do my best to respect his wishes." The Black Bandit rowed on, the only sound that of his oars splashing in and out of the water. I must have drifted miles away, for the minutes that followed are a blank, but I was brought back to the boat by the sound of rushing water. My gaze, having returned to the here and now, searched in vain for its source across the vast lake. “What you can hear is the Immense Waterfall,” growled the Black Bandit.

“The Immense Waterfall?” murmured I. The Black Bandit put down his oars, stood up, and rubbed at a crick in his back. “These waters may look still to the untrained eye but do not be fooled. The current that runs just below the surface runs *fast* towards the Immense Falls.”

“But I see no falls …”

“They lie not one hundred metres away,” said he, glancing in their direction.

“And … are the falls dangerous?”

“Yes. As their name suggests, they are *immense*,” growled he, rubbing his neck.

“Then you shall see just how immense!” cried I, jumping up and, catching him off balance, shoving him for all I was worth. When it comes to shoving seven foot fiends who have killed your one true love over the side of boats, I must be worth rather a lot for he fell, head first, into the water. As the swiftly-moving current carried him towards the Immense Falls, his head returned to the surface just long enough for him to cry out in a voice that I not only recognised but longed to hear: “Truly! Is that your heart’s desire?”

“*Edward*?!” The next moment, I had launched myself over the side of the boat. The current below the surface was indeed fast moving, a fact for which I was grateful when I felt a rush of breathable air in my face, before plummeting towards the lagoon below. Initially, I was pleased to discover that the water in the lagoon was deep enough for me not to hit the bottom. But my relief was replaced by the fear when I remembered something pertinent: *I cannot swim. I wasn't written that way …*

Sometime later …

Sometime later, I opened my eyes to behold not only the most welcome but also the most hoped for sight imaginable. “Edward?” murmured I, for it *was* him.

“Yes, my love,” said he, welling up and then smiling that smile of his that used to make me faint from famishment.

“… You’re *alive*?”

“I cannot deny it.”

“I hoped you would not. And you rescued me?”

“Yes.”

“But …”

“But?”

“I came here to rescue *you.*”

“A truth for which I shall always be eternally grateful. But since you saw fit to shove me into the water and then join me, what choice did I have but to return the favour?” said he, brushing a hair tenderly from the corner of my eye.

“But why did you not tell me who you were? And how have you grown so *tall*?”

“Lifts,” replied he, pulling off one of his knee length boots and removing the extraordinary wedge within. “You see,” continued he thoughtfully, “I seized upon an opportunity to escape from the cage that the Black Bandit had locked me in."

"Well done you!" said I, squeezing his arm.

"It was nothing really, I just utilised some of the lock picking skills that the little lamb taught me."

"The little lamb taught you how to pick locks? I had no idea. I knew that it was he who taught you how to read and how you used to hop, skip and jump as you did so … it explains why you have such a bad …" At the sight of Edward's raised eyebrow, a subconscious sign of his that lets me know when I'm babbling, I closed my mouth.

"So," continued he, "once free of my cage, I crept up behind the Black Bandit and, having availed myself of a large water jug, I brought it down upon his head with a force that I judged would render him unconscious."

"And did it?"

"It did."

"And he did not see your approach?"

Edward shook his head. "You see, at the time he was sitting with his back to me, stirring a pot above a fire."

"And what was in the pot?"

"Baked beans," replied Edward, stifling a burp.

"So, then what happened?"

"Using his own ropes, I tied him up."

"*Tight*?" said I, squeezing his arm tenderly.

"Very. And when he came around, he was none too happy as you might imagine."

"I'd rather not," said I, with a shudder.

"Quite so. Having felt the large bump on his head, he swore that when he was eventually free of his bindings, he would track me down and kill me."

"No!" said I.

"Yes. In fact, he told me that there was no place in Wonderland that I could hide. And that it was a just a matter time before he made good on his promise to end my life."

"Oh, Edward!" said I, glancing about us for any sign of the fiend.

"So you see, I had to disguise myself, for if the Black Bandit caught us before we were able to return home, and made good on his promise, I could not risk you having to suffer the grief of losing me twice."

"So, you believe there is a way home?"

"There's always a way home."

"And the perfluous characters?"

"Will all be safe and sound in the fictional real world with Alice."

"But how did you arrange all that?"

Edward stood and offered me his hand. I took it and, as we began to walk into the surrounding forest, he said, "Having availed myself of the Black Bandit's copy of *their* book, and having read it thoroughly, I deduced that the white rabbit was not only the key to Alice finding her way home to safety, but also any other characters who happened to be with her."

"So, what did you do?"

Edward reached out and held back a low hanging branch so that we might pass and said, "I felt certain that should the white rabbit be led to believe that reaching Alice's home was a matter of some urgency, and knowing that his character was written in a way that made him determined *never* to be late, that he would be able to summon a conduit that made the journey possible."

I stopped walking and gazed up at him. "That's awfully clever," said I.

Edward brushed a hand past his face as if to say it was nothing really. And then, using words rather than hand gestures, he said, "It was nothing really. All there in the book for anyone to discern."

"But how did you contact Alice's father to demand the ransom?"

"I didn't. It was all part of the ruse to trick the white rabbit into opening the conduit. Shall we?" said he, motioning to the way ahead, "for our journey is not inconsiderable and the Black Bandit, not to mention the Queen of Heart's army, will be tracking us as we speak."

We began walking again. "We're on a journey then? I mean, you have a destination in mind? Somewhere where we might find sanctuary?"

"Yes, my love."

"Where?"

"The palace of the White Queen. It lies on the western fringes of these very woods."

"The White Queen?"

Edward pulled the Black Bandit's copy of the book from his pocket and, as he flipped through its pages, I said, "And you don't think she will want to kill us? Only my experience of queens in lands such as these is that they should to be avoided if possible."

"The White Queen is the exception to that rule."

"How can you be so certain?"

"Because she was written that way."

"Music to my ears," said I.

"Indeed. It would appear that the author of *this* book wrote her as a foil to the Queen of Hearts."

"Foil?"

"Yes. As a mirror image. That's to say in reverse. Which is why he imbued the White Queen with all the kindly qualities that the Queen of Hearts is so sadly lacking."

"And you believe she will offer us sanctuary?"

"Yes, I'm quite convinced of it," said Edward, showing me an illustration of the kindly queen in question.

"She's very beautiful ..." said I, lifting the book so that I might see its title, "Alice Through the Looking Glass," murmured I.

“Indeed. It is the sequel to this one … Alice’s Adventures in Wonderland,” said Edward, taking that very book from his pocket.

An hour later …

An hour later the sun had gone down below the canopy of the trees, and the shadows had begun to merge into darkness. “It's time …” said Edward, glancing above us into the canopy.

“Time for what?” said I.

“For us to seek sanctuary in a tree,” said he, reaching out to touch a sturdy specimen of oak beside us.

“Is that really necessary?”

Edward took a step backwards and craned his neck to see up into the tree’s furthest reaches. “Perhaps it's time I told you the name of these woods.”

“Perhaps it is,” replied I, uncertainly.

“They are called The Woods Where Crazed Carnivorous Toads Roam After Dark.”

“Talk about a mouthful,” said I.

“Which is what I've been given to understand we shall become if we are not out of hopping range …”

“Ours?” said I, hopefully.

“Theirs,” said he, with a shake of his head. “Indeed, if the rumours are to be believed, then the hop of the Crazed Carnivorous Toad is considerable.”

“How considerable?”

"About three quarters the height of this tree. Which is why there is no time to lose," said he, cupping his hands for me to step into. And so it was, that by the light of the moon, I found myself climbing a tree with Edward in the Woods Where Crazed Carnivorous Toads Roam After Dark. We climbed almost to its top where we found a crisscrossing cluster of branches capable of supporting our weight. It was here that we lay on our stomachs and looked out over the woods for any sign of the bloodthirsty toads. "It may be a ruse," said I, squinting to scrutinise the woods below.

"A ruse?" said he.

"Yes, you see, in my efforts to reach Wonderland and rescue you …"

"Something for which I am forever in your debt."

It was my turn to brush a hand past my face as if to say it was nothing. My hand brush, however, was accompanied by an awkward snort. And I knew I must be blushing for Edward's face, so close to my own, was splashed with crimson. "How is the charming little fellow?" asked Edward.

"Awkward?" said I.

Edward nodded.

"The last I saw him he was fine."

"I will see you reunited with all your dwarves if it is the last thing I do."

"I very much hope that it is not the last thing you do."

"You were saying?"

"I was?"

"Yes. I believe that you were about to expound on a theory about these woods?"

"Oh, yes. You see, in order to reach Wonderland, it was necessary to pass through another wood called the Woods of Utter Despair."

"That cannot have been easy."

"Indeed, it would not have been had the woods not been given a fake name."

"Fake you say?"

"Yes. The woods had been given that name only to deter characters from the south crossing it to reach the north where they might have been meddlesome."

"That cannot have been easy for you to hear."

I nodded. "The news gave me cause to shudder. How well you know me."

"How is Meddlesome?"

"Well, I hope," said I.

"I hope so too. As regards these woods, I fear they have not been given a fake name simply to deter travellers."

"And what makes you say so?"

"I have no desire to alarm or make you fearful for my person but …"

"But what?" Edward motioned with his eyes in a way that suggested I sit up and look at his person. Doing so, I beheld a toad the size of a lap dog with its face buried in my true love's buttocks. Much crazed gesticulation from myself followed, this met by a stoic acceptance from Edward of the need for me to pull the toad free from his person. Doing so was not easy, indeed it required all my strength, as the toad had buried its fangs deep and was keen as mustard to remain where it was. But I persisted and, no sooner had I tossed the toad away, had it bounced up again, almost to our height, in its eagerness to reach Edward. As it bounced, it croaked in such a way as to alert the other carnivorous toads of the woods to the presence of a great delicacy in their midst. And, so it was, that Edward placed his arm around me, and we lay awake watching the army of carnivorous toads as they tried valiantly but in vain to reach the delicacy that lay upturned beside me in the farthest branches of that tree. As reunions go, it was unusual to say the least.

The following morning …

The following morning, as we climbed down from the tree, I for one was thinking about how unusual our night together had been. This had been due, in no small part, to my applying a makeshift bandage of leaves to Edward's savaged area. As we made good our descent, I might have broken the silence by reflecting on how I'd been forced to grasp at his buttocks for over an hour to stop the bleeding. But Edward had requested that I not bring that up. At least, not until the smarting had desisted.

Once back on terra firma, where the sun dappled woods were now mercifully free of carnivorous toads, Edward broke the silence when he said, "We must make haste, and reach the other side of these woods before nightfall."

"You are not wrong," said I, "particularly with such a great delicacy in our midst."

Edward looked closely at me for the hint of a smile but I was able, somehow, to maintain a serious expression. Then, having satisfied himself that my comment had been well intentioned, he took my hand and we sprinted west towards the promised sanctuary of the White Queen's palace.

It was sometime later, whilst thus engaged, that we were startled by the sudden appearance of a man on a horse. And while Edward skidded to an impressive halt, I tripped and fell flat on my face. I felt Edward's strong grip about my shoulders, lifting me back onto my feet. I wiped the soil from my face but hopes that I had removed it all were dashed when the rider of the horse drew a cutlass and, having swished it back and forth, pointed its tip at my face and snarled, “You missed a bit.”

In a flash, Edward had drawn his own cutlass and stood with it raised between myself and the rider whose identity, it turned out, was no mystery to Edward. “Fear not, for it is only the Red Knight,” said he. Indeed, with my senses returning, I beheld a superior looking fellow dressed in a suit of red armour. He lifted the visor on his helmet to reveal a ruddy, moustached face. “I mean to capture her, so stand aside, *sir*, or suffer the consequences,” said he.

“Consequences?” smiled Edward, uncertainly.

“Of my blade running you all the way through!” replied the Red Knight swishing his blade.

“Never!” said Edward, standing firm.

“What do you want with me?” I asked the Red Knight over Edward’s shoulder.

“To capture you.”

“Why?” said I, stepping in front of Edward.

The Red Knight looked at me in way that I recognised only too well, it said ‘you do not belong in this story.’ Then he stated: “Because *you* are the new white pawn.”

“I'm the new *white pawn*?”

“Let me explain,” said Edward, once again stepping in front of me. “Alice was originally meant to be the white pawn. Is that not so?” said Edward, raising his voice and sounding rather commanding as he directed his question to the Red Knight.

"She was," replied the Red Knight, his horse stomping back and forth impatiently.

"And ..." continued Edward in that same commanding tone that had given me goosebumps, "because Alice was forced to return home a little earlier than the author of this book had originally planned, you decided to make Snow White the new white pawn."

The Red Knight nodded. "Without a white pawn to capture, I would have been superfluous to the story. I am pleased to discover her hue fitting."

I stepped around Edward. "The fact is, I am visible from space most nights."

"That I have no trouble in believing. And now, white *pawn*, I am going to capture you."

"Never going to happen!" barked Edward, stepping in front of me.

I clasped hold of Edward's shoulder. "You sound awfully confident."

"If you cock an ear to the east, you will hear the reason for my confidence approaching." I cocked an ear to the east.

"Other east, my love," said Edward. And indeed, no sooner had I cocked my ear to the other east, did I hear the sound of approaching hooves. And, looking in that direction, I had mixed feelings at the realisation that the hooves were attached to the legs of a horse rode by a knight.

"Who's this then?" murmured I.

"Unless I'm very much mistaken, it is the *White* Knight,"

said Edward.

I nodded. “He is wearing a suit of white armour. What's he doing here?”

“He too is intent on capturing the white pawn.”

“Me?”

“Yes.”

“Then why do you smile so? After all, was not one knight intent on capturing me bad enough?”

“On my command run like the clappers …” said Edward under his breath.

“On your *command*?” said I.

“You’re right of course. Poor choice of words. On my say so, run like the clappers.”

“They say that the clappers run exceedingly quickly.”

“Precisely,” said he, taking my hand.

“You shan't take the white pawn! Not while I still have breath in my lungs!” barked the Red Knight at the approaching White Knight.

“You took the words from my very mouth,” replied the White Knight drawing his sword.

“I found her first! She's mine to take!” said the Red Knight.

“It seems that you are not familiar with the rules of chess! It's therefore time that someone taught you a lesson!” said the

White Knight, charging forwards with his sword raised high.

"Now!" said Edward, darting away like the clappers and pulling me with him.

As we ran, we heard the sound of steel crashing upon steel. "They are well matched, and it will therefore be some time before they decide to call it a draw," said Edward.

"A draw?" panted I.

"Yes. They will doubtless decide that the best course of action will be to share the spoils."

"The spoils?"

"Yes, my love. You."

Some considerable sprinting like the clappers later …

Some considerable sprinting like the clappers later, we exited the woods and beheld the fortress of the White Queen. Indeed, we did so in the nick of time, for a great thundering could be heard from behind us. “That sounds like an awful lot of noise for *two* knights,” panted I.

Edward nodded. “I suspect it’s the Queen of Heart’s army. It’s time we upped our game.”

“Upped our game? How?”

“By running like the *crazy* clappers.” And so it was that we ran like the *crazy* clappers towards the castle's lowered drawbridge. As our heavy footfalls fell upon the comforting sound of the wooden drawbridge, I glanced over my shoulder to see an army of playing cards thundering down upon us. As the drawbridge began to rise, we found ourselves running down an increasingly steep incline towards the palace’s entrance. We stumbled off the drawbridge and through this entrance, and somehow managed to remain on our feet. We turned to see that several playing cards had leapt on the top of the rising drawbridge. A great commotion followed as the palace's guards rushed to apprehend them as they tumbled down on our side.

An official looking man with a white beard and tall staff hurried over to us. Without any introductions he said, “I take it that *you* are the replacement white pawn?”

“Yes, I believe that I am.”

"And you name is?"

"Snow White."

The man tutted. "I suppose you're aware that you're in the wrong land?"

"Of course, I am. I'm not stupid."

Sensing my irritation, Edward said, "We have come here seeking sanctuary from the White Queen."

"Of *that* I am well aware. As is the White Queen who awaits an audience with the replacement pawn in her throne room."

We followed the man, who banged his staff upon the ground with every stride, through the palace until we reached the throne room. Here, we discovered the White Queen pacing up and down before her throne in a most agitated manner. Even in the midst of her agitation, the queen's beauty was not diminished. Whereas the Queen of Hearts has an inflated head that comprises most of her loathsome person, the White Queen is more conventionally shaped, only her neck, pure white and swan like, looked longer than perhaps a neck should to be considered 'normal'. Indeed, the White Queen is a great beauty and this beauty radiated from within. A truth echoed by the first words to leave her lovely white lips. "You made it to the sanctuary of my palace just in time. Welcome!"

"Thank you, your Majesty," said I, curtsying.

"It *is* you. Snow White. The fairest in the other land …" said she, stepping towards me.

"Yes," your Majesty, it is I. And this is Edward, my betrothed."

"We thank you for your kind offer of sanctuary, your Highness," said Edward with a bow.

"I do not believe that I've heard of you, Edward."

I glanced at him. "If you've heard of me, then maybe you've heard of Edward's father?"

"His father?"

"The woodcutter."

"The kindly fellow who let you go rather than killing you as your stepmother had ordered?"

"Indeed, they are one and the same."

"And has the kindness of the father been inherited by the son?"

"Oh, yes, very much so," replied I with pride. "But how have you heard of me and the woodcutter?"

"I have an extensive library here. My late father, the king, was a prolific collector of books. He sent out emissaries to a great many other lands, emissaries tasked with bringing back books for his library. He read fairytales to me as a child. And your story was one of my favourites."

"I'm very flattered, your Highness."

"And has our book made it to your land?"

"I have never come across it. But my stepmother's library is said to be extensive. And she must have a copy otherwise how else would she have known to banish Edward here?”

As the queen nodded sadly, a page rushed into the throne room and handed her a note. As the page backed away, she read, “The army of the Red Queen is amassing outside … it is led by the Ace of Hearts …” The queen read on in silence and, as she did so, her beautiful face assumed a grave expression.

“What is it?” said I.

“The Ace of Hearts, *your fiancé*, is threatening to lay siege to my palace, preventing all supplies from getting through, in effect, starving us unless …”

“Unless?” said I, horrified.

The queen looked at Edward. “Unless you go out and engage him in a sword fight to the death … the winner takes all.”

“All?” said I.

“You,” said the queen.

“And if I defeat him?” asked Edward, bravely.

“Then Snow will be free to marry whom she chooses.”

“And the siege?” asked Edward.

“Will be over.”

“Then there is nothing else for it,” said Edward, “I must meet the Ace of Hearts in battle.”

“No!” cried I, grabbing his arm. “There must be another

way."

"I am afraid that my own army is no match for my sister's," said the queen.

Edward placed a comforting hand upon my shoulder. "A battle would result in a great many deaths and, knowing you the way I do …"

"You know my very soul as I know yours," murmured I.

"Quite so. And knowing your very soul, I know you would seek to avoid the bloodshed of anyone who did not genuinely have it coming."

"I cannot deny it."

"It is therefore beholden upon me to face The Ace of Hearts in combat." Edward gazed into my eyes and, having seen the distress therein, said to the queen, "Would you mind if I spoke to Snow in private?"

"By all means," replied she.

Edward took my hand and led me to a quiet corner. "There really is no need to fear for my safety," said he.

"But how can you say so? If the Ace has challenged you, it can only mean that he's an expert swordsman."

"As am I, my love."

"You? But you're just the poor son of the woodcutter."

Edward shook his head. "You are aware of how the little lamb taught me how to read and pick locks."

"Yes, of course."

"Well, reading and picking locks were not the only things he taught me."

"They weren't?"

"No. He also taught me the ancient art of fencing."

"The little *lamb*? Are you joking?" Edward pointed to his uber serious expression. Quite unnecessary really as my eyes were already glued to it. "But what does the little lamb know of fencing?"

Edward smiled and brushed a stray hair from my cheek. "You know what They say, don't you?"

"On the subject of the little lamb's skills as a fencing instructor? Actually, I have no idea."

"That never was there a more proficient teacher of the ancient art of sword combat."

"Really? Is that what Frank said?"

"Really." Edward rubbed at the small of his back. "It was not easy wielding a sword whilst hopping, skipping and jumping about my yard. But I persevered, and I'm glad that I did."

"That makes two of us."

"So, you trust me then?"

"I trust you."

Some thirty minutes later …

Some thirty minutes later, Edward had been dressed in a silver breast plate and helmet, and I had been led up to the battlements. I gazed out over the army now amassed outside. Indeed, it spread all the way to the setting sun. The Ace of Hearts sat at the head of this army upon a black steed. He looked without a care as he awaited the poor farm boy from the other land, now being sent out across the drawbridge. I had to stand on tiptoes and lean over the battlement to get my first view of Edward. As the Ace dismounted his horse and drew his sword, my heart pounded in my chest. All I could do now was hope that the little lamb was as good a fencing teacher as They say he is. "I trust you Frank," murmured I.

What happened next surprised me, but not nearly as much as it surprised the Ace who stumbled backwards, swishing his blade. You see, as Edward drew his sword, he leapt into the air as though stung by a bee, landed on one leg, and hopped from side to side as though trying to avoid further stings. The Ace edged tentatively forwards until the two were standing opposite each other. Well, I say standing, but Edward's hop had now been joined by a skip and a jump and, no matter where the Ace attempted to stab at him, he missed wildly, while Edward's blows rained down hard and fast, and from every which way except the way the Ace expected. All of a sudden, the Ace's sword was sent spinning from his grasp! He fell upon one knee in submission where, for the first time, Edward stood perfectly still, and held the tip of his sword to his throat. "Give way!" commanded he.

"You're offering to *spare* me?" stammered the Ace.

“Gladly. But only if you agree to give up your claim on Snow White and *never* trouble her again.”

“Then … I agree!”

“And you give you word before all present?”

“I give my word!” shouted the Ace.

“Then I will remain true to mine,” said Edward, reaching down and lifting the Ace back onto his feet. It goes without saying that I was bursting with pride, not only at Edward’s swordplay, but at the mercy he had shown that odious playing card. Indeed, I wondered if I would have been quite so merciful. I promised myself that, if Edward and I found a way home, I would ask the little lamb to teach me his extraordinary fencing style.

“How else will I ever know if I can be as merciful as Edward?” murmured I, as I watched him walk back over the drawbridge.

A minute later …

A minute later, I had run down a flight of winding stairs and flung myself at Edward who caught me. "You have spared me from becoming an exhibit in my own exhibition!" cried I into his shoulder.

"It was nothing. You would have done the same for me, or any other innocent character, of that I have no doubt."

"Maybe so. But would I have been so merciful to one so undeserving?"

"Let us hope you are never faced with such a choice," said he, putting me down (physically for he would never do so in any other way).

Soon after, we were back in the White Queen's throne room. She was seated upon her throne and smiling as we approached. She stood up, and extended a gloved hand for Edward to kiss. "Your bravery and skills with a sword, while unusual, have done us a great service. Ask anything and, if it is in my power, I will grant it."

Edward took her hand and kissed it. "My only wish is that Snow and I can be together for the rest of our days."

"Then you may remain here for the rest of your days," said she. I glanced up at Edward and, although I was smiling, the queen must have noticed that my smile was tinged with sadness. "Is there nothing else I can do?" she asked.

I looked at her. "You are very kind. There would only be one thing better: returning to our own land. You see, we have many friends there and miss them dearly. But it may not be possible. And even if it was, I fear that only They would know how to go about it. And we have no means of contacting Frank."

"They?" asked the queen.

"You've never heard of They?" said I.

"No, never."

Edward cleared his throat. "*They* is the fount of all knowledge and wisdom in our own land, your Majesty."

I nodded. "He's a groundhog called Frank."

"They is *singular*?" said the queen.

"Very much so. But as he explained to me once, if he called himself 'I' then he would sound like an English gentleman every time someone quoted him."

The queen nodded thoughtfully and lowered her bottom down onto her throne. "We might not have *They* in Wonderland but …"

"But what?" said I.

"We do have Ancient Chinese Proverb Says." The queen beckoned to one of her courtiers who stepped forwards and bowed. Where is Ancient Chinese Proverb Says now?" she asked.

"The last I heard he was burrowing beneath the White Rose Garden, your Majesty."

"Burrowing?" said I.

"Yes, it's his favourite pastime," replied the queen.

"It's his *only* pastime," added the courtier.

"And Ancient Chinese Proverb Says possesses great wisdom?" asked Edward.

The Queen smiled. "What Ancient Chinese Proverb Says doesn't know can be written on the back of a postage stamp."

"Is that what They say," murmured Edward.

"If Frank were here perhaps he would," said I hopefully, before adding, "If it's not too much trouble, might someone show us to the White Rose Garden? We desire a word with Ancient Chinese Proverb Says."

As it turned out, Ancient Chinese Proverb Says was an earthworm called Janice. At first Janice seemed none too pleased at being plucked from the rich soil of the White Rose Garden by the courtier but, as soon as I mentioned that we needed her help in the absence of They, Janice's wriggly demeanour softened considerably.

"How is Frank?" wriggled she, as the courtier lowered her down upon a tiny cushion in the palm of his hand.

"You know They?" said I, peering down at her.

"We're cousins. Several thousand times removed."

"Really? Well, the last I saw him, Frank was in fine fettle."

"Then why the long round face?"

"It's just that the possibility of never seeing him again, not to mention all our other friends ..."

"Your melancholy is understandable. Home is a place where the roots of the tree receive nourishment from the soil."

I nodded. "They say that home is where the heart is."

"That sounds like Frank," wriggled Janice. "Always did like to simplify things."

"So? What does Ancient Chinese Proverb Says say about returning to the land of fairytales?"

Janice raised her head. Or maybe it was her tail. Who could tell? "Ancient Chinese Proverb Says that the water that carries migrating salmon up stream is purer than that which carries them down."

"That sounds awfully profound," said I. "But how is it useful in helping us return to our own land?"

"It isn't," wriggled Janice, "but luckily for you, I'm only just getting warmed up.

I smiled. "You remind me of your cousin."

"I'll take that as a compliment. Ancient Chinese Proverb Says that you must seek out and pass through the looking glass."

"The *looking glass*?" said I, for it rang a bell. Edward took one of the books about Alice's adventures from his pocket and read the title aloud, "Alice Through the Looking Glass."

"Would this be the looking glass to which you refer?" said I, taking the book and holding it face down over Janice.

"That's the one."

"But," said Edward thoughtfully, "would not this looking glass deliver us to the fictional real world? More precisely, the parlour in Alice's home from where she began her second journey to Wonderland?"

"My my, you are the scholarly one," wriggled Janice.

"Indeed, he is," said I beaming at him, "but why should we wish to travel to the fictional real world? It sounds further away from home than ever."

"It is further away. But the well-trodden path is not always where the cherry blossom tress grow the tallest."

"Pardon?"

Janice tutted. "The conduit that will deliver you back to the land of fairytales, awaits in the fictional real word."

"Where in the fictional real world?" asked Edward.

"The Old Curiosity Shop. The conduit you seek is a neglected item in that establishment."

"And what's the book called that brought the Old Curiosity Shop into being?" asked I.

"The Old Curiosity Shop," wriggled Janice.

"Makes sense, I suppose. And its author?"

"Charles Dickens."

"So, apart from the obvious, what's his book about?"

"It's about a girl called Nell. She's not quite fourteen. And lives with her lovely grandfather in his shop."

"His Old Curiosity Shop?"

"That's right," said Janice.

"Well, I'm pleased to hear that life in the fictional real world is kinder than in our own," said I, feeling relieved for Nell. My relief was short-lived, however, when Janice shook what I presumed to be her head. I folded my arms. "So? What horrible fate has the author of *this* book …"

"Charles Dickens," murmured Edward.

"Yes, what has *Charles Dickens* got in store for poor Nell?"

"I'm afraid that her grandfather, whilst well meaning, loses all his money gambling at cards."

"That doesn't sound so bad. Far worse fates occur to those in our land on a regular basis," said I, looking at Edward.

"That's not all," said Janice.

"It isn't?" said I, swinging my attention back to her.

"No. Their shop, which is also their home, is taken away from them by a malicious moneylender."

"So where do they live?"

"Nowhere. They have nowhere to go. And the guilt of what he's done causes Nell's grandfather to lose his wits. Nell loves her grandfather dearly, and so takes him away from the cruel Victorian city of London, with its noisy streets and terrible pollution, into the countryside. Once there, she relies upon the kindness of strangers and fresh air to aid her grandfather's recovery."

"They are to become beggars," said Edward, quietly.

"Yes."

"Well," said I with a shrug, "surely the fresh air does them both the world of good. And doubtless they meet many kind strangers along the way?"

Edward squeezed my shoulder and asked Janice, "So, to cut what sounds like a long story short, what becomes of Nell and her grandfather?"

"Nell dies from the sheer exhaustion of helping her beloved grandfather on their travels north. Help is on the way but arrives too late only to find Nell's grandfather sat beside her grave. Soon after, he too perishes from the grief of losing her."

"That's too horrible!" exclaimed I. "I won't allow it!"

"Not much you can do about it," said Janice. "It's just the way their story was written."

"It is, is it? Well, we'll see about that. So where is the looking glass that we must pass through to reach the fictional real world?"

The courtier cleared his throat in a way that suggested he wished to get our attention. "I believe I can answer that question. It is in the royal viewing gallery," said he, motioning back to the palace.

Ten fraught yet hopeful minutes later …

Ten fraught yet hopeful minutes later, Edward and I once again entered the throne room, where the White Queen sat with a straight back, her face filled with expectation. "Well?" enquired she, "did Ancient Chinese Proverb Says know the answer to your conundrum?"

"Indeed, she was most helpful," said I.

"Then pray tell, what did she say?"

"Ancient Chinese Proverb Says or, to use her proper name, *Janice*, told us that there is a conduit that will deliver us home. But that it exists in the fictional real word." The queen leaned back and looked thoughtful.

"Your Majesty," said Edward, "the conduit we seek is located in an establishment called The Old Curiosity Shop. It's in a town called London, in a land called England."

"England? Is that not where our own Alice hails from?"

"Yes," said I, "which is why we would like your permission to pass through *the* looking glass."

"The looking glass of the title of the book in which we all exist?"

"Quite so, your Majesty," said Edward.

"But will that not upset the settled order of things?"

"The settled order of things has already been *thoroughly*

unsettled," replied her courtier.

"If I may, your Majesty," said Edward, "our returning to our own land can only serve to *restore* the settled order of things. After all, the longer we remain here, where we were never supposed to be, the greater the unsettlement." Edward's words must have struck a chord for the queen stood with some urgency, looked at her courtier and said, "I'm inclined to agree. Convey our friends to the looking glass, and see them safely through to the other side. I wish you both a safe journey back to your own land, where I hope with all my heart that you shall live happily ever after."

"We'll certainly do our best ..." said I. It would be no exaggeration to say that we were rather unceremoniously hurried from the throne room towards the location of the looking glass. "All and sundry appear as keen as mustard to help restore the settled order of things," said I, glancing at the hand of the courtier that clasped my shoulder.

"Quite so," said Edward, glancing at the hand that clasped his own. The Hall of Mirrors was some considerable distance from the queen's throne room but we found ourselves crossing its magnificent threshold in two shakes of a lamb's tail. And once the lamb was done shaking its tail, it exited stage left. The room was long and narrow with a polished wooden floor. Ornate mirrors of all shapes and sizes ran its entire length. As we were hurried along the hall, I said, "It's a good thing this Hall of Mirrors is not located in our own land ..."

"Indeed, my love," said Edward, "for the pronouncements on your beauty would come thick and fast."

"It'd be quite the delusional cacophony, I should imagine."

Midway along the hall we were spun about to face a window size looking glass with a beautiful silver frame. Edward lifted the book, Alice Through the Looking Glass, and held it up so that we could see the illustration of the glass on its cover.

“This appears to be the one,” said he.

“It is the one,” said the courtier.

Edward looked sideways at me. “Would you like me to do the honours?” By this I presumed he was offering to pass through the mirror first. I nodded, only to find that my presumption had been correct when he stepped into the mirror and disappeared, the book falling to the floor.

“The book cannot make the crossing,” said the courtier, clicking his fingers at another who rushed forward to pick it up. I glanced over my shoulder. “Goodbye Wonderland …”

On the other side, I found myself standing on a ledge atop a fireplace, over which the looking glass hung. The room was splendid and grand, like the dining room of a very small palace. Edward was standing by a set of veranda doors, beyond which I beheld a well-tended garden. He made his way around the dining table in the room's centre, stood before the fireplace, and opened his arms so that I might climb down into them. "What took you so long?" said he, lowering me down onto the polished wooden floor.

"You are mistaken; I followed you through the looking glass immediately."

"I see," said Edward, thoughtfully. He took me by the hand and led me back to his vantage point at the veranda doors. "I believe you are overdue for your first good look at the fictional real world …"

"Indeed I am. For I have never laid eyes upon it before. The fictional real world is a *very* beautiful place," said I, taking in the scene of the lovely lawn and garden, and beyond the rolling hills of the countryside.

"Do not be fooled," cautioned Edward, "for the perils of the fictional real world are easily a match for our own."

"Having heard of poor Nell's fate with her grandfather, should they lose their Old Curiosity Shop, of that I have little doubt."

"Do not forget that the portal we seek to deliver us home is located in that very establishment."

"I have not forgotten," said I, returning his gaze. Edward's attention was taken by something outside and, placing his arm about my shoulder, he led me into the shadows at the side of the doors.

"What is it?" whispered I.

"Look, yonder …" said he, pointing. I followed his finger and spied a party coming through a gate at the farthest end of the garden.

"Alice!" said I, for it was she who led the party. If not for Edward's grip on my arm, I would have thrown open those doors and rushed to her. "How well and happy she looks!" said I, as the dodo, the mouse, the white rabbit, and finally a tall, willowy lady followed her through the gate.

"That must be Alice's mother," said Edward.

"And what a pretty lady she is …"

"Indeed. And clearly understanding."

"Understanding?"

"Yes. To have taken three such curious characters as the white rabbit, the mouse and the dodo under her wing. For while such characters are commonplace in the fictional lands, they are *never* to be found in the fictional real world."

"And why is that?" enquired I.

"I believe the clue can be found in the words 'real world.' You see, while curious characters may be created in the real world, or *fictional real world*, they certainly have no place living and breathing in it. Do not look at me that way, my love. You see, curious characters, such as those that Alice's mother has taken under her wing, simply *do not* exist here."

"I beg to differ," said I, watching said characters make their way to a garden table that contained a jug of lemonade and 5 glasses.

"Indeed, our friends that accompanied Alice from Wonderland are unique. Doubtless they are the *only* such characters to have lived and breathed here. Alice's mother must know very well that a talking rabbit with a fear of being late, a gigantic talking mouse, and a talking dodo are *beyond* curious here."

"You mean outside of books."

Edward nodded.

I gazed out at the woman now pouring lemonade for her curious wards. "How very understanding she must be …" murmured I.

"The precise point I have been endeavouring to make. And what is more …" Edward paused as the dodo accidently knocked over his glass of lemonade, and Alice's mother rushed to comfort him and refill his glass.

"You were saying? What is more what?" said I.

"What is more, if Alice's mother were to meet you, it would surely stretch her credulity to breaking point."

"Why? Am I really as curious as all that?"

Edward brushed a hair tenderly from my face. "Truly, you

are the stuff of fictional legend in this land."

"Well, you are the woodcutter's son. And the woodcutter is an important character too."

"My father is but a minor character. As for me, I was unknown before you rescued me from my enslaved fate." There was a grandfather clock in the room and it began to chime. This reminder of the passing of time brought me to my senses.

"We must make haste to the Old Curiosity Shop. I feel it in my water that Nell's grandfather is soon to gamble away their home." I sighed, placed my hand on the window, and lapped up the sight of the friends I hoped with all my heart I would see again.

"Come," said Edward, "a grand house such as this must have a conveyance in the form of a horse and carriage."

"What? You mean to steal their horse and carriage?"

"Steal? Never. We must borrow it in the pursuit of a good cause," said Edward, heading towards the door.

Several minutes later …

Several minutes later, Edward and I had successfully tiptoed our way past several maids dusting, and out of a door onto a path that led to the garage. Edward opened the garage door to reveal a fine coach. He opened the coach's door, and held my hand as I climbed inside. He told me to make myself comfortable while he went to the stable across the yard to fetch a horse. He returned with two fine looking horses, and attached them to the carriage. Not long after, we were on our way to London of the Victorian era. Edward was sitting up front holding the reins, while I poked my head through the window and enjoyed the rush of fresh air on my face.

Some hours later, following a nap, when I tried the same thing again, the air outside was anything *but* fresh. Indeed, it was full of thick black smog and, casting my gaze forwards, I saw its cause: a great metropolis where many thousands of dwellings and countless factories belched smoke into the air.

“London?” cried I, above the sound of the horses' hooves on the road. “London,” replied Edward, cracking the reins.

The sights that greeted us as we entered the narrow-cobbled streets of the city made me want to leap out and provide comfort to the wretched urchins who sat in doorways, or begged a penny from passers by in frock coats and tall hats. The smells too were pungent and, as I pressed my sleeve to my nose, I thanked my lucky stars that those who had penned the stories of my own land had not written about it having such a terrible stench. I witnessed a wretched little boy on crutches lose his balance and fall flat upon the road. Seeing that no one had paid him the least bit of attention, I opened the carriage door and cried out, “Stop the carriage, Edward!”

“We are almost there,” replied he over his shoulder.

“Now, Edward! Or I shall jump!” Edward pulled hard on the reins and the carriage came to a juddering halt. I leapt out and ran back to assist the boy who lay so still that he might have been dead. “Young man?” said I, clasping his shoulder. “Young man!”

At first, he did not respond but then, much to my relief, his eyes slowly opened. “*Miss*?” said he, lifting his head and blinking at me. “Do I *know* you, miss?”

I shook my head. “No. I was passing and saw you fall. And I could not for all the world continue on my way without seeing you safely on yours.”

Edward was suddenly crouched beside me. “Come, let me help you up and away from the road,” said he, lifting the boy to his feet while I gathered up his crutches and handed them to him. Having steadied himself, he gazed up at my face in the most peculiar and open-mouthed fashion. “I *do* know you.”

“As I said, you are mistaken. The fall must have scrambled your senses. But fear not, they shall return to you presently.”

“If you say so, miss. I’m Archie, Archie Smith, and *you* are?” asked the canny young fellow.

“Snow, Snow White,” said I. Archie's bottom lip dropped so far from his top that, for a moment, I feared he’d dislocated his jaw.

Edward crouched down and said, “We would consider it a

personal favour if you would not draw any undue attention to the celebrity in your midst."

"There's a celebrity in his midst?" said I, casting my gaze about the gloomy, foul smelling street.

"As I live and breathe, *Snow White* ..." said Archie.

"Oh, *right*. You've heard of me in the fictional real world."

"Course I 'av!" beamed Archie, whose cheeks were now mercifully aglow.

Edward brought his mouth close to my ear. "Not so much of the *fictional*, my love, like Alice, these characters have been written in a way that has them believe they are inhabitants *of* the real world."

"Point taken," murmured I. "And this is Edward," said I to Archie. "Edward is none other than the son of the woodcutter."

Archie gazed up at Edward, and scratched his head.

"Oh, come now," said I, "surely you've heard of the woodcutter and his family?"

"Maybe. Look, I was just off to see my friend Nell at her shop. *Please* say you'll come along? She'd be *chuffed to bits* to meet Snow White. And you too Edward."

"You're very kind," smiled Edward.

"My friends call me Snow," said I, "and funnily enough, we were just on our way to see Nell."

"No, *really*? At the Old Curiosity Shop?"

"Yes, really. For we have been led to believe that that is where she lives."

"Great! Come on then," said Archie, hobbling away down the street.

"Is it far? Only we have a carriage?" said I.

"Na," said he, "it's just around this corner."

Just around the corner …

Just around the corner, at the centre of an intersection, two roads ran down either side of a squat, crooked looking shop. The shop had three stories, and was made from broad, dark wooden beams that sagged miserably with age. Indeed, it was this sagging that gave the shop its crooked appearance. In the shop's window were arranged a great many old curiosities. "The establishment is aptly named," said I, gazing up at the sign above the door. Archie, to whom my words had been directed, had not heard them, for he had already hurried through it on his crutches. I glanced behind me to see Edward pulling up in the carriage across the road, and followed Archie in.

Inside, the shop was chock-a-block with things for sale: chairs, tables, paintings, cabinets, stuffed animals, musical instruments and many more curios besides. All these encroached upon a table in the room's centre. Indeed, the area around the table was just large enough for a person to navigate. A girl was sitting at the table with her back to me. She was buttering a slice of bread from a freshly baked loaf. Archie, for whom I hoped this bread was intended, was standing beside her, propped up on his crutches. The girl handed him the buttered bread and said, "Dear Archie, your hunger has clearly rendered you delirious again." Archie, after somehow managing to shove the entire slice into his small mouth, mumbled between excited chews, "Well, see for yourself!" and lifted a crutch in my direction. The girl climbed out of her chair and, having brushed the crumbs from her threadbare green dress, turned and gazed at me with the same befuddled, open-mouthed expression that Archie had. I had been told to expect a girl of not quite fourteen but, so pale and waif-like was she, she might have been nine. I supposed she must have been written that way, and sighed. But my spirits were lifted when she walked determinedly towards me and, gazing up at me (for I was at least a head taller) murmured, "You can't be her. You simply *can't*."

"If you tell me to whom you refer, perhaps I can answer your question?" My words seemed to fall upon deaf ears for she reached out and felt my hair.

"Even *saying* your name would, well, it would sound *too* strange," murmured she.

As you're well aware reader, I am supremely practised in the art of sounding too strange, and so announced myself thus: "My name is Snow White. The fairest in the other land. Or so the reflective surfaces delight in telling me."

Nell released my hair as though stung by it and stumbled backwards. "*No*."

"I assure you that I am she. And what's more, I have travelled all the way from Wonderland to make your acquaintance."

"*Wonderland*?" said she, gazing over my shoulder as if half expecting the next person to enter her shop to be Alice.

"Allow me to introduce Edward," said I as it was he and not her.

"Edward?" murmured she.

"Edward's the son of the woodcutter," said Archie between

chews.

"The woodcutter who let you go?" whispered Nell as though confiding a secret.

"Indeed, they are one and the same."

Nell wobbled on her skinny pins. "Do you mind if I sit down?" said she, distantly. I stepped past her, pulled a chair a little way from the table, and turned it about so that she might lower herself into it. Then, crouching, I took her tiny, pale hands in my own, and believe me when I say that my own hands looked plump and ruddy in comparison, I said, "I realise that I'm a curiosity here. And how I came to be here is a long story." Nell glanced over her shoulder at Archie. "I've read your story to Archie many times."

"Not this one you 'aven't," replied he.

"Archie is right," confessed I, "for I am making this one up as I go along."

"Are you allowed to do that?" said Archie, reaching for another slice of bread.

"Strictly speaking? And technically? No. However, there are a great many lands and many more injustices besides."

"And?" murmured Nell.

"And *someone* has to do something about them."

Nell lifted a hand and felt my hair again. "… *Extraordinary* … I've never felt anything so silken."

"Too kind. Although you should see me when I'm caught in the rain."

“Frizzy?” murmured Nell.

“You have no idea.”

“Time is of the essence, perhaps we should explain the reason for our being here,” said Edward.

I drew a breath and said, “We, *Edward and I*, arc on our way home from Wonderland.”

“As in Alice *in*?”

“The very one.”

“I do love that book. In fact, we have a copy of it here somewhere,” said Nell, glancing about fretfully.

“Please do not trouble yourself. There are two reasons why we sought you out. And your copy of Alice in Wonderland is neither one of them.”

“*Two* reasons why you sought *me* out?

“Yes. Firstly, we have it on good authority that your grandfather, kindly though he is, is soon to gamble away this shop in a game of cards.”

It was clear that Nell had her own suspicions on the subject for she trembled horribly. “It’s my worst fear. This is our home and we have nowhere to go.”

“Fear not,” said I, comfortingly, “for I am here now and one of my dwarves isn’t called Meddlesome for nothing.”

“One of your dwarves is called *Meddlesome*?” said Archie.

“I'll say. Things in the land of fairytales are not all you’ve been led to believe."

"I'll say," echoed Archie.

"Do you mean to say there's something you might do to stop grandfather's gambling?" said Nell, "only his habit is of the most severe kind."

I sighed. "It's just the way he was …" I was about to say 'written' when Edward cleared his throat in such a way as to remind me that our new friends are unaware that they are written.

"Just the way he was what?" enquired Nell.

"Made," said Edward.

"You're not wrong," said Archie.

Nell sat up straight. "You said there were *two* reasons why you sought me out. If there's something I can do for you, it would be an honour."

I smiled. "Edward and I have it on good authority that somewhere in this shop is a conduit that will deliver us home to the land of fairytales."

Nell rose slowly to her feet. "I know every nook and cranny of our shop, and I have never come across anything like a conduit. Who told you it was here?"

"Janice," said I.

"Janice?"

"You may know her by her other name, Ancient Chinese Proverb Says," said Edward.

“I've heard of Chinese proverbs,” nodded she, “indeed, I found one in a fortune cookie just yesterday. But I couldn’t make head nor tail of it.”

Archie burped. “That’s because it was absolute gibberish.”

“You still have it?” murmured Edward.

“I believe it's in my room,” said Nell. “Grandfather he …” At the mention of her grandfather, Nell shuddered.

“Is he here?” asked Edward.

“Yes. He’s asleep upstairs,” said she, glancing at the ceiling. “But I fear that despite your good intentions, *nothing* can be done to cure him of his habit.”

Edward placed a hand on his chin. “I believe I know of a way.”

“You do? If so, that would be awfully helpful,” said I.

“I do. Although, it will only work if Nell’s grandfather agrees to submit to it.”

“What is it?” asked Nell, breathlessly.

Edward clasped his hands behind his back. “Snow is aware how the little lamb taught me how to read, pick locks and fence.”

“Indeed, Edward is a most accomplished reader, lock picker and fencer,” confirmed I.

“But what you do not yet know is that the little lamb also taught me the art of hypnotism.”

“Hypnotism,” said Nell, brightening.

“Quite so,” replied Edward, “and, although it was not easy hopping, skipping and jumping about my yard while the little lamb taught me the precise mechanics of swinging a pocket watch, I persevered,” said he, rubbing the small of his back.

“Do you think that hypnotism might work on Nell’s grandfather?” asked Archie.

“If he agrees to submit, then of that I have little doubt,” rubbed Edward.

I smiled at Edward and then looked at Nell. “What is your Grandfather's …” I had been about to say ‘name’ when Edward cleared his throat in such a way as to suggest that he would prefer that I did not finish my question.

“Might I have a quiet word in your ear,” said he, motioning to the door.

“Hope you don't mind,” said I to Nell and Archie. They shook their heads and I accompanied Edward to the door where he whispered, “It's important that you do not enquire after her grandfather’s name.”

“Why ever not?”

“Because the author of this book never gave him one.”

“Oh, I see. Like the miller's daughter in our own land.”

“Quite so.”

“But how do you know?”

“I read it in The Almanac of Nameless Fictional Characters.

It's a short tome, but interesting nonetheless."

"How well read you are. I had no idea that such an almanac even existed."

"Is something the matter?" asked Nell.

"No. And you know what They say?" said I, making my way back over to the table.

"No. What do They say?" replied Nell.

"That there is no time like the present. Have you a pocket watch that Edward can use to demonstrate the skills that the little lamb has taught him?"

Nell nodded. "Grandfather has one. He keeps it on his person."

A few minutes later …

A few minutes later, Edward, Nell and I were upstairs and huddled around a door. Nell tapped on the door, opened it and went inside. "Grandfather?" said she, "wake up, we have visitors."

"Visitors?" said he, blinking into the gloom of his small box room.

"Yes, grandfather," replied she, drawing open the curtains. "Come in," continued Nell, beckoning to Edward and I.

Nell's grandfather sat up in bed and looked at me. He rubbed his eyes and looked some more. "I must still be asleep," said he.

"Grandfather, may I introduce Snow White?"

"Snow White? Yes, of course."

"And her beau, Edward. Edward is the son of the woodcutter who set her free. You remember? You have read me their story many times."

Nell's grandfather raised a hand in greeting and grinned the toothless grin of one who imagines they must still be sleeping. "Curiouser and curiouser," muttered he, running a hand over his white stubble.

Edward stepped towards the bed and said, "I expect that a fine gentleman such as yourself has a pocket watch?"

"Oh, yes, yes indeed," replied Nell's grandfather, reaching

into his waistcoat's pocket and drawing it out.

"May I see it?" said Edward.

"See it? Why not. For Edward son of the woodcutter? Anything, anything," said he, handing it over.

Nell placed an arm around her grandfather's narrow shoulders. "Edward is going to hypnotise you, grandfather."

"He *is*? Why?"

"To stop you gambling away our home."

"Well I never, this is *quite* the dream. Oh, yes, quite the dream indeed!"

"You have no objections then?" said Nell, squeezing his arm.

"Objections? Oh, goodness gracious me no. Objections you say? I have been in mortal peril of such a thing happening for some time. I can't stop myself you see. Not when it comes to the cards. Just don't have the willpower."

I smiled at the kindly old fellow. "That's because you were made that way."

"God in his infinite wisdom?" nodded he.

Edward began to swing the pocket watch.

"Watch the watch, grandfather," said Nell, propping him up with pillows.

"Happy to! Hypnotised by Edward son of the woodcutter? The woodcutter who let Snow White go? Who'd have thought it? Certainly not I. Not in a million dreams! I only hope I can remember so I might tell you about it when I wake, Nell." Nell smiled and pointed at the swinging pocket watch. As she did so, Edward began to hop as he swung the watch. Nell's grandfather's eyelids grew droopy. "Things just keep getting curiouser and curiouser …" murmured he.

"I believe I've heard that expression curiouser and curiouser before," whispered Nell as her grandfather fell under the trance.

"Yes," said Edward, switching his hopping leg, "it was originally Alice's saying but, doubtless due to the cross contamination, it appears to have become your grandfather's instead. Now please remain silent while I …" Nell and I nodded. "You no longer feel compelled to gamble at cards," said Edward.

"I no longer feel compelled to gamble at cards," repeated Nell's grandfather.

"Now your compulsion lies elsewhere."

"My compulsion lies elsewhere?"

"Yes. In flying kites."

"Oh, how I love to fly a kite!" said he.

"Indeed. And, what's more, should your hands ever come into contact with playing cards, the cards will scold you as though on fire."

"Scold me? Yes! Cards are such hot things."

"Quite so. And now I will count to three and on three you will fall into a deep sleep … one, two, three." Edward stopped hopping and rubbed at his back.

"It's done? Really?" said Nell. "Grandfather will no longer gamble at cards?"

Edward nodded.

"I don't know how I can thank you!"

"That is easy," said Edward, "by helping us locate the conduit that will deliver us home."

"But I don't know where it is. It could be anywhere," said Nell, casting her gaze about fretfully.

Edward opened his mouth but closed it again when I pressed a finger to his lips. Over my shoulder, I said, "Please fetch the message you found in that fortune cookie yesterday."

"But why? It was gibberish. At least it was as far as I …" A penny must have dropped for she hurried from the room to fetch it.

She returned with a small, crumpled piece of paper. "Give it to me, please," said I, returning Edward's smile. I unfurled the paper and read the following aloud, "Ancient Chinese Proverb says: when two digits of equal weight are placed in the balance, all things are possible."

"You see. I told you it was gibberish," said Nell.

Edward's lips parted but closed again when I pressed my finger to them. "Have you a pair of scales for sale in your shop?" Nell lowered herself onto the bed where her grandfather was sleeping soundly. She gazed into the middle distance as though doing a mental stock take. "… The only scales I can recall are with other trinkets in the window … in a hat box."

"Trinkets?" said Edward before I had a chance to silence him with my finger.

"Yes," said Nell, standing.

"Sounds like they're quite small then?" said I.

"Very," nodded Nell.

"Small enough to hold a *digit*?" said I, lifting my finger from Edward's lips and gazing at its print. The pennies were dropping thick and fast now for Nell as she made for the door. "Follow me!" said she, disappearing through it.

Two minutes later …

Two minutes later, Nell, Edward, Archie and myself were gathered around the table downstairs and gazing at the smallest pair of silver measuring scales you've never seem. "You reckon they're what you came to find then?" said Archie.

I lowered my head and studied the scales. They were bronze and just large enough to place a sugar cube on each side for weighing. "I suppose there is only one way to find out …" said I, hovering an index finger over one side of the tiny scales. Edward did the same on the other. "On three?" said I.

"On three ..." repeated he.

"But what about us? What should we do?" said Nell.

"Shield our eyes perhaps," said Archie, his own eyes wide in wonder.

"I do not think that will be necessary," said Edward. "I believe that when Snow and I place our fingertips down on either side of the scales, that a conduit will be opened to our own land."

Nell reached out and squeezed Archie's hand. "You mean to say that we might see into the land of fairytales?"

Edward nodded. "On three then," continued he, his own finger hovering above his side of the tiny scales. And so, on the count of three, we lowered the tips of our fingers so that they rested on either side of the measuring scales and, with the sounds of Nell's and Archie's gasps ringing in our ears, we beheld the scene of our wedding that now occupied the entire side of the shop. In this frozen scene, Edward and I were standing side by side at the altar preparing to say our vows in that splendid cathedral. My wedding dress was of the sort that you'd expect for the wedding of a fairytale princess: white, figure hugging, and with a train that reached to the bottom of the dozen steps that led up to the altar. Likewise, Edward was wearing the type of tailored uniform with medals and sashes that are common in fairy stories such as these. We were a sight for sore eyes, and that explains why our mouths snapped closed when Archie murmured, "Blimey."

"Language please," Nell admonished him, herself loath to draw her breathless gaze from the scene as just described. "Oh, look … is *that* your evil stepmother?" said she, pointing to my stepmother seated in the front row of the congregation.

"That's her," sighed I. "But on a more positive note, the beauty sitting just over her left shoulder is my dear friend Cinders …"

"Oh my *goodness*, so it is," said Nell.

"I know. She's lovely. And seated on either side of her are her sisters. They must have prevented her from coming to my aid with Little Red when things took a turn for the worse."

"Her sisters? They don't look ugly," said Archie.

"Their ugliness lies within," said Edward.

"Talking of Little Red, isn't *that* Little Red Riding Hood," said Nell, pointing at her.

"Yes, that's her. What splendid eyesight you have."

"All the better to see Little Red Riding Hood with," giggled Archie as Nell tickled him.

I lowered myself into a chair. "I suppose this means that she will not remember *anything* of our adventure with Gretel?"

"You suppose right. It will never have happened," said Edward philosophically, "but," continued he, "you can always tell her about it in a diary."

"I *may* have made one or two notes to that end," said I, feeling for them in my pocket.

"I somehow thought you might. And now it's time. We must return to our own land."

Archie spat on a palm and, having rubbed it against his trousers, reached out to shake my hand. "Thanks for everything, for coming to my aid, for *everything.* I only wish there was a way I could thank you properly," said he as I shook it.

"Snow came to you aid?" said Nell.

"Archie fainted in the street," said I.

"Is that true, Archie?" Nell asked him.

Archie shrugged.

"Then you must come and visit me more than once a week! Do you hear?"

"Wouldn't want to be a burden."

"Burden smurden," said I, "you *can* thank me properly by promising me you'll do as Nell asks."

"All right, I will! Thank you."

"My pleasure," said I, bending down and kissing his cheek. As Archie touched a hand to his blushing cheek, Nell said, "That goes quadruple for me. For without your kindly meddling, my grandfather and I, well …"

"It's true that things were not headed for what I consider to be a satisfactory conclusion," said I. It was at that moment that Nell's grandfather came down the stairs, smiling in a way that reminded me of the Cheshire Cat.

"Grandfather?" said Nell.

"Still dreaming am I, Nell?" said he, taking in this most curious of scenes.

"Yes," said all present to him.

"No matter, no matter …" said he, searching behind a collection of stuffed birds and drawing out a kite. "Here it is! I'm off to Hyde Park," continued he, making for the door. "Toodle pip!" And with that he disappeared through it.

"Blimey," said Archie, "he had all the troubles of the world on his shoulders yesterday. Has he had a personality transplant?"

"In a manner of speaking, yes," said Edward. "Now, shall we?" continued he, gesturing to the cathedral, "For our wedding awaits …" And so it was that, having exchanged hugs with our new friends, we stepped into the cathedral. Looking back, I saw Nell and Archie watching us, rapt, from within the clutter of that shop.

"It seems that the proceedings cannot get under way until we assume our positions at the altar," said Edward. And indeed, the many thousands of spectators in that cathedral were still frozen in time.

"My stepmother's going to be none too pleased when Alice does not show up …" said I, smiling in her direction. Edward raised an arm for me to hold onto and, as we made our way towards our frozen selves standing before the altar, he said, "I for one will have no objections to your glancing in her direction at the moment you say, 'I do,' for I believe that I was transported to Wonderland just at the moment that your lips parted to do so."

"Ditto," said I.

"As much as I'd like to see her thwarted expression, the congregation may think it peculiar if we both look at your stepmother at such an important moment," said Edward as we prepared to step back into our frozen selves. And, as we did so, the spectators came to life, and the sound of coughing and shuffling could be heard. My heart sank when I realised that Nell and Archie had vanished but rose again when I felt a trinket in my hand. I knew instantly that it was the scales. I had no recollection of taking them, but scales such as these that could potentially open portals to other lands? My meddling heart smiled at the possibilities. Not long after, I beheld something that made my face smile as I said, "I do," to Edward. Then, looking in the direction of my stepmother, I watched her expression go from expectant, through puzzled and perplexed, to out and out furious. I looked back at Edward whose own expression could not have been more different.

I write these words on the evening of our wedding. Edward

and I are to spend our wedding night at the top of the magnificent tower that my grandmother promised us but never expected we'd be able to use. Unlike Rapunzel's tower, where my grandmother had hoped I would spend eternity, this tower has not only windows but a door. A door through which Edward will soon be joining me. If you cast your mind back to the start of this diary, you'll remember how Edward had told me that I would not need to keep a diary once we were married. I believe his exact words had been, "Do you really think anyone in the real world is going to be interested in a diary about someone living happily ever after? It might easily be summed up with day after day of smiling faces." But, as I sit here at this writing desk, looking out over the land where the sun has just begun to set, it occurs to me that a life of smiling faces may not be the life for me. Indeed reader, *friend*, you are the first that I have confided these doubts in. And the embryo of a plan: a plan that would see Little Red, Gretel, Alice and myself forming a little troupe: The League of Fairytale Heroines. Imagine the wrongs of heartless authors we might right? And with the tiny scales, it may be possible to travel to any land of our choosing. I have no idea if my plan will come to pass. But if it does, I shall keep another diary. So, keep your eyes peeled, for you are more important than you imagine in the scheme of my things. *Our* things. Until then, keep your chin up always, and a goodnight to all. Snow.

The end

Thank you for reading! If you enjoyed these diaries you might also enjoy the latest novel by the same author *The Scratchling Trinity*. The opening pages of which follow here …

Book description: *The Scratchling Trinity*

No one knew the importance of the Scratchling-born, until now.

When orphan called Eric Kettle scratches a desperate cry for help into a wall in 1840, little does he know that it's about to be answered by luckless Max Hastings in 2016. Both Max and Eric are soon to discover that they're Scratchling-born, and that along with the Ellie Swanson, a no-nonsense Scratchling veteran, they are destined to form the Scratchling Trinity. With an evil headmaster, a flying boat, two vengeful giants and a clutch of ghostly helpers along the way, they are off on an incredible adventure!

One
Max Hastings

London, England, 2016

Max Hastings was leaning low over the handlebars of his bike, and pedalling like he'd flipped out. The distance from his school to his home was two and a half kilometres, and Max *had* to smash his personal best time. The reason was written on a scroll of parchment, held closed by a black ribbon and jutting from his blazer pocket like a piston powering him towards a new school-to-home record. He sped up his drive, leapt off his bicycle and sprinted, arms flailing, towards the front door. Once through it, he darted into the living room, unclipped the strap on his bicycle helmet, and cast the helmet onto the couch. Max was twelve years old, of average build if a little on the chunky side, with a shock of white-blond hair that grew every which way except the way Max would have liked. Max drew the scroll from his pocket, gunslinger style, straightened his back, and announced his extraordinary news to his parents: 'I've finally *won* something!'

Mr Hastings looked at Max over the top of his newspaper. 'There must be some mistake,' he said.

'That's what I thought when Miss Hale announced the name of the re-cip-ient.'

Mrs Hastings, who was holding Max's one-year-old sister Maxine, put the baby down in her walker. 'Congratulations, Max! So what have you won?'

Max gazed at the rolled-up parchment in his hand. 'It's a grand prize,

Mum. They picked *my name* out of a hat during the last assembly of term.'

'You've broken your duck, then?' said his astonished father. 'If memory serves me correctly, you've never won anything in your life. Not even when you went through that annoying competitions phase.'

'I know, Dad. I was there.'

'So *what* have you won, exactly?' asked Mrs Hastings.

'No idea.'

'Well, then, I suggest you untie that ribbon and find out.'

Max glanced from the parchment to his mother and back again. Mrs Hastings placed her hands on her hips. 'Whatever is the matter with you?'

'It's just so …'

'So what?' said his father.

'Official-looking.'

'Which must bode well for the prize,' said Mr Hastings, putting down his newspaper. 'Give it here, son. I'll open it.'

Max shook his head. 'I'll do it.' He untied the ribbon and unfurled the parchment. His lips moved slowly as he read it, and his brow furrowed.

'Well?' pressed his mother.

His father leaned forwards in his armchair. 'What are you the recipient *of*?'

'Of a life-time membership …' murmured Max.

'A life-time membership of *what*?' said his mother testily.

Max read the words slowly. 'The Ancient Order of Wall Scratchings.'

'Of *what*?' said Mr Hastings.

'Of *wall* scratchings,' repeated his mother helpfully.

'But what does that even mean?' mumbled Max, his eyes glued to the parchment for some clue.

'Oh, for pity's sake, give it to me,' said his mother, sliding it from his hand.

Mrs Hastings scanned the parchment. 'Oh, my goodness. Max has been invited to a private viewing of their wall scratchings tomorrow, at Mansion House!'

Mr Hastings cleared his throat. 'What? The place where the Lord Mayor of London lives?'

'Yes!'

'There must be some mistake,' asserted Mr Hastings.

Mrs Hastings shook her head. 'No mistake. The Ancient Order of Wall Scratchings, Mansion House, City of London, London.'

Max sighed. 'Trust me to win a grand *booby* prize. Tomorrow's *Saturday,* not to mention the first day of the Christmas holidays. I'm not going.'

'Not going?' echoed Mrs Hastings.

'Why would I? Since when was I interested in *wall scratchings*? I don't even know what they are!'

'They're scratchings on walls, presumably,' said Mr Hastings, happy to apply his keen insight to the problem at hand.

'Well, whatever they are,' said Mrs Hastings, glancing at the parchment in her hand, 'it says here that they have the world's largest collection of them.'

'Not helping, Mum,' said Max. He went to the dining table and opened his laptop, muttering absently to himself as he typed *the ancient order of wall scratchings* into the search engine. He sat back in his seat and breathed a sigh of relief. 'Just as I thought. There's no such place. It doesn't even exist! ... What are you doing?' Max asked his mother.

'There's a phone number on here. I'm calling them.'

'But—' said Max.

'But nothing. I intend to get to the bottom of these ... these *scratchings*.' She tapped her foot impatiently as the phone rang at the other end of the line.

A woman with a cut-glass English accent answered. 'Thank you for calling the Ancient Order of Wall Scratchings. How may I help you?'

'My name is Mrs Hastings, and my son Max has just won a free membership to your organisation.'

'Hearty congratulations!' said the woman.

'Be that as it may, there's no mention of you on the internet. No mention whatsoever.'

The woman drew a deep breath. 'Ours is an ancient organisation, Mrs Hastings. As such we frown upon all modern conventions.'

'Alright. But your address appears to be the very same as the Lord Mayor of London's.'

'That's right.'

'And the Lord Mayor?'

'What about him?'

'He's happy to share his residence with your organisation?'

'The Ancient Order of Wall Scratchings has been located at this spot for over a thousand years, Mrs Hastings. Since the year 1065, to be exact. The first Lord Mayor didn't move in until some seven hundred years later, in 1752.'

'*And*?'

'And since then we've had no complaints from any Lord Mayor in office.'

A man's voice came on the line. 'Max is going to benefit greatly from his membership, Mrs Hastings,' he asserted.

'*Max is going to benefit greatly from his membership*,' repeated Mrs

Hastings, as though in a trance.

'And he'll meet a great many important people.'

'*And he'll meet a great many important people*,' echoed Mrs Hastings.

'People,' the voice went on, 'who will be able to help him in his chosen career.'

'He wants to test video games for a living,' murmured Mrs Hastings.

'*Help him in his chosen career*,' said the man, raising his voice.

'*Help him in his chosen career,'* repeated Mrs Hastings obediently.

'Tell Max he's welcome to bring a friend tomorrow. Goodbye.'

'Goodbye!' said Mrs Hastings, putting down the phone. She turned to Max. 'You're welcome to take a friend tomorrow,' she said, grinning terrifically from ear to ear.

Max scratched absently at his left cheekbone, just below his eye, where there was a birthmark that looked as though someone had signed their initials in black ink. 'O-kay. Are you alright, Mum?'

'Never better,' she replied. Mrs Hastings's smile then did the seemingly impossible and grew wider still. Max had never realised his mother had so many teeth.

Two
Eric Kettle

Yorkshire, England, December 1st, 1840

Inside a carriage drawn by two horses, a frail boy sat shivering beside a giant of a man. The man was expressionless and granite-faced, and indeed any onlooker might have thought him cut from granite. The only clue to his being flesh-and-blood was the smile that curled his lips whenever the carriage hit a pothole and the boy yelped. The man took up most of a bench designed for three adults, squashing his young companion against the carriage door like an item of worthless baggage. The boy's name was Eric Kettle, and Eric looked so fragile that he might break in two every time the carriage lurched over a bump in the road – of which there were a great many, and many more potholes besides. Despite these hardships, Eric's saucer-like brown eyes gazed with extraordinary hope from a face gaunt with hunger.

It was gone midnight when the carriage came to a halt at its destination: the St Bart's School for Boys. The school was a crumbling mansion that rose from the Yorkshire countryside like a vampire's abandoned lair. The carriage door was opened by the driver, who was hidden by an entire closet's worth of coats, scarves and gloves. The brute heaved himself out of his seat. 'Fall in behind, sir,' he grumbled at his young ward. Eric followed as quickly as his shivering legs would allow. He hugged himself for warmth, and stumbled towards the promise of heat beyond the door that now opened for them. Once through the door, Eric wondered if it hadn't actually been warmer outside.

They'd been admitted by a pale and hungry-looking boy swaddled in a threadbare coat several sizes too large. He was carrying a paraffin lamp, and, without uttering a single word, he illuminated their path across a cavernous entrance hall and up a sweeping staircase. Two flights up, he lit the way down a long corridor before finally stopping outside a door, on which a gold plaque read: *Headmaster. Augustus Mann*. Augustus took a key from his pocket and unlocked the door. He turned to the boy carrying the lamp, now hastily lighting a candle by its flame, and snatched the lamp from his grasp. The boy scurried off on bow legs, and Eric watched the candle light until it disappeared from sight at the end of a corridor. 'Fall in, sir!' came the gruff voice of Augustus Mann, from inside the study.

The headmaster placed the lamp on a desk piled high with books, and pointed to a spot on the wooden floor before the desk marked with an X in chalk. 'Stand there, arms at your sides, chin held high. That's it. And stop your shivering.'

'I'll try, sir, but it's just so …'

'Say the word *cold,* and as God is my witness, I'll thrash you where you stand. Perhaps you think that I should light a fire for you? Waste good wood? Is that what you think?'

'No, sir.'

'Speak up when I address you!'

'No, sir!'

'No what?'

'No, I don't think you should waste good wood on me, sir.'

'Spoilt! That's what you've been. Spoilt to the core.'

Eric shook his head. 'They work us very hard at the orphanage, sir.'

The headmaster sat down and opened a folder on his desk. 'It says here that your father went off to seek his fortune the day after you were born. Wherever he went, he must have liked it there.'

Eric smiled. 'Do you think so? Why do you say so, sir?'

'Liked it more than he liked *you,* anyway.' Eric's smile vanished as the headmaster grunted and went on, 'I see your mother went looking for him soon after, and whether or not she found him, nobody knows. Never seen nor heard from again. But whatever she *did* find, she must have preferred it to you.' The headmaster observed Eric through narrowed eyes. 'What is it about you that so vexes others, *boy*?'

Eric's gaze dropped to the ground. 'I'm sure I don't know, sir.'

'After so many years in an orphanage, I dare say you thought your ship had come in, with your name chosen from a hat to receive a scholarship to attend a fine Yorkshire school of good repute. Thought you'd get yourself a proper education, eh? Those abominable do-gooders, passing their laws that say the likes of *me* must look with charitable eyes upon the likes of *you.* The paltry compensation I will receive for your keep will barely cover my costs.'

'I'm very sorry, sir.'

'You will be. The fact is, you are worth more to me *dead* than you are alive – a fact that doesn't bode at all well for you,' said the headmaster, rising from his chair and turning to face a collection of canes hanging on the wall. He stroked his grey moustache thoughtfully, smiled, and then reached for one.

'Please,' implored Eric. 'I don't know why my parents left me. I did nothing wrong. I was just a baby, and that's the God's truth, sir.'

The headmaster turned and swiped the cane back and forth to gauge its suitability. 'I would strongly advise you not to take the Lord's name in vain. Not in this establishment, *sir*, or God help me …'

As Augustus Mann made his way around his desk towards him, Eric closed his eyes and willed himself back at the orphanage. It didn't work, although the heavy blow that struck his face might almost have launched him back there. Eric's legs gave way beneath him, and he collapsed to the ground, groaning and clutching a cheek that felt savaged by a thousand bee stings. Augustus Mann loomed over him, cane in hand. 'Down at the first lash? Pathetic! That is what you are, pathetic. Is it any wonder your parents left you?' The headmaster yawned, ambled back around his desk, placed the cane back on its hook and walked towards the door. 'You can spend the night there on the floor, like the dog you undoubtedly are. Although I can assure you that your life expectancy is considerably shorter than a dog's. A truth I intend to take *considerable* comfort from,' he yawned. Augustus Mann stepped through the door, closing it and locking it behind him.

Eric dragged himself into a corner, where he huddled miserably for warmth, trying to remember a legend he'd heard some years before at the orphanage: *If a child of kind heart and noble mind is ever in mortal danger, all he needs do is scratch a message of help into a stone wall, and help will find him.* Eric fumbled down his side for one of the safety pins that kept his clothes from falling apart, and with it he scratched the following words in tiny letters into the wall: *If ever a boy was in mortal danger, it's me. Please, if anyone's there, help me!*

Thank you for reading! If you enjoyed this sample, *The Scratchling Trinity* is available from Amazon.

Made in the USA
Middletown, DE
04 November 2018